About the Author

Johan Stiel was born in 1977 to two book enthusiasts who at the time worked as a schoolteacher and a social worker in Karlskrona, Sweden, where he grew up and where he now works as a librarian. Before moving back to his hometown, he studied English translation, then library information science, at Linnaeus University in Växjö, and in 2008, he took a class at Gotham Writers' Workshop in New York while living in Queens.

Dawning Wonder

Johan Stiel

———————————————
—

Dawning Wonder

Vanguard Press

VANGUARD PAPERBACK

© Copyright 2024
Johan Stiel

The right of Johan Stiel to be identified as author of
this work has been asserted by him in accordance with the
Copyright, Designs and Patents Act 1988.

All Rights Reserved

No reproduction, copy or transmission of this publication
may be made without written permission.
No paragraph of this publication may be reproduced,
copied or transmitted save with the written permission of the
publisher, or in accordance with the provisions
of the Copyright Act 1956 (as amended).

Any person who commits any unauthorised act in relation to
this publication may be liable to criminal
prosecution and civil claims for damages.

A CIP catalogue record for this title is
available from the British Library.

ISBN 978 1 80016 729 2

This is a work of fiction. Names, characters, businesses, places,
events and incidents are either the product of the author's imagination or
used in a fictitious manner. Any resemblance to actual persons, living or
dead, or actual events is purely coincidental

Vanguard Press is an imprint of
Pegasus Elliot Mackenzie Publishers Ltd.
www.pegasuspublishers.com

First Published in 2024

Vanguard Press
Sheraton House Castle Park
Cambridge England

Printed & Bound in Great Britain

For Karin.

Part I
Summer Sunrise

-1-

Niels squinted up at the lime-green hot-air balloon that at last stood ready to board. Newly filled with heat, it had the look of a thing about to burst. A thing of beauty. One he'd used his inheritance to construct, as the Scholars' Society had only agreed to cover the costs of the meteorological instruments.

He smiled then at the freckled grinning face of his twin sister, Aurora, nearly a mirror image of him if you took away her softer features. Her big blue-green eyes flicked to his, then back to the balloon, her every look sparkling approval, while her flashing motion – turning her head so fast her chestnut braids whipped – came with dependable vigorous enthusiasm.

While his chest puffed out like a balloon, she now dashed through tall, hunched straws that had stretched their full lengths to the burning blue sky to drink fresh summer light. He tried to keep up with his twin's near-frenzied pace as she reached the mule-driven wagon on which she'd come at full dust-raising speed. With bouncy liveliness she went straight from the wagon to the ladder hanging from the side of the wicker basket, now shadowed by the inflated balloon, and... did she carry a tiny furry thing in the crook of her arm?

His voice came out high-pitched. "What is *that?*"

"Why, my guinea pig, of course. You've been working so hard on your balloon, having twenty different craftsmen working on the gas bag alone, that you missed that I got two little ones months ago. One is coming with us on our maiden flight, and then, if all goes well, on the ex—"

"No. Not a chance. In no way or form will you bring a guinea pig with you on my expedition."

"I told you I would take him with me."

"When?"

"In the letter."

"What letter?"

"Well, I haven't sent the letter to you yet, as I have been too busy preparing for our departure with Hoodlum."

"Who the hell is Hoodlum?"

"My bravest guinea pig. It's all in the letter. Here it is." She pulled out a sealed letter from her chest pocket. "My terms for coming with you."

"I don't *want* you to come with me if you're doing this."

"That's because you haven't read my terms yet. You can read it on the way. It's mostly about Hoodlum. You'll find that what he lacks in ways he makes up for in form. Bandit had to stay at home, as he has a nervous disposition. Could I have the honour to untie the anchor lines?"

He rolled his eyes. Sighed. "Wait. First, sparkling wine."

"Should you really be drinking right before flight?"

"It's not for drinking. For the naming ceremony."

"*Ooh!*" She rapidly clapped her hands. "She's got a name!"

"She'll bear our mother's name. Here's to you, *Nita.*"

*

Almost a year had passed since Aurora, who used to chide her mother for neglecting sleep, for the very last time had urged her to go to bed, the night before her surgery. The surgery that would claim the life of the one who had given life to Aurora. "Mother, you need your rest. Turn out the light after this page. You can continue when we get back."

"Here we go again. You know, you usually call me by my name. It's ironic how you only call me Mother when you speak to me as though I'm a child."

Yet at that moment, Aurora did see the girl her mother once had been. A glimpse of a spell over Nita's face, an open-gazed, unguarded glow of lost innocence, her humour lit with childlike hope for all pain to wash away. Aurora had dropped her eyes and screwed them shut to stem the tide of tears, then quickly looked up, and hid the pang with an outwardly cheery smile.

"You're reading his favourite exploration novel again, aren't you, Nita?"

"No. *Wilderness Howls* was the dearest book to him."

"Niels would be happy to hear that."

"He loves it, too, I know. The one thing the two had in common, I suppose. How did he fare today?"

"An overwhelming reaction, far different from yesterday."

"I should have known that the mercantile financed scientists would be kinder to his balloon project."

"Today, if there were boos, they were quite drowned out by the eager applause of the members who wanted to make it deafeningly clear that they weren't like the royal researchers and so wouldn't mind to be daring and give an atmospheric scientist a fighting chance to test his wild hypotheses. But as we walked home, he said he feared he couldn't live up to their hopes and expectations. Then he divulged that he had already abandoned his idea to use the balloon to prove that our world is protected by a magnetic force which can't be seen, except near the north pole, in the celestial phenomenon after which I'm named. With a shaky voice he said that instead of measuring magnetism, he would be the first to come back with a map of the Forbidden."

"If that is what his heart truly desires, then let him. Though I will fear for him, I know he won't be living a full, happy life if I don't allow him to risk it. He has my blessing in this foolish, foolish, endeavour, should he one day pursue it."

"He's a foolish, foolish young man."

"But you must promise me to never, ever go with him if that is where his heart takes him. Because that place is where science and faith both crumble. It's the edge of the chaos beyond creation. Promise me you won't follow him into it."

"I promise so."

Hours earlier, walking home with her brother from the auditorium of the Scholars' Society of Kullum, funded by the city's merchant guild, she had said to him, "Take me with you."

"I'd like to, but Mother won't want you to be sucked into it. It's hard enough to ask for her financial support."

"I told her you were worried about that and she said, 'If it makes him happy, then no cost is too high'."

"That doesn't sound like her."

"Well, I can't do her voice. I'm asking you again. *Please* take me with you. Promise me you will, or I can't help you, and if I can't, then I can't be the same sister you know and love."

And he'd said, "I promise so."

*

After their toast, Niels swallowed the strawberry wine slowly, wondering what his sister was thinking about.

His eyes dropped from her flushed face to the sky-blue summer dress she wore for the occasion, a luxurious flowing fabric following her dancelike movement light as air—his suit appearing cheap and his posture an unintended joke in comparison. Then, as she woke from her reveries, having sipped with faraway eyes, she said, "We hereby name you Nita," and smashed the bottle against a steel anchor with eager swiftness. And right then, a happy, bright memory of her flashed inside. That time at the posh club of the Scholars' Society when a fresh-faced student, just barely old enough to be granted entrance in this establishment, had struck up a conversation with her. Aurora had talked faster than the fellow could follow. The fellow wore, along with an overthought, fashion-fixated dapper suit and tie, a perpetually confused look on his face, like a man who didn't speak the language and translated each word separately before putting it all together in a sentence, by the time it was several sentences later.

As she'd paused in her lively sharing of her love of aviation, the young fellow naively inquired, "Say, shouldn't you have a flag on your balloon to show from where you hail?"

He'd turned his gaze her way in time to catch sight of her calmly shaking her head, a devilish glint in her eye, and in the left corner of her mouth, he'd seen a shadowy hint of one of her lopsided smiles.

"All flags are a waste of perfectly good cloth." She'd been clearly amused by how the inexperienced lad seemed to hiccup at this assertion. She'd smiled a warm, kind smile then, though looked like a she-wolf grinning over a skittish cub whose shyness she found endearing. "We all hail from the same tiny globe," she'd then said, waving for the bartender to fill the first of many glasses of wine for the young fellow. "Whether the same air we breathe is produced by trees here or on the other side of it."

Another vivid memory immediately followed. The moment when he'd been certain that his sister had felt his pain as though it had been her own. It was just after he broke up with Merinna, who he'd wanted to fall in love with but hadn't. Merinna, his study partner at the time, had agreed when he'd said he thought they worked better as friends. When he went to study with her later that same day, she'd smiled as she'd opened the door, yet there were black streaks under her kohl-painted eyes. A melancholy mess, like a snowdrift, melted to the ground. She wiped it away and smiled on, there in her doorway, but there were still traces of it left. Hard to look at. The pain of it, seeing her carefully painted eyes ruined like that. It made a mess of him. But then, there it was, the bittersweet ending to that memory. He remembered sitting on his sister's bed that day, remembered crying, remembered her comforting him. Her arms had been around him. With her warmth, she'd taken away his pain, and for as long as she'd held him, it had been the only thing that mattered to him.

What had happened to him since then?

What was this thing he had set in motion, that had pulled his sister into it as well, this thing he couldn't stop?

They would both have safety lines attached to their waists at all times up there. If ever she fell out of the basket and couldn't haul herself back up, he promised himself he would climb down to her and add his strength to hers to bring her out of harm's way. It was either both or neither of them. Should she fall out of the sky at the edge of the known world, Nita's basket would reach the unknown empty. Apart from Hoodlum, that is.

Though he didn't believe in heaven, he loved to picture Nita there. He imagined her smiling now, reading his mind.

-2-

Leina Greenbow, light of hair like savannah grass and innocent as a cub discovering its fangs, had filled her girlhood with wildness.

Years before her adolescence, her wild heart had ached to express that burning within which craved adventure, in the hope that somebody would recognise it as their own fire.

Before she'd learned to read and she'd been with her playmate Juniet, she would speak incessantly, always looking for words, always stumbling as she spoke words that never seemed big enough. Even when silent with Juniet she seemed to speak, with her glances, her blushes, her heart as fast as a young bird's wingbeat, beating with an insistent longing too big for her chest. An unvoiced fondness, loud with her sprinting pulse, her silence had held the expectancy of a folded note pushed under a door.

She grew bigger, grew wilder still, always looking for what she couldn't find, what she had felt in the wildness of her dreams.

She had been a breathless girl, lost to raptures of play and dreaming. She had invented games and dances for her and her friends to play and dance, and she had come up with stories and jokes to make them gape and laugh. She had imagined feverishly, dreamt up things beyond what even far-knowing divinities could have foreseen.

And she had been an adolescent given to fits of blushing, her cheeks flushing as often with embarrassment as with lust, chasing after thrills that slipped out of her grasp like fish.

She had loved boys fiercely, felt broken when they didn't love her back and felt mended in the arms of girls who lent their shoulder to cry on, as she shared her ardour with their heat.

But then, over the threshold of womanhood, it all ended.

On entering her youth, she'd lost sight of her happiness.

Was it that she came to know too much about the world and how disappointingly inadequate it was, compared to all it could and should have been?

Was it that she no longer could see herself clearly, like she could as a feral child of dirty pale-gold hair and daring blue eyes?

Or was it that the dreams she once had, once clung to with a passionate strength bigger than her, now seemed unattainable?

Was it just life?

All she knew was that something was sorely, achingly missing. That she had lost her spark. Her eyes no longer shone like the sky. Left was but a faint glow, and she feared it would go away, too, that even the yellow colour within her blue irises, radiating in hair-thin streams like captured sunrays, would fade away like dying embers.

She dreaded that even the colourful memory of it would soon be lost – this lust for life she'd loved to death – irretrievably.

And so all through her youth, she had waited for its return.

She had grown taller than all the other girls in the plantations and had welcomed it, hoping fulfilment awaited at her full maturity, hoping it would come like blooming beauty.

On and on she'd grown. Eventually, she'd surpassed the height of every girl in the village of Dophra, where she had studied under private tutorship with five other privileged girls, who had looked like small children when placed next to her. And she hadn't stopped growing. With each new inch added to her height, it had seemed she had inched one step closer to the happiness she'd waited for since her naive girlhood had faded.

When her growing finally levelled out, after sixteen years since her birth, she stood possibly taller than any woman in the world. At her full height, she'd reached six feet and four inches. Which intimidated all boys. This didn't bother her, as only men, and only the tallest kind, found their way into her fantasies. Her sheer fifty-inch legs, almost two-thirds of her body, gave her an appearance of a young giraffe. And her towering body would make even tall boys shy. She had loved this about herself.

But even this love hadn't been enough. What she'd waited for hadn't come.

She had woken and stood up in the morning sun, her room flooded with light like hope, and had cried without knowing why.

She had fallen in love with music, and all had paled next to the sunburst elation of a song that spoke to her heart because it knew her heart intimately. She felt it close, but it hadn't come.

She had kissed a well-built, dark-skinned stable boy whose height was level with hers. Her heart had flamed with excitement and her skin colour had almost changed to mirror his with her passion – as of course happens to girls like her when pleasure overwhelms them completely – and yet it would not come.

She had had sex with this same boy, and the colour of her skin and eyes did change to his, as his emotion became hers. But soon after, she'd felt empty again, because it wasn't it. Though he'd been heavenly and though the two of them had come on the same shuddering beat, what she'd waited for hadn't come for her.

She had been desperate for it to come, and had done that which scared her the most, defying her intense fear of heights as she had climbed to the very top of the highest oak in a nearby grove. Doing it on a dare, a challenge that *she* had initiated. Climbing towards high courage, for a wild rush. Hoping this was what she'd longed for. It hadn't come.

She had succeeded in getting perfect scores on tests at the end of the last semester of her tutorage. It hadn't come.

She had drunk herself to various stages of drunkenness on many occasions after that. She'd run with dogs, scaled walls, howled at the moon, touched roses no one else could and felt kissed by the sky and touched by muses, and still the thrill of mayhem and raising hell didn't outlast the night. It never came.

She had even gone out on an adventure with her best friend, had felt her small, taut waist held tightly as she'd ridden her father's racing horse as if death chased them, had braved a strange forest until hunger got her and urged her home, and her friend had cried with relief. But even that didn't bring it to her.

And so here she was, at the very height of her youth, aged eighteen, and she was desperate to have what she'd waited for since growing into womanhood for the past six years.

And this was why she, at the zenith of the summer, as heat and light inundated the world, came to hate her father more than ever and went against all he stood for.

Why she would love to break his heart.

*

Kyra had grown up experiencing far too many fearful nights. Agonizing dreams of being chased, echoes of a fever dream from when she'd shaped her first memories, the barking hound that had hunted her until she'd woken up screaming. Sporadically throughout her girlhood, the nightmares came, releasing chasing beasts which she had no name for. Later she would call them demons, of the terror they made her feel, such as you aren't supposed to suffer so early in life. A recurring nocturnal torment she had trouble forgetting, it had made her sick, too ill to eat. Only when she managed to forget her nightly suffering did her appetite return. But when hunger came, it was ferocious. Like a feline animal she would live for food, never have her fill. But then, another dream of horror, and she was sick again. Her body seemed to refuse to let her swallow anything down that would feed the badness inside that she couldn't translate into words.

With time she had grown thinner, having at some point lost her voracious appetite before she ever knew satiety. At the first signs on her girl's body of the woman's physique she would slowly acquire, she had chosen to dull her senses by making herself throw up, to feel in control, to empty her body to be empty of emotion rather than mad with fear. Only as puberty fully set in did the terrible demon-dreams go away, and the unfair pain they'd brought her ebbed, slowly letting her dare to feel safe.

These days, she often felt an immense relief that her fragile girlhood was over. Now old enough to be her own person, she only needed money to emancipate herself from her father and move out of his farmhouse. To then feel *invulnerable*.

*

It was plain that to Leina's father, her protests were that of a child that would come to her senses. That Leina would later thank him for having guided her to her destiny, the title of consequence, a name echoed at each mention of the title bearer's land. Anything other than this equation were childish miscalculations, and if she didn't submit to this, she wouldn't be who he thought, couldn't be the daughter of his heart, whose well-being depended on him.

He'd probably had plans for her all her life, yet it was only this summer, in her last year as a pupil to her carefully chosen tutor, that she knew for certain what these plans entailed. It was his wish that she, unlike her two older brothers, wouldn't go away to pursue higher learning at one of the realm's most prestigious academies. He had decided she should soon marry, and he had already selected with whom: a merchant son from a family as rich as hers. Their impending marriage would merge their dynasties. A final decision he couldn't withdraw. For her to be a loyal wife, and dutiful mother, this and nothing else, for the rest of her life. This, though he knew how she'd yearned to choose her own path as a student of music, to discover the secrets of masters who she couldn't wait to learn from. And yet he did this to her.

He utterly humiliated his wild-dreaming daughter.

She rebelled in a way he would utterly hate.

She did it as soon as he and her mother left. They would be gone for the rest of the summer, travelling to meet landowners in neighbouring provinces whose land he wanted, leaving her alone with their servants while he expanded his business. She told the supervisor of the banana field workers that her father desired her to work in the fields for the rest of the summer, as punishment.

"Punishment for what, Milady?" the supervisor asked.

Stone-faced, she replied, "An offence of a private nature."

He knew better than to pursue it further. Being who she was, she already had him in the palm of her hand.

And this was why she found herself in the wagon going into the chlorophyll-shimmering, life-booming fields she had only seen from afar. Heading into the fields that stretched out farther than the eye could reach, all of which belonged to her father, all of which her family deemed beneath her to set foot in, let alone work in. She'd always dreamt of becoming a banana girl, for her body to be an instrument useful to the world rather than a useless ornament. But for a noble girl like her, this would be scandalous, unheard of. Her parents would be appalled if word reached them that she'd subjected herself to the grime of physical labour. Willingly covering herself in sweat and filth. She imagined them seeing her now, imagined their disgust. *How could she?*

Not long before they left, they'd been talking about her, loud enough for their daughter to overhear it in the other room. The lord and lady of the manor took more care to be discrete if others were close by. Had the maids been there, they would have heard their lord say, *"She thinks she can manipulate me with tears. I simply won't have it!"* She had nothing to say to him after that.

For many other girls, it would be enough to simply be born into her family, heiress to a rich landowner. But to only have and never give left her empty. So, she had followed her passion to where its heat led her and had taken lessons from vocalists this year to one day give the world her songs. If war struck and they were to lose all, title and land and they'd be scraped bare, she believed she could survive as a taverna singer. Her father had mocked this idea. He could never understand. She could live with this. What truly hurt was that her mother hadn't stood up for her.

But now, bouncing along with the others at the back of the wagon in the thickening heat of the morning, she almost smirked. The only girl in the wagon full of young men who were brawny and bronzed from labouring hard in the southern sun. The first girl to go and work in the fields in ages. It was rare work for girls for a reason. To carry and load the banana bunches required raw strength. But if they'd started with little strength, it gave them more of it in return, no less so for girls. No less so for the girl whose father owned these fields of bananas, melons and dates in the south of Kalid. Yet the only women who had come to work in the fields of this plantation had been broad in build.

Leina wasn't. She was made of other stuff.

But she could change. She could surprise them, and wipe the grin off their faces. She would be sharp, alert, and attentive when they carried out their tasks, to learn faster than they had when they were new. That would teach them not to dismiss her so easily, which they already did, indicated by the open mocking and condescending looks she received. Their exchanged glances seemed to say, *I know, man. She won't last a day.*

*

Kyra balled her deep-tanned hand into a fist, her other hand aggressively pushing a glossy, sweat-slicked strand of jet-black hair away from her hot face. Her brother had ruined her young life before it began in earnest, but the soldiers had absolutely no right to do this, taking him away from their farm. Now and then he looked back over his shoulder with pathetic puppy eyes. Her parents' presence behind her was an old, grim silence.

She didn't care what her farther would say. She was going to let these men know exactly what they were worth to her.

And in a fiery blaze of having every right, she let it out, and in the shout erupting through a tight throat that felt like an overstrained muscle, she heard her emotion. Outflashing the words that tore out of her, the blaze was the sound of a voice breaking apart to be heard. "I'd spit in your face," her shout flame-lashed at their uniformed backs. "If it hadn't meant I had to look at you! To call you fools would be an insult to fools! Fools don't stoop as low as you bullying, buggering sadists who take pleasure in following senseless orders, jailing us farmers whose yield you depend on, while you yourselves produce *nothing!* You're a bunch of cowards, preying on those you perceive as weak, and because you hate everyone but yourselves, you want our world to capsize, just so you can point your finger, while the rest of us are trying to get everything back on an even keel! In a just world, you would either undo this or perish from shame!"

*

On Leina's first day out in the fields, the field they took her to was treeless, yet full of wild tangling shoots. An old man waiting there was untying ropes attached to fallen rods, which had been used to prop up the tallest banana palms last season. The trees in this section had been cut down to make way for new trees to be planted this fall. They were tasked to tear the heavy iron rods out from under thick clinging weeds. To then lift the rods up on the cart, using only the power of their arms. It was beyond gruelling work. She had to carry and lift as much as them, and they gave her no quarter, gave her only the least possible amount of help.

"You never told them whose daughter I am, did you?" she said to the supervisor, out of earshot of the others.

He gave her a slanted smile and a wink. "Should I have?"

"No. You'd be the last to know why I'm punished."

Right now, she didn't feel bad that she was lying to him, letting him believe she was being punished, while she only did this to satisfy her curiosity and to make her father furious.

It was starting to feel like a real punishment all too quickly.

Before the end of the first hour, since they'd gotten out of the wagon's shelter and shade, she was covered in dirt and soaked with sweat. The sun beat down on her relentlessly. But she refused to show them how tired she was.

By the end of the day, she was on the verge of fainting.

It was a fatigue she could never have been prepared for. She hadn't known a person could be this spent.

After they left her off at the gate of her manor, physical exhaustion made her stagger as soon as she was out of their vicinity. She stumbled to bed without bothering to take her clothes off and slept as soon as her face hit the pillow. She woke up at midnight with her stomach screaming for nourishment, a loudness inside her that was only outmatched by the deafening ache in her muscles that seemed to bust out of the seams of her sinews. Stiff like the rods she had hoisted up on the cart all day, she could hardly lift a finger, there in her bed. Her arms shook as she made an attempt to get up to get something to eat. She closed her eyes and found sleep take her easily again.

Her eyelids remained shut until the cock crowed at dawn.

This was the day they counted flowers, which drooped crimson with the budding fruit that would ripen for the picking a month away. As they taught her how to use the blue strings to tie around the trees that had flowered, they seemed reluctantly impressed that she hadn't given up. She began to look for flowers above her on her designated path, squinting hard. The sun pierced through powerfully, her lashes nearly sealing her gaze to the intensely green world around her. It disoriented her, the colour, the light. It became ever harder to think, to recall anything but this intensity. The flowers had to look a particular way, had to have a certain size, a specific crimson colour. She found it honed the eye.

Four hours of this, then it was time for the primary backbreaking feat of working in the banana fields. The supervisor and another middle-aged, grey-haired fellow, the same man who had gathered all the rope from the rods yesterday, got out their machetes. Selecting trees marked with red strings from a month ago, they cut off the ripe bunches for her and the boys to carry. On some trees, there were yellow strings, trees whose flowers had been counted early in the season and would yield even bigger produce. She couldn't imagine how muscle-breaking those bunches would be to carry a whole day, as the ones she had to take were as heavy as a six-year-old kid. They'd shown her how to balance the bunches on her shoulder, and the juice spilt down on her shirt and dripped in under her belt. It stung the scrapes on her shoulder muscles, where the hard, green bananas cut into her skin like blunt knives. The gloves they'd given her quickly stiffened from the dirt and the juice, and she hated how they felt on her hands. Already toughened, she bore it in silence.

But she loved the smell.

When she got home, she slept an hour, then showered until she almost shivered. Then, in the dining hall, she ate alone, and felt like a sleepwalker as she moved with her tray full of food. Her biceps were taut, an inner strength waking up, stinging swollen, a raw power bulging so fast it seemed fit to rip her skin open.

Back in her room, she found that the juice from the cut stems of the trees had stained her underwear beyond rescue. She put them in the waste bucket. She would have to wear nothing underneath her work clothes tomorrow.

Her sleep unbroken, she woke up refreshed to her third day, proud to have lasted longer than they'd thought. It made her cocky enough to look up from the table in the shed in which they sat and ate breakfast, and wrinkle her nose at the decoration on the wall. Old drawings of naked women in lude positions. She glared at these images with unmasked disgust, until she saw that at least one of them noticed it. Of course, he snickered.

This time, she did smirk.

On the fourth day, heading to the field with the biggest bunches, the boys sang in unison, a song that was popular now in the old barns they called dance halls. They didn't care how they sounded or looked, lazed on their backs on the cart, their voices both soft and loud, silly, carefree boys. She found herself singing with them. They smiled at her then. She was one of them, and she surprised herself at how it felt. She didn't hate it.

But something was still missing.

At the end of that day, she'd carried such heavy bunches that her body seemed upset with her, her muscles trembling as if afraid that she was trying to kill her body.

On the mare-pulled cart, going back to the stallion-pulled wagon that would take her home. That was when she dared open her mouth and ask them, "What happened to that girl you spoke of on the first day? The one you laughed about. Who was big and tall and ate so many eggs at each breakfast?"

"Amaida," said Hanosh, who was broad-chested and washboard stomached like a boxer. "Yeah, she went crazy."

Later that same afternoon, after what Hanosh had said made her quit work before the others, she left the fields of green-gold heat. To see Amaida. She needed to know what had happened to the last girl who, like her, had worked her body to utter exhaustion in the banana fields.

There was a basket full of clothes on the porch as Leina knocked on her door, and Leina recalled that the boys had said she now worked in the laundry. *Did she bring the work home?* Leina joked to herself, smiling, hoping her buoyant mood would hold.

Amaida didn't seem deranged or even daft. Her unkempt frizzy hair did give her a crazy look, but her eyes were sharp and moved with intent. She offered Leina lemonade, and they sat down on the porch, Amaida waiting for Leina to state her errand.

"Why did you quit?" Leina asked.

Amaida hesitated. Cagily, she said, "I told them things they didn't want to hear. Especially the supervisor."

"Oh."

So, she hadn't quit. The supervisor had fired her. Had he fired other girls who had tried to switch from their duties in the plantation's kitchen or barn? Leina knew milkmaids who'd love to have a go of the fields, to be relieved of worn out tasks whose monotony every now and then left them feeling emptied. Had it been fear stopping them from asking?

Amaida unhurriedly said, "Everybody hates being assigned to the laundry. It's not so bad. And I'm on a rota now, so I'm switching with a kitchen maid every other—"

"What did you say that rubbed them the wrong way?"

"I just told them who I saw in my vision, not what this being told me."

"They said you had sunstroke and never came fully back."

"Maybe I did. But I saw a goddess from another world."

*

Many times, Kyra's mother had seen Kyra direct her worst anger inward, against her complex over her unusual tallness. It had been there to see in how Kyra occasionally stooped, in how she this way tried to make herself appear less looming. Her mother, a tall woman herself, always told her to straighten up, but she'd rather have a weak posture than draw unwanted attention to her mannish height. And now, seeing those men in uniform turn their eyeballs at her with a hint of amusement, Kyra wished for that anger to possess her again. So that the more hurting anger, against a world she couldn't change, would stop.

But no. She had to fly in the face of them all, in front of the woman who'd brought her to this unfair world.

She hurled a new husky yell, "Don't look at me, you bastards!"

And now her mother said her name softly to calm her, as though she thought that it was herself Kyra hated most, that she couldn't stand to be evaluated by male eyes, which no longer was true. Yes, she did shout at them not to look at her, but it wasn't because she was self-conscious about her outlandish height.

If they went on looking at her like that, she didn't know what she might do.

She went silent all the same.

Beginning to shake with storming thoughts of violence.

As her mother mistook her rage.

As her mother stopped her from picking up a stone to throw at the soldiers taking her brother away.

Silent all along as her mother said, "Steady your tongue. When they bark at trees, the trees don't bark back. Don't look back at them. Steady now, as that ash tree, the pride of my garden. See how tall trees flower only at reaching their full height. When you're full-grown, the sky will open, the rain will fall, and all of this will fall off with the dirt, and then you'll find it."

"Find what?"

"What you're looking for. You don't have words for it now, but you know what it means when you reach it."

"What did it mean for you, when *you* were searching for it?"

"You." Her mother's eyes filled up with the fullness of her emotion that suddenly shone with liquid shivering. Behind her mother's back, her father turned and aimed his steps to the barn, where he quite possibly would whip the trespassing creature that her brother had come home with, bewitched. Her mother seemed unaware, now saying, "But every heart is *different,* and so your meaning might be found in a place as blessed with childlessness as my place has been blessed with you."

But it wasn't enough to have and know only instinctual love. She wanted a chosen love. Would she have loved her brother if they hadn't had the same blood? She'd never chosen him to be in her life. But she had loved him, and because she had, she hated what the female beast had done to him. Making him forget that he was a corn farmer with responsibilities to his family, making him flee the real world. In parts of the real world, vile, abhorrent liaisons such as this were punishable by stoning.

Only a demoness can make a man risk such pain, such shame.

A demoness that had utterly changed Kyra's life along with his. Kyra used to have more time to tend to their chickens and ride Lopo, her beloved horse. But after Remin had changed, she had to work in the field in his stead. The demonic beast in the barn was to blame, and in her angriest moments, Kyra hated and despised this beast so much that she wanted to see her stoned.

These creatures didn't belong here and should be driven away from the human realm, to where they couldn't be seen, to be forever gone, forgotten. She'd told her brother this, told him she was sickened by his taboo, but that it wasn't his fault.

He had looked at her with stricken eyes full of bewildering meaning, which she couldn't decipher in a thousand years.

*

The word *'goddess'* echoed over *'from another world'*. And it rang even as Amaida took a breath and continued to explain. She told Leina she had truth in her heart, imparted by the goddess. A truth she feared to tell in its whole because it was undeniably dangerous. She said that she had a very bad feeling as if she might die if she told this truth. She couldn't say why.

Leina didn't know what came over her. She put her glass of lemonade down, leaned forward until the porch creaked, and said she would have her fired if she didn't tell her the secret.

And in the fading light, sitting there on her dusty porch, the dry air full of the first chirping of crickets, Amaida whispered the secret. She said that at next summer's zenith, in the middle of the day, the sky would turn purple and the Forbidden would vanish.

Hearing this, Leina opened up to what opened like a flower unfolding, a secret promise, bigger than anything.

And just like that, at long last, that nameless thing she had been striving and hoping for, dying to have it for so long.

It came.

-3-

The first soldier in his troop fell to the sun-drenched, hard steppe ground a second after the hail of arrows began.

Two more in the vanguard fell in the following second.

One of them yelped like a kicked dog, the other not making any sound at all, at least not anything that reached Kruso's young ears and keen hearing in the chaos of it all.

He saw their bodies fall, two young men in their mid-twenties, like him and Edeline. His breath froze to a stop in his chest at the thought that his fiancé might've been hit. But no, she had her shield up. Relief washed over him, to see in the shield's shadow the oval, dark-brown face he loved more than anything. She now squatted to present as small a target as possible, and he blinked, seeing her through a thick heat haze that made all in his large-eyed wide-open view undulate as if about to evaporate.

Stars flit like fireflies before his eyes. So lightheaded now, every fear fading—yet every thought as well. And then, just like slipping between two dream states, he wasn't there any more.

He was thirteen, awash in blinding sunlight and exploding chlorophyll, heading again to the river with same-aged Drein, the first person in his life he'd lost himself in completely, loving him like joy, because Drein *was* a joy. Seeing again Drein run ahead, dark of hair and eye, light-brown of skin, a freckled thin face, hued by sun and thrill, casting back a challenging grin. Drein was teaching him about courage, and now they were diving together, smiling underwater at each new record of breath-holding, punching fists up through the surface and hugging in exuberance. Two boys with a sweet secret, that they'd go to the ocean, to dive for oysters and sell the pearls for boards, to ride waves so big that they could kill you if you weren't made for them if your lungs didn't measure up to the size of their devastating seduction.

And suddenly, inside the moment when their secret began, he was twelve, standing on a faraway beach with Drein whose eyes glittered abundant with light like the sea that day. "Would you dare?" Drein had said, the two of them seeing waveriders for the first time. "Dare me."

Somebody shook him. Kruso said, "What happened?"

Edeline's hands, pulled him up, to share half her shield. He was back amidst the chaos of being under attack. As his awareness came fully back, all he knew and could see was *her*.

She, the second person he'd ever lost himself in.

The girl who'd roused his pulse and awakened his heat.

The only one who could really hurt him, but who hurt as much as him—he saw and knew it now, too late.

He should've told her that he trusted her when she said she had her drinking under control, that it won't happen again, that she won't let it. Why hadn't he given her more, when having all the world's gold wouldn't come close to what he had in the looks she'd given only him? All past hurts gone, the repair of just one smiling look that can only be understood by the heart.

Now, flashes of when she'd been new to him and she'd looked at him with furtive eyes, eyes that said she wanted him for what she saw in him. The time he walked on clouds when she first told him she was in love with him, making him just as new.

When did he see it, that those who give us our deepest happiness in life are also the ones who can give us our deepest wounds? For all she hurt him, he feared for her life more than for his. He could've left her, to ensure that he wouldn't feel that hurt again, but then he'd ensured that he'd never feel the sweetest happiness he'd ever had again. Unbidden, a question came to him. *Is this what we see before we die? How true happiness is born of true love and true love is born of true risk?*

Wide-eyed and unblinking, he stared at her in the shadow under her round shield, praying this wouldn't be his last look.

Her jet-black tight-coiled hair stood springy as heather in a round short-cropped arch over her fine-boned countenance.

Her small yet strong pointed chin and the narrow tapering jawline slanted with the exact corresponding degree on each side.

Her sharp-featured symmetry, the fine-boned brittleness, not a hint of a capacity to harm in that innocent softness.

How some appearances deceive.

An arrow hit her shield now, almost going all the way through. He pushed the shield so it covered only her. As long as she was in that crouching position, she'd make it. He, on the other hand, was shieldless, and he couldn't see where the arrows were coming from. Open steppe all around, but for the ridge ahead, with a scattering of thorn bushes amid the sparse yet dense tufts of grass. Presently, a new wave of arrows, now arcing above their heads, now falling steeply directly at them, hailing down on them, hitting whom they may. Yet the largest number of arrows seemed to strike down on those in the front.

To his right, Hanid, a new friend and confidante of his fiancé, took an arrow to the chest, and as he thudded to the hardpacked sand between steppe tufts, the last oxygen in his lungs bubbled out of his mouth with the blood he coughed up until his eyes stilled a second later and moved and blinked no more.

Three more soldiers fell – two of whom were young women who Kruso had only known for a few days – before the captain gave the order in a hoarse yell, *"We yield!"*

The white flag came immediately from the last forerunner left standing. Kruso turned his eyes to the dying faces of the fallen female soldiers, a memory flash lingering: those two girls braiding one another's hair this morning. He presently saw their eyelids close, and his own eyes blinked, before his gaze flung up to the lance from which a white flag waved over their heads.

And the hail of heavy, razor-sharp arrows stopped.

The steppe had a smell of burnt grass, a smoky thickness to the heat. A shrill cry pierced the torrid, heavy air, sounding not much different from the war cry that had preceded the onslaught.

All along the ridge, half-naked, red-painted tall warriors arose from behind the thorn bushes. Their skin glared pale where it wasn't painted, unlike the dark-skinned peaceful tribes who these nomads had pushed away on their sacred journey from northern to southern permafrost. As they one by one, one redhaired head after another, came into view, Kruso saw that they were all male. None of them were young, unlike the men and women of Kruso's troop who lay killed or severely wounded.

Captain Brind was gagged and bound. Everyone else in the decimated troop was trusted not to run or protest, as there was not one warrior among the small nomad army that didn't have their bows aimed at their prisoners. The heavily bleeding ones were put out of their misery. Those with flesh wounds and narrowly missed arteries, a few young new-recruits, were patched up and pushed onto the backs of who among the survivors stood closest. As they were shoved on their way, Kruso took Edeline's hand and she squeezed it, then let go. She seemed to be too angry to cry. Hanid, who she got close to when she'd needed somebody other than Kruso to talk to, was gone. Kruso suspected Hanid had favoured men rather than women, but he supposed he would never know now. He wondered what his fiancé was thinking, but then decided, seeing the way she looked at their captors, he didn't want to know.

None knew the language of these barbarians who wandered from polar region to polar region. Yet ... The more he strained to really listen and focus on it, the more he recognised it. A dialect of Rya, the one nomad language he had chosen to study, due to the botanical knowledge of their shamans. His deep interest in potent subpolar flowers had indeed been the reason why he had set about learning their tongue in the first place. But these men, though clearly belonging to the deeply superstitious Rya tribes, wouldn't know about the magical healing properties of different floral specimens. They were hunter-warriors, with an abundant, never diminishing supply of beef from the wildebeest that proliferated the borderlands on their migration from the southernmost to the northernmost edge of the two continents. They wouldn't know, would they, about the unusual effects of the blue pimlocks of these outlands near the subtropics? Flowers he'd collected and put in a dense pack on the top of his rucksack.

Once, he'd made Edeline's smile with tender wonder, sitting up straight in bed, listening with attentive yet pensive eyes while habitually pinching her plump openmouthed lips. As he'd told her botanical facts that fascinated him. He'd felt safe then that she wouldn't look at another man that way. She'd touched his elbow and her dark-brown skin had deeper darkened with passion, as welcome as a raincloud to a desert.

He wouldn't give up hope that she would make him feel like that once more. If only he had it in him to properly forgive her. He needed to survive to find out.

Kruso moved closer to the chieftain, who wore a headdress of red feathers and was the only one not covered in black and red war paint. At the chieftain's side, one of the tallest warriors presently said in that odd dialect what amounted to, *"They can't understand a word we're saying. They must think that you are the head of the clan."*

And the man who apparently wasn't the chieftain said what Kruso understood as, *"Let them think that. Send a bird to my father. He shall return tomorrow and see them bled dry in the Blood Ceremony. I tell you,"* and here he said unfamiliar words Kruso couldn't string together and give meaning.

But then he did understand what followed, as the son of the chieftain said, *"They are lucky. If my father hadn't been on a hunt, he would have bled them himself on this very battlefield. My only worry is that bringing them to our homestead will bring bad luck."* And then the other man said something Kruso didn't understand, before the chieftain's son retook with, *"Rya-Sih-Ro."* Apparently the name of the secret interpreter. *"Don't for one second let them suspect that you know their language. You used to be our emissary in their lands, and now, as soon as we reach camp, you shall guard their leader. Listen to what he says to these ridiculously dressed warriors. Before my father returns and will have them all killed, I intend to learn as much from these foreigners as I can."*

Then they spoke about things he didn't understand at all, and so he fell back to walk by Edeline's side again. But a man right behind her was shoving his spear onto her back and she increased her pace just as he decreased his. A sharp spearpoint came at him from behind then, hurting him without piercing the skin on his back. This was accompanied by a guttural growling word he couldn't interpret, yet which sounded like a swearword.

Kruso said, "Charming folk. Of the Rya tribe, I gather."

"Polar nomads, following migrating wildebeest. Every other year their warriors attack the peace-loving Azide river-tribes." Again, by the looks she shot the war-painted men, he felt that the harm she wished them would scare him if he could look inside her head. "And now these brutes attacked *us*, unprovoked, and they killed Hanid. If they're taking me to hell, I'll take at least one of these bastards with me."

From up ahead, he heard encouragements from his captain and replies of many men half-shouting with one voice. *"Stay strong!"*

"Yes, Tan!"

"We mustn't lose our spirit!"

"No, Tan!"

As they neared the tents of leather hides of the camp, about half an hour later, he once more felt the spearhead prodding at his back and another hissing word from the middle-aged, seemingly short-tempered nomad behind him. His brute force flared up every time Kruso's pace slowed more than he liked.

An idea had grown inside Kruso for the past half hour, making him feel as hopeful as his fiancé appeared to feel enraged.

She didn't know that he understood most of what these men were saying, that nomad languages had been a fascination of his in his school years, along with hard-to-find botanical knowledge. He couldn't risk losing his advantage by letting her in on it, but he could let her know that his spirit was strong. "Hey," he said, smiling at the old women herding goats and pigs in the middle of the camp that was one big dusty mess of hides and all sorts of domesticated animals. "I like what you haven't done with the place." Then, as the man behind him pushed him and spoke another litany of what sounded like the most vulgar swearwords he could think of, Kruso told his fiancé, "Is he angry, or just flirting? I can't tell with this fellow."

"I think you're one more joke away from getting your head chopped off."

"So you *do* think he's angry."

"I wasn't talking about him. I meant by me."

Again he was shoved forward. The man who kept pushing him barked words Kruso didn't understand, but it was a good bet that the imbecile was telling Kruso to shut up. Fed up with him, Kruso couldn't help biting back with, "The upside of being you, I suppose, would be that you never have to play stupid."

At that moment, he felt an itch between his shoulder blades, right at the place where a cruelly aimed arrow would've lamed him. For the first time, he feared being shot, thinking it could happen if one of them didn't like his smile. He wasn't afraid of pain. Pain always went away. But paralysis, this he feared more than death. He had to act now, or that fear might consume him. He looked over his shoulder, having an intense feeling that somewhere, among the nearly hundred barbarians with bows, one arrow pointed right at the place on his back that itched. That target, his spine.

In the corner of his eye, he saw Brind's mouth uncovered.

And so it was at this moment that he urged his fiancé with him to the vicinity of the man who knew the language of the civilization of Hanair's Reach. And spoke in a low voice to her.

"Listen carefully," he said. "I will tell you something very important. None of the others in the troop must know."

He saw her eye the tall man in front of her suspiciously.

"Don't worry," he said, even as he saw the secret interpreter slip back to walk in closer range. "These ridiculously painted barbarians don't understand a word we're saying. Now, you know how I threw away my best jacket, the only civilian garment I carried with me. The wine-red one. You called me 'Grape', because I looked like a red grape to you in it."

"Where are you going with this?"

"I threw that jacket away to make room for pimlock flowers in my rucksack. Once plucked, for days afterwards they will emit a scent that means five seasons of the worst kind of luck for anyone who, unlike us civilized people, eats meat. It doesn't matter if they throw it away, the long range of scent will reach the meat eater. The only way to stop the bad luck, of long seasons with absence of prey and failed hunts, is to burn the rucksack before the dangerous scent reaches their noses."

Hardly had he said that before the man who knew their language spun around and tore the rucksack from Kruso.

Minutes later, after the man had explained to the chieftain's son what he'd heard Kruso say, the son, as superstitious as the low-born among these folks, went straight to the rucksack. And threw it in a big fire outside the biggest tent, probably his father's. He called for all the people of his clan to gather. Smoke rose to the sky as the sun coloured the steppe gold and orange.

Kruso whispered in Edeline's ear. "They'll soon all be within its long range of fragrance. At my signal, take a deep breath, pinch your nose as hard as you can, then walk slowly backwards, away from the smoke."

As the first ring of people near the fire slumped like dropped bags of grain, Kruso winked at Edeline. She took a deep breath. The smoke reached the chieftain's son and the interpreter—they both fell. The rest of the gathering began to scramble away from the smoke. If they covered their mouths, the scent still entered the nostrils, and the scent was everywhere, the smoke lidding the camp. Even those who ran didn't get far before they stumbled to the ground, instantly unconscious.

Kruso found the reeds in the pond by a stroke of luck. He'd planned to get inside a tent and hope the smoke wouldn't seep in. But this was by far better. He broke the roundest reed in half, gave the longer one to Edeline, and then jumped into the pond with the other.

He'd just put it in his mouth and begun to breathe through it under the surface, his nostrils sealed by water, when he heard the splash of his fiancé following his lead.

It was maybe three-quarters of an hour later that they dared to emerge from below the pond. By then, the smoke had cleared.

Not a single soul could be found in the camp that wasn't heavily asleep. And he and Edeline looked at each other, shivering after a small eternity under water. Unspeaking, she took his hand, brought it to her trembling lips and kissed it.

The two of them tied up all those they'd seen in the tribe who had obviously had some role of authority or important function. They bound and knotted, bound and knotted until they didn't have any more rope to tie with. Then they filled a wagon with spears and bows, and drove it to a sweat lodge by the nearby river. They couldn't be sure that they would have time to destroy the weapons. Time was getting short. They needed the captain to be the first one awake. A bucket full of water poured on his face was just barely enough to wake him up.

*

It was on the day that followed, the day after they had buried the fallen, that Captain Brind called for him to wade alongside him through the shallow part of the river they were crossing. Having reached the other side, they let the sun dry them, watching the others come across the water slowly.

"You'll get a medal, as I already said after you woke me."

Kruso forced a smile. Why was it so hard to pretend now? "Thank you." For a second he forgot that Brind was his superior and should be addressed as such. "That is, I thank you, Tan."

"Let me speak to you as one man to another. You haven't seemed yourself in a while. You used to laugh all the time."

"Our spirits have their seasons, I suppose."

Not long ago, on the evening of Edeline's twenty-fourth birthday, before he had to leave her for two days of stealth training, he'd made her laugh. Such a sweet sound, larchlike, he'd laughed just from hearing it. It had been like before when he lived to think up things to make her laugh, and so he'd seemed to laugh through his days. Then, back from his training, the day before their deployment, he came upon her laughing with another man. How she then with guilty haste told him she'd made a mistake with that man the night before.

Why did he keep on thinking about that? He wasn't the jealous type, so why was he falling into that irrational trap?

The captain held a hand aloft to stop the ones approaching until he had finished what he had to say. His focus returned to Kruso, impatient to be satisfied.

"As you saved all our lives, we heeded your one wish, that we should only make a bonfire and destroy their weapons and leave their camp without harming them or taking prisoners. I see now the barb of that. As warriors without weapons, they'll be castrated, and humiliated for life. But how did you know that they didn't know about the flowers?"

"Do you know anything about what flowers can do?"

"I'm afraid not. What's your point?"

"Warriors and flowers don't go together. If you'd caught me picking those flowers, you'd made me into a laughing stock and would have tried to whip some toughness into me."

"Not if you'd told me about that narcotic power."

"You wouldn't have believed me. Those flowers are so rare that the knowledge about them comes from the sparsest of sources. It might even be that I found the last place in the last valley where they grow, that they're all but extinct. The ones that only emit scent when burned, whose seeds I had planned to save and plant, might very well have been a few of the last of all time."

"Well, we all owe you the cost of our lives. In one's lifetime, a man must know when it is his time to give to those who truly deserve it, so as not to die with debts unpaid. I know I wouldn't forgive myself if I didn't try to repay you in any way I'm able to. You're a shrewd, scholarly man. I know you see through the charade of titles and medals. Tell me what I can do for you. I know

I can't give you as much as you gave me. Nothing is as dear as life. But at least I can narrow the huge gap in my debt."

"In that case, all I wish is for you to grant me freedom if I ever can convince Edeline to begin a new life with me in Aura."

"That I can easily do. Is there really nothing else?"

"Just this: I know our mission is so secret that only you, the cartographer and the second and third-in-command know of our true purpose in this territory. Once we reach the borderlands to the Forbidden, scouts will be sent out to certain points near it that you've marked on the map. What is it they'll be tracking?"

"When our march stops at our destination, everyone will be told what the king of Albad and his council have decreed, why our troop will be sent forth far outside the king's domain. Are you sure this is all you seek to know? In two days, at our march's end, you'll find out anyway, along with the others."

"With respect, Tan, I can't wait two days."

"Very well. The king's council have voted, and the king has little choice but to carry out their will, as the council represent the merchant guild, whose support is where his power rests."

"Voted on what?"

"I see in your eyes that you already suspect what."

"Tan, even so, please tell me. What matter did they decide on, that touches on why we're sent into the borderlands?"

"That the beasts that have been sighted in the southern border territories are to be shot and killed on sight. Now that it's the church's position that the mythical beings are God's enemies, it was just a matter of time before the first troops were sent to track the beasts who enter our world. Once we have fresh tracks, we'll send a bird to General Urun, whose older and more experienced men will take over, finish our job, finish it all."

"I don't understand. Most half-human creatures in Kalid have gone back inside the Forbidden. So why now?"

"The plague. It is destroying the south, and the king is haemorrhaging money from the loss of taxable lands. Those who survive are desperate for a scapegoat. And many of them believe the mysterious beasts of the Wilds outside the realm are demonic carriers of the disease that is the devil's work. By killing what the public sees as a threat, the Crown will consolidate its power and the southern population will accept to be serfs and pay the taxes as recompense for the king's men waging a war on the plague."

"Does the king himself believe that the beasts are demons, sent from hell to bring pestilence to our world?"

"It doesn't matter if he believes it or not. The church feeds on the public's fears, and if the Crown can profit from fighting ghosts, then the truth doesn't matter. Not to powerful men."

So this was why it was difficult to pretend with Brind. Brind was generous with sharing his thoughts though he didn't need to. Such openness deserved honesty in return. And Kruso honestly wondered, "And you, Tan? What do you believe?"

"I believe I envy you. It is too late for me. I'm too old. This is the only life I know. Besides, with my history, I'm bound to the Crown for life. Allow me one piece of advice. Don't wait for her too long. Right now, she may want to prove her loyalty to the realm rather than prove her love of freedom. You can lead by example. There's a time for patience. That time isn't now."

-4-

It really came to Leina, on that porch, all fulfilling and all at once.

All that had made her, came back and became new as it remade her. All her emotions, all the most moving moments and thrilling marvels of her life, her childhood's all warmth flooding her freezing adult world. A secret feeling, overwhelming and true and all hers. Such was the fulfilment filling her with wonder.

She rose to her feet, went to the edge of the porch, and gazed up at the vivid blue sky, imagining, air trembling in her mouth that still hung open. It was so delicate to her that she was afraid to breathe, lest it would break the spell. She didn't ask Amaida another question. All she said was that she wouldn't breathe a word of what Amaida had told her.

That the sky would turn purple in broad daylight. That it would change into that colour for just a few moments, but that in that brief time the Forbidden Forest would disappear.

Nothing was known for sure about that forest. Yet Leina seemed to recall a tale of a nymph, Sangaris, with hair like the reddest sunrise and such a strong connection to the forest that if a branch was severed, it felt to her like losing a limb. And when this nymph died, the trees she protected would die with her.

Leina could hardly bear waiting for what came next.

She went directly from Amaida's porch to the plantation's guest house, bought a pie, and a bottle of wine, and sat back. Waiting for darkness to settle, for the hour when the musicians came, the ones whose songs made her heart storm with passion. She took a small sip, swallowed slowly, and thought that the thing about wine wasn't that it got harder to do the right thing. It was that it got so much easier to do the wrong thing.

Leina didn't get up until they began to play, and went then to the front row. Pilgrims, most of them, stayed at the plantation on their visit to the nearby shrine of Valeida, this crowd lived for this. Paid for by her father, to make them, his valued well-paying guests, eager to come back on next year's pilgrimage. None of them, she would wager, knew this duo. Unlike her. She had heard them once before, and it had been all love, so genuine.

Tonight, the music was louder than its source.

Why had she bought the wine, when she had this?

*

Unseen in the tall grass, Edeline strung and launched an arrow at the nearest deer. Hit in the neck, the hind gave a jerk, began to flee, yet in an instant fell, succumbing to the pain, the trauma.

Unlike the tropical and subtropical societies and all populations of the continent across the sea, they didn't have the luxury to feast on a diet free from meat. Here, with scarcer resources, despite what Kruso had tricked the nomads into thinking, they needed meat, needed good hunters, and she was the best one in the troop.

Her focus on tracking and bringing down her quarry had given her a long welcome reprieve from what weighed heavy on her heart. But no sooner had she found the path back to the camp at the edge of the flat, high-growing grassland, carrying the small hind on her back, than a nettling memory came back.

All through their military training, she'd stuck up for him.

Had he ever thanked her?

She washed the hind's blood off her hands in a bucket filled with hot water, while the cook skinned it. Having dried her hands, she went to their tent. Kruso nowhere around. Lightly, she pinched her pouty lower lip, disappearing into her thoughts.

She remembered how it had been in the beginning, when she first saw Kruso. How full of promise that moment had been. How he still could have been anything she imagined him to be. How he'd surprised her in ways she found she loved, as few people had in her life. So improbable, but it *had* happened.

Before he'd become her fiancé and all uncertainties and possibilities had frozen into familiar, unchangeable things, how he'd made her heart race. At her first sight of his strong upper body naked, as he and the boys he'd run with had savoured a summer day and dove into their river back home, she'd been lost in the frenzy of her heartbeats. Her mind had been gone in the lostness of pulsing breaths short and fast, melting in the taut tension of his gorgeous blocky chest, to later have fantasies about pressing herself against it, before she'd set out to find out if it would feel as good as she'd dreamt. It had felt even better. He'd been unaware of it, but she used to love to steal glimpses of him, keeping what she saw to herself, close to the downhill-tumbling thing that was her heart. He had green eyes, uncommon among dark-skinned people. The deepest, most soulfully expressive eyes she'd ever seen, a deeper sun-hazed emerald shade than could be found anywhere else. How she had loved how he always seemed to squint as if the sun lived on in his yellow-green eyes even when it was cloudy. How even his fidgety nervousness that rarely left him was dear to her. How could she have lost sight of him? How had she, somewhere along the way, lost *herself?*

Long ago, she'd dreamt of becoming a songwriter, like the duo Drive who she'd once heard in Cabra, their lyrics precious, naked, divinely powerful in their vulnerability. To write songs like theirs, lyrics that would make him thunderstruck, hearing such eloquent passion come out of her as he'd never thought she'd had in her. But since signing the contract that would make her a soldier for life, she hardly ever wrote any more, and couldn't remember the last time she'd written a lyric to soothe her soul.

She hadn't thought she would be this person.

She needed to feel like somebody else.

She needed a drink.

Antsy, she fiddled with her anklet, then her bracelet. Tokens to remember her mother by, like the book she took with her everywhere. It was there in her big back pocket even now. Her mother's best gift to her was that book. Through her mind now came the voice of her mother, saying, *"Keep an empty head, and soon enough you'll sleep in an empty bed."* Alcohol emptied her head, but she'd told herself so many times that she needed it, to get away from herself because her head was so often too full, so crowded with unhealthy thoughts that she couldn't stand it.

After they'd eaten the meat she'd provided with her bow, the march resumed. As the sun sank low enough to look at without shading their eyes, they stopped at the last palm tree grove before the plains and the desert took over. Here, after they had pitched camp, she waited until alone in hers and Kruso's tent, so small you couldn't stand in it. In a feverish, breathless hurry, she threw herself headlong into writing a letter to herself.

A vow.

Inheld breath vibrating in her lungs.

Ink losing itself in a manic dance of calligraphy.

I hereby swear that I will never drink again. I will make it up to everyone I've hurt because of my addiction. And on the last day of this summer, I will tell Kruso that I'm an addict but that I have made this vow and that I've been sober since the day I made it. I will be so proud of myself!

She wrote the date on the top of the page, folded the letter, put it in her diary, to serve as a bookmark for every new day.

Then, at dusk, Kruso was out on scout duty, loneliness frazzled her. She made a deal with herself. She would gamble, and if she won four times in a row, she would allow herself just one little drink. Reasoning that if fortune smiled so on her, it would be a sign from heaven that she could do it. That she could celebrate and treat herself, just a little bit. An unlikely winning streak like that, it would be fate.

An hour later, she'd lost nearly all she had to gamble with. The dice only rolled in her favour when she tried to win it all back. And then the dice fell again as if a demon had cursed them, and it was all over. A heavy rock in her stomach, and it was a heroic effort to smile though she wanted to die. But she couldn't stop her eyes from wildly casting around, scared to see Kruso appear inside the cramped tent, back from his scouting only to find her gambling. Though it was punishable by twenty humiliating lashes. Though she'd told him she'd never do it again. So she felt so bad, she had to hurry out, then came back to them with the book her mother had given her, the one she loved like she'd never loved any other gift. Feeling she didn't deserve it any more. They offered her to raise the stakes with the book as a deposit, tried to tempt her to win one last time before she called it quits. But no, she refused. Instead, utterly debased, she agreed to the price of all their shares of the rationed wine, and the cook took the book for himself and handed some coin to the others.

A voice inside said she'd let herself down, betrayed her self-trust by breaking her promise to herself. But she defied this voice. As if to spite whichever god had given her a life of unfair misfortune that didn't allow her to be happy. And the stone lodged in her stomach was so heavy that she knew that it would stay there for days, and only alcohol would make it immediately dissolve and allow her to escape it all.

She sat in the fat cook's tent, drinking alone with him, listening to him talk of the pastry shop he would open someday.

Then listened not at all, brooding over the riddle of her life.

Once every day, for as long as she could remember, she had needed mischief, or she would lose her mind. If days went by when she didn't do something naughty on the sly, something bad for her, the tedium of falling into routines made her desperate to make all sorts of interesting new trouble. She'd lived for the thrill of doing things that weren't part of the conduct of *proper* girls, those small moments of misbehaviour that felt bigger than anything. All through her youth, she'd tirelessly sought out novel thrills. She had often thieved in her teenage years to fill her need for danger and daring. Slyly stealing mostly nuts and sweets at the market, she took only so little that the vendors wouldn't know it was gone. Only sometimes trinkets, and then only cheap ones, which the wealthiest sellers wouldn't miss anyway.

She still needed to be bad to be happy and true to herself.

She no longer stole.

She drank.

And she had lost control over it.

It had become all the more delicious the more it had felt like a rebellion, one she threw herself into both openly and privately. She had been smoking a lot, too, this only in secret, because it was a sin, and because everyone who thought they knew her would be shocked if they saw. But most of all, she always drank. She couldn't drink her fill. And when at her drunkest, she'd done the most reckless, callous things, because, at those times, she genuinely thought there was no tomorrow.

And when she'd been so drunk that she'd slept with that other man without her fiancé knowing where she was, it had been stupid, senseless, utterly thoughtless. But it had also given her so much pleasure in its novelty and its bad danger. Because it was forbidden. Because it made her heart pound with the rush of nervous energy.

Because it gave her a feeling of being young and alive and adored again, the world being reshaped and made just for her.

Then, when she'd told Kruso, her heart torn between prideful justification and compassionate regret, he'd said, voice breaking, "I'll never hate what you meant for me. You changed, and now that this happened, now that you did this to me, you don't mean the same as before. But no, I can't hate you."

"I haven't changed!" she'd protested, desperate for him to have mercy on her, shaking her head while her eyes clung to his.

"Would you have slept with him the night after the first time you and I slept together?"

"No. I mean—Something *superficial* has changed. But all that matters, deep down, these things about me are the same."

She'd tried to take his hand.

"Don't touch me. I'm not ready for that yet."

She'd felt her lower lip tremble, and tried to stop it, but the hurt overpowered her. She hissed ghostly, "Am I ugly to you now?"

"What? No, you can never be that to me. What's beautiful is rare, and none is rarer than you. It's what you *did* that's ugly, not you. I forgive you, but if you do it once more, I could never look at you again."

Lying inside a stuffy small tent now, oh, with Pavlo, the troop's cook, in charge of the liquor. Vaguely recalling owing him money, and was this why his hands were on her breasts? Why he was trying to get her clothes off, kissing her neck wetly and all out of breath? She heard him moaning, "You're so soft, so soft."

What am I doing?

She pushed him off and sat up. "Wait. Stop. I can't do this."

"Don't test me. The deal, remember? I wouldn't tell Brind you've drunk four times your share on this march, and I'd pay for all you drank tonight. Only a frigid bitch would back out now."

She had a flashback of kissing him. Her stomach turned.

She didn't know what she said now, only followed her body's movement as she got out of his tent, suddenly revolted by the thick smell in there. A throng huddling in the firelight ahead, too distant to make out their faces. But as she got up from her hands and knees and closed the flap to the low tent behind her, she could hear somebody moving towards her from that throng. Dry palm-bark crunching under somebody's feet.

She turned fast and reeled, nearly losing her balance. Her eyes could barely focus on the face of the man approaching. She blinked and saw that it was Kruso's. Frowning hard at her, like he had so much to tell her that it didn't find its way out, leaving him just standing there, incensed, fists clenched.

"Nothing happened," she said.

"Why should I believe you?"

So dizzy now. The world seemed to spin faster around her the more she tried to be still. Which told her she had to move to be steady, and it made sense to her, though she couldn't say how.

Her mind so cloudy, moving woozily slow now, she set her lips, let go of his eyes—and walked as fast as she could straight past him, to their tent. "We'll talk about it tomorrow."

Because tomorrow felt like eternities away, happening to another person, somebody she could ignore again, the next time she got drunk.

And why shouldn't she treat herself and drink again? Nobody could forbid her. Not even herself. So bugger all dull sober inhibitions and prohibitions, censoring her and taking all the fun out of life! She could do anything, whatever she felt like.

Their tent in her line of vision, bobbing closer with her bouncy yet unsteady walk, concentrating hard to keep a straight course. "Hey," Kruso said, his hand on her shoulder, and she shrugged it off, amazed at her reaction, how instant, how easy. Yet it threw her off course, her leg snagging on the tent line, the peg attached to it flying out, as she slammed down.

"Damn," Kruso said in a whisper so silent it could be his thought she heard. "Are you all right?" Offering her a hand up.

She didn't take it. Crawled the last paces, shooting pain in her elbow, dust all over her. "I don't need anybody's help."

The next morning, as memory returned a few moments after waking up with a splitting headache, the shame and guilt made her want to be punished. The pain only abated when she had fantasies about giving up a limb to pay for how she'd hurt Kruso, again. Like the fairytales, she'd been told as a little girl, about a witch wanting to eat children limb by limb. Even that early in her childhood she had felt that if it came to prove her courage and strength, she would be like the heroic girl who had offered her leg to save her brother. But Kruso wasn't her brother. He wasn't bound to her by blood, their closeness was never predetermined by nature, his love for her not merely instinct. He had chosen her, again and again, and had wanted to believe in the best in her, to give her *his* best. He never had to. And she had ruined it. Being unfaithful to him. Being untrue to herself.

She washed her face in the brook by herself. Couldn't wash it off. She'd brought her bag with her soap, lotions, balsam and makeup. But after she'd scrubbed and soaped the smell of sweat away and washed her hair, she found herself with a towel in hand, staring at her box of makeup. She couldn't open it and pick up the small mirror in it, once her mother's, found it impossible to look herself in the face for even a second.

She dropped to her heels and sobs racked her body.

She came back to the camp with her face undone, unpainted, a mess. Coming inside hers and Kruso's tent, seeing him in there, reading the letter she had written to herself. Her solemn vow to herself that she would never drink again. She stared at him with eyes so wide open she thought she couldn't blink any more. It was evident he had read it more than once.

What she had planned to say to him. How she hated herself, how she wanted to die, how she'd do anything to take back what she'd done. It all ran out like sand in the upper half of an hourglass. The last grain of sand falling irretrievably into the lower half, leaving her empty, unguarded, a glasslike frailty.

And when the pain of realization hit, it nearly killed her.

He slowly looked up at her, pain stark as blinding snow in his eyes. "Why didn't you tell me?"

She opened her mouth and what came out was a voice she didn't recognise. At all. *"Give it to me."*

"Edeline. Please. Talk to me."

Her voice broke, shook. "I said give it to me."

He said nothing, held her eyes until he saw something in them that made it too painful for him to look on, and his gaze dropped to the sheet of paper he held in his hands. She fought tears of feelings too wild and complex to ever be named. There was a growing swollen ball of brokenness in her throat.

Time slowed down with his slow movement, as he finally lifted his arm and held out the letter. She took it, but didn't look at it, couldn't look away from his eyes, as he now met hers again.

"I know I shouldn't have read it, that I had no right. But after last night—You said it would never happen again."

Now she could tell that he was fighting tears along with her and that it took all he had not to crack.

She had no words, and at this moment, between two stumbling heartbeats, she wondered if she had been struck mute and could never speak again, no matter how much she wanted to. Never able to tell him all she should have, long ago.

He said, "I know you want to burn it. I can do it for you."

"No."

"Don't do this. It's not your fault."

She said nothing.

"I can help you."

She folded the paper neatly, carefully. She had no strength at all to tell him what she had to do. But said it anyway—a miracle, as she knew in her heart that she had no power left to speak. "I'm sorry. For everything. The only thing I don't regret is this letter to myself. I owed it to myself to write it, and now I can't, won't, burn it. I will write a new date on it. Today."

She was about to leave when he moved closer and gently caught her by her arm. His careful touch, the care in his eyes, was enough to make her muscles let go of some of their tension.

But far from all of it.

His voice unsteady, he said, "We have the chance to leave the army, to migrate, begin life anew in another land. Don't you want that?"

She couldn't look him in the eye, as she said, "It's too late."

"It's never too late. You once told me you'd always nourished a dream. To write. Songs. Poems. Even a book. Have you forgotten that?"

"Sometimes, it's a matter of self-preservation, forgetting."

He looked away, thinking. She needed space. Time to go. But hardly had she begun to motion out before she heard him say behind her, "Sometimes, so is remembering."

*

They were two fiery girls calling themselves Drive, taking turns playing guitar and drums, both singing. Their vocals often overlapped in countermelodies; strings of notes braided together into feelings as complex as falling in love with somebody entirely unexpected. *Driven as Pure Snow* always gave Leina goosebumps, the one song they had contributed to equally in every sense.

Nervous, stuttering and fanning herself as she spoke to the couplet after the show, Leina told them that one of their songs made her think of what she'd just heard an eccentric woman say.

Neida, the guitarist, wondered who that woman was, and when Leina told her, Neida said, "Amaida? I grew up with her."

And the drummer, Tunni, said, "Didn't she go crazy?"

"She did."

Leina had up until now been open to believing in Amaida.

Now, doubt seeped in. She asked, "How can you be sure?"

The guitarist said, "Ask her to tell you about the curse."

Then the drummer veered to a different topic, wanted to go smoke some soothing herbs and unwind, and Leina couldn't go with them and get a clue about the mystery of the curse.

Leina had to talk with Amaida again. Tomorrow. Right now, sleep beckoned, for her to crash into a dream of music. To follow the echo of songs bringing back her girlhood soul.

In the morning, approaching the wagon, she heard them talk inside in odd, weighty tones, heard Onil, a big voice to match his big body. When he said the word "murdered," she slowed down. Then she stopped in her tracks, hearing the name of the victim. At some time after midnight, just a few hours after Leina last saw her, a swordsman had run Amaida through, the murder witnessed by Amaida's sister. To hear this, Leina's blood froze.

Less than half an hour later, the cold shock had worn off, enough to give way to hot anger. The surreal madness of it, to hear the boys laugh it away as they rode into the banana fields. The seven boys then talked about other things, acting as though they'd already forgotten Amaida. For her to just sit there while they talked as if she wasn't there, as if they didn't consider her to have anything important to say. That was when she knew.

She wouldn't rest until she'd shown them all.

She'd put up with crude jokes at her expense, with snide remarks, with rough posturing, and their endless underlying contests.

She'd been patient, saving her energy.

She now knew what that energy was for.

She would find the mysterious swordsman and make him tell her why he'd come to Dophra, why he'd taken Amaida's life.

Amaida had last been seen at the market, and so that was where Leina would go, after another day of defiant hard work.

They would never underestimate her again.

-5-

The short, stocky mercantile administrator, Baul, rose to signal that the meeting was over. With a hanging head, Niels stood up on the shining floor. The tiles he stood on must have cost more than the expedition Baul wouldn't fund and was shutting down.

Niels felt his blood begin to boil. Overfrustrated anger, it seemed, would be his last resort. "People have *vanished*, brothers and sisters never seeing one another again. I want answers!"

"*My* answer is still no. Prior funds have vanished, too."

It all became too much. He left Baul's overlarge, lavish office slamming the door behind him, could scarcely picture anyone having thrown a door shut with greater force. It wasn't enough. All he couldn't stand, he wanted to see it all fall down.

*

At the market, as the afternoon light softened into the evening, Kyra saw her. The rich girl she'd heard about, the one her schoolmates claimed had more money than common girls like them could spend in a lifetime. Most importantly, this girl, Leina, was described as freakishly tall. A designation she shared with Kyra, yet she clearly walked taller even than Kyra's six foot and two inches. Leina's other differences were more eye-catching still, with that perfect skin, those gold-flamed blue eyes, that naturally wavy honey-blonde hair and that noble high-bridged nose. Features that were painfully enviable to Kyra, who fought a losing war against oily skin and pimples and whose eyes were nearly as dark as her black hair that hung straight as a curtain. But what truly set her apart could be sensed in her movement.

Skirting this dusty market, Leina carried herself like a woman who felt that life was too short for shame. Like somebody who had never bowed and cowed. Somebody very much Kyra's opposite. Kyra never wore high heels and had often wished she was petite. Out of the men who could muster to even *like* tall girls, a fair number wouldn't want to be seen walking by their side and appear small in comparison. But Leina seemed unconcerned by others' perception of her, her own love for herself was enough by far. A breezy smile played on her lips, a natural comfortability to her mouth's soft stretching that let Kyra know that smiling came easily to her. Not to please others. No, Leina rather smiled, Kyra thought, because others amused her, as she could afford to amuse herself. A fiercely fearless girl, strong of body and mind, could smile like that, thinking, *I'll give them hell.*

Despite herself, Kyra burned to have what Leina had. If she'd had Leina's pride and money, emancipation would be possible. Instead, her fate seemed tied to shame, to a demoness.

It had been shortly after Kyra's father had locked the demoness in the barn that her brother had tried to break the lock, driven by this *temptress*, the mythical *seductress* that had ensnared him. When the soldiers broke up the fight between her brother and her father, anger had swallowed Kyra whole. Which was why her mother had to stop her from throwing stones at the men arresting her brother. Then, looking at the deceivingly innocent face in the barn, that was when Kyra had seen her chance to harden her heart. As she rummaged for the key to the barn, and rode to a smith to make a copy of the key, all through that, she'd held on to her anger, seizing her chance to harden herself. To unlock the barn, and to take her father's whip.

With a heart of stone, she'd thought, *No shame can break me.*

Since her brother's incarceration five days ago, she had used the whip on the deviously captivating beast in the barn. Not to hurt her, like her father had, but to frighten her. Once a day she had lashed the air over the creature, staring at its cowering shape, which was only human from the waist up, the rest of her a mare. A mute miscreation, this silent half-human, half-horse that stood responsible for her brother's fall from grace. The only consolation for the shame her brother had brought upon her family was that her father had taken the female creature captive to punish her. Tying her to a beam in the barn or to the plough, using her as a slave. And by hardening her heart, Kyra could learn to enjoy making the whip snap over the creature's head, a punisher, like her father. Why shouldn't she? Only the innocent suffered deep-cutting wounds, due to their sensitive thin skin, and their softness. Those at the top, like Leina's family, toughened with their guilt, in order to live with themselves, desensitized by trampling rivals down. Kyra had steeled herself in the past, but this was different. She had to be hard as a rock, overcome her fear of the beast, her innocence a sacrifice she had to live with, turning her pitiable bleeding heart into stone. Then she'd be free from all old, lingering painful feelings, all shame. She wouldn't have to fear losing that which was good and frail inside. Feeling nothing, there'd be nothing to take, if the bad nights returned.

Yet now she felt *some*thing. A troubling thing. It shouldn't be possible. She had relinquished all, even love, to feel safe from all hurtful feelings, and had hardened herself by abusing her four-legged slave. But after she'd seen Leina, she felt… mourning?

Her eyes now swept over the crowd's faces, none known to her. And she longed for familiarity, for a place she knew well, for the sanctuary of her stable, for the pleasant smell of horses and hay, for the peace and contemplation found in there, before—

There Leina was again, still just outside the edge of the market, her head staying visible even as the rest of her came in and out of view as people shuffled by, their eyes on the wares. Kyra's eyes were only on Leina. Did she know how desirable she was? She looked newly-made, appeared to have come into the world this way, this piercingly blue-eyed and with these high-cheeked even features, only ever drawing attention like this, never having been a baby. For how could a tiny, clumsy baby know how to grow into such big precision, with every gentle wave of hair and every fine bone seeming so carefully intended?

Kyra burned even more now, as Leina had properly caught her big-eyed gaze. She had never been jealous like this before. If it was love, it was the strangest kind. It very nearly felt like an obsession. And she welcomed the feeling because it took her mind off her troubles. But no sooner was Leina out of sight again than Kyra's thoughts returned to her brother, in jail for the taboo of having been seen kissing a disease-spreading centauress, the creature her brother had called Chyanne. No matter how many times Kyra whipped the air above Chyanne's head to frighten her, it wouldn't erase the shame. And with Remin gone and Kyra working near her every day, she couldn't escape her, her devil-red hide a constant burning reminder of his evil sin. Kyra longed for the beast to be gone, longed to have it back, what she'd loved, to tend the bees and poultry. But no, now she had to be out in the dirt, tending the soil in her brother's stead. She didn't think she could ever forgive him. The thought of him made her fingers itch to hold the whip again.

The air was too dusty here, at the canopied market stand where her father's workers sold his fresh corn. So: "Move legs." And her legs led her away from the place where dust stuck to her hot bronzed skin. But not until the temple yard did the air clear of dust. Her mother was still praying to the Saint of Lost Children. Kyra didn't need to ask for whom she was praying.

"Mother."

"What are you doing here? The hallow ground is no place for a girl like you. Go to your father and make sure he isn't throwing more of our coin away."

She was back in the dust, and then the different, burnt smell stirred up at the racing ground across the market. She quickly found her father shaking a fistful of coins at the dogs he'd bet too much on if his history was anything to go on.

"Father."

"What did I tell you about coming here? The racing ground is no place for a girl like you. Go to—"

She stopped listening as she turned, her legs now taking her as far away from Dophra as her options permitted. The problem was, her options were limited.

"Sometimes," she said to herself aloud when the din of the market grew faint behind her and she was alone again. "I wish there was a saint of the whip. Whip or be whipped; that's the world in a nutshell. I'm going to teach her to wake up to pain, like I did, until I release her and she'll run straight back to the Forbidden, forgetting Remin in a hurry. That way, the only one I'll have to whip, to exchange the dullness of melancholy for the sharpness of pain, is myself."

Her mind cast back to the day before when she received the message that the same soldiers that had come for her brother would come for the centauress. And the beast's life wouldn't be spared. She saw how she then, at this very hour yesterday, had ridden up to the gate of the baroness, the current provincial vassal, who'd sent her soldiers as soon as the priests signed their sanction of the king's missive. The gate had opened to a square courtyard, neatly planted with mangoes, the farthest trees shading the main door to the sprawling castle's great hall. To the left, a leafy passage led to the stable. To the right, a walk of equal length took you to the pavilion that was the baroness' private retreat. She knew she should want the mythical being dead, but for some reason, it didn't seem right. Was it that she didn't believe the official explanation for the plague? If these beings spread disease, she should've been dead by now. True, some appeared immune, but even if she was, there were other workers employed by her father who still lived, though they'd worked near the centauress for many days before the plague struck.

"No," the baroness had said after Kyra had pleaded with her. Kyra had called on them to postpone the execution until they'd interrogated the creature. If these

mythical creatures really had caused the plague that reaped lives all over the realm, Kyra could understand the desperate measures. All such creatures had to be eradicated, the king and his council had decided. But something she couldn't put her finger on had bothered her, and the baroness' answer had left her dejected. Why? She'd done all in her might to avoid pain. Yet, knowing the centauress shortly would be put to death, for some reason this had hurt.

Presently, while making her way back at a canter on the old farmland road, her face stilled as though she'd come inside the eye of a hurricane. Realization flashed. She didn't want the soldiers to take away the strange being, didn't want it gone from her life, and couldn't stand to see it killed. She wanted to know that strangeness. In the hope that that otherness was so far from her experience that in it she could entirely forget herself.

Half an hour after riding away from the market, Kyra reined in at the small plot of land they leased. In the faint light amid swiftly thickening dusk, she swung her leg over the saddle outside the barn. Not yet knowing what she would say if the centauress was awake. She only knew that she had to, *needed* to, look at that face again, the face of the being that her brother had chosen over the dignity of his family name.

Inside, Kyra's breath caught in her throat and she stood startled and stiff. And in the shocking gap as her heart skipped a beat, what her eyes saw stilled her every muscle so much that she wondered if this was how petrification would feel like. Standing so still, staring in utter disbelief, she seemed to turn into a stone.

Chyanne wasn't alone. There, at the centre of Kyra's field of vision, in the black shadows at the other end of the large barn, a centaur was rearing up and stretching to a place Kyra's father had to use a ladder to reach. Clothesless, unhumanly smooth-muscled red, the male human-horse was untying the female one from the ring out of her reach, loosening the rope attached to the leather collar around her neck. Setting the female beast free.

Faint light came from where Kyra stood, and she saw it hit the male horse-human's eye and saw his left front hoof stamp.

Chyanne turned and said something Kyra didn't catch.

The two creatures set off for the barn's open exit, where Kyra stood riveted to the ground. She barely had time to throw herself to the side as the four-legged red-hued pair stormed past.

Seconds later, panting to recover the air taken quite out of her, she pulled herself up from her stomach with shaky arms. She dusted her hands off, rushed for the whip, unhooked it from the wall. Then ran flat out, lifted and swung herself into the saddle, saying to her horse, *"Come on, Lopo."* And urgently yet gently she tapped her heels against his flanks, the air soon streaming past her, cool on her skin, fresh with night.

She sensed she would think of this for the rest of her life. The night she turned the table on her fear and chased demons.

*

The last day out in the banana fields of her father's plantation.

Two days after Amaida's dead body had been found, with no clues anywhere that could explain why she'd been murdered.

Two days to go before her father would return and she would have hell to pay.

The day after the harvest season's big market, where she hadn't found the woman who she'd hoped would give her a clue.

The day before she'd have to tell the supervisor the truth.

This day was beginning so strange, so detached.

Making her hands learn what her father's hands never had, the muscles in her dexterous fingers moving to a new memory, how to prepare the bunches for shipment. She'd already learnt how to use the hooks to hang them on the wheeled posts and how, as a stacker, to place them in neat stacks on the cart. Now, in the rising morning sun whose light slowly shifted from red to orange to yellow, the supervisor himself taught her how to make a loop and tighten the rope to the absolute maximum around the bunches, and what knots to use where. She found herself drawn to this part of being a banana girl more than anything.

On her breakfast break, resting on a bed of straws a dozen strides from the shed, closing her eyes in the shade, under the now lemony sun, she dreamt of knots. For a blissful spell, she forgot the sight of Amaida carried on the main road in an open casket. Gone from her mind now, the slow funeral procession walking to the sound of the temple bell's chime of finality. Gone, the maddening puzzle of a strange woman slayed by the sword of a killer who'd vanished without a trace. And gone, all worry that came with thinking about her father. As she tied and untied in a dream, breathing in and out.

After Hanosh woke her, she soon stood over the spring tap by the shed, filling water containers that she and the boys needed out in the blistering sun. And suddenly remembered, stiffening. She would face her father the day after tomorrow. How would she meet his anger? What if he took away all of what was left of her freedom? She could no longer go out to hone her muscles in the sun. But could she still sing, still learn to play the guitar, or would she be caged by duty? How much time did she have left?

Breaking into Leina's nagging worry, a wide-eyed girl with tiny, dirty feet came to stand in the shade some paces away. Half-shy, half-bold, the barefoot girl smiled with unblinking curiosity. Leina returned her gaze to the flow of fresh water slowly increasing the weight of the container. Silence persisted, aside from the hiss of the tap, and the girl didn't move. Leina glanced hastily over her shoulder to get a measure of her. A head shorter than Leina, skin warm-toned brown, hair black and tousled. The girl looked up with a glint of humour in her sloe-eyed gaze as if waiting for Leina's heart to lift. As if tired of waiting but had learned to hide it. Appearing spunky, eager to learn, itching for new experiences, like a collector of novelties. Leina recognised that look, and it hit too close to home, too close for comfort.

"Do you want anything?" she asked while facing the tap in front of her. Any second now the container would overflow. She couldn't look away from the tap, or much water would spill before she had time to close the vault. To be wasteful was a sin.

"I've been wanting to do this for a long time."

"Do what?"

"Find the nerve to ask you to bring me with you. I've always wanted to be a banana girl, but I never had the—"

"No."

The water touched her finger that curled round the rim. She turned the handle and the smooth liquid hissing stopped.

"No?"

"It's buggering hard work. How old are you?"

"Sixteen, Milady."

"Don't call me Milady. What's your name?"

"Katanya. But my family calls me Anya."

"I'm not your sister."

"I don't have a sister. But I want my few chosen friends to call me Kat because it makes me happy."

"Yeah, I'm not going to call you either of that. I'm not your friend." Leina turned her attention back to the container and screwed on the lid. "Come back when there's more meat on your bones. This work is for grown-ups. Go back to school."

"We're on a break for the harvest month."

Leina made an irritated face. The girl didn't know how to take a hint. She didn't seem particularly bright. Leina turned and left with two full containers in each hand. She knew before she turned around that the girl would follow in her footsteps.

*

Leina couldn't figure Katanya out. One minute the girl could be timid and cautious with her words and demeanour. The next minute there could be something untameably feral about her smile. As if too in love with mischief to let her shyness stop her.

Leina was supposed to be at home, yet she was waiting to hear what Katanya had to say.

"Well?"

"You really think he might be the last one to see her alive?"

"Yes."

"He didn't open up much. These people are so *disrespectful*, it really gets to me. They act as if I just moved here."

"You did just move here."

"Yes, but they don't know that."

Leina's eyes went skyward. "But he opened up a *little?*"

"I asked him about Amaida and looked for any signs of discomfort, and he gave nothing away. He doesn't seem to be hiding anything. But he did provide me with some new details. The lawkeeper told him that a black-hooded stranger had been seen riding out of the plantation on the night of the murder. The witness couldn't see the rider's face but can describe the pattern of his speckled horse in detail. The horse is white with three distinct brown patches on each side of its rump."

"I don't understand why anyone would want to kill her."

"How did she die?"

Leina lifted her knife to Katanya's line of sight, and pierced it through the air. "Only, imagine a sword, not a knife." She sheathed the knife, which she'd used for cutting off leaves that prevented sunshine to reach the bananas, and for 'cutting hands'—cutting off small clusters of bananas the size of fingers, to give more water and nourishment to the rest of the bunch.

"Why did you suspect the supervisor knew anything?"

"He knew I was heading to her after I asked about her."

"He has an alibi."

Leina groaned. "Why didn't you say that before? That eliminates him, doesn't it?"

"Don't look at me that way. I'm new to this."

"It all ends soon anyway. My parents are coming back, and I'm afraid they won't let me out of their sight."

"Don't give up that easily, my friend."

"Don't call me that. The summer is nearly over and I'm nobody's friend."

*

Sweat-soaked, labouring to staple the bunches firmly onto the cart, with the other workers leaving her to it on her own at her request, she vaguely heard Katanya drone on, while massaging her muscles with coconut oil. "For a good four minutes he picked it apart, the sequenca I love, pointing out details that don't make sense. But if you look closely, his complaints have holes in them."

"Such as?" Leina said before she remembered she shouldn't encourage the girl to babble on.

"He said that it doesn't make sense that the hero's mentor tells Rex's sweetheart, Lope, to ride with him. This critic said, 'Why put her in danger?' But it would've made no sense *not* to let her ride with him.

Lope would never have forgiven the mentor if he hadn't given her a chance to save the hero's life."

"Are you really nitpicking his nitpicking?" She shook her head, and wiped the sweat off her brow. Then sighed, as she remembered what she wished she wouldn't. "Head back, Katanya. I have one last page of a letter I've waited all day to read. I intend to read it here in the shade before I ride back with the cart."

Katanya protested, and a big argument ensued.

When at last Katanya left, Leina went to the thick shade by the side of the road, took a deep breath and unfolded the last page of the letter.

Reading it, it felt like God or destiny had written it.

It was her future, there in black and white.

She swallowed.

Exhaled.

And tore the letter into pieces.

-6-

On her grandfather's sunlit balcony, Aurora looked up from the foxboard, outfoxed again. Her grandfather, Cliff, was putting the pieces back, both hers and his, the strategic game of fox newly over with him the winner as always. It was touching, really, the quiet humility he would muster, never fully basking in the glory of being the reigning champion. Still, he would never let her win. He hadn't even gone easy on his cherished daughter, not even when he and Nita had played the game after the failing health of her kidneys meant that Nita had to play it lying down.

"Cliff," Aurora said tentatively. "There's something I have to tell you, but I don't quite know the right way to say it."

"You don't have to." With brow still furrowed after the cerebral battle, he knocked his tobacco pipe on the railing of the yellow balcony that held for her countless happy memories.

Sidetracked, peeved, she said, "Don't you think there are enough troubles in life without tobacco polluting one's lungs?"

He chuckled, relit the pipe, and shot her that old cheeky grin that bunched up his left cheek and gave him a boyish look just a shade away from smug, maddeningly both infuriating and endearing. "Well, I'm getting tired of my troubles, which isn't a problem any more, because my troubles are getting tired of me."

She threw up her hands in mock surrender. Then remembered. "Look, about what I do have to say, it's not easy."

"Niels has already let me in on your little secret."

Taken aback, because the secret was hardly little at all, she blankly said, "He *told* you?"

His old eyes held hers, and for all the concern she saw in them, she found strength there, too. "He was quite determined."

"I just don't want you to worry. I can promise you that we'll return in one piece!"

There came a faraway look to his eyes. And he said slowly and quietly, *"Return."* Saying it as if the word had gained a flavour he hadn't tasted in ages. His eyes regained focus as if he came awake from a puzzling dream. "Look. There's nothing that can prepare you for it. Returning home from a distant land after what feels like an eternity. The capsized feeling of it, the reversal of perception. Everything looks smaller than you'd remembered it. At the same time, those distant things you'd imagined bigger will grow in size in your mind with the memories you now have attached to them. What once was strange is now made familiar, out there, and coming back here, what once was familiar now is strange. I'm telling you this because I want you to be careful and not take anything for granted, whether here or in the unknown."

"I think I know what I'm in for."

"It's good that you say that you *think* you do. It's when you say you *know* you do that you're in trouble."

*

Kyra hated Chyanne more than ever, now that the slave was getting away.

Chyanne hadn't paid for all the shame she had led Kyra's brother into, which had made even Kyra's friends stop talking to her or wanting to be with her.

She would never have paid enough.

Branches of oak and hornbeam lashed Kyra, as she tore through the woods on Lopo, knowing a shortcut that would close the distance between her and her quarry, the beast that she would face and finally speak to as she would to a human. Coming out of the woods in a moon-bright midnight hour, she saw them on the path she'd expected them to take, only farther away from her than she'd thought possible. On the one path ahead that ran along the margins of the grassland between the Forbidden and the canyon leading to the desert.

For hours and hours, she rode after them.

Not long after the first light of dawn, having ridden in the moonlight through plains and fields, she saw Chyanne for what she knew was the last time. Away from the rolling golden fields and into the emerald green Forbidden Forest the centauress galloped, waving her last goodbye to the centaur who'd saved her. And this centaur, for some reason didn't go with the one he'd rescued. No, he loped for the red sandstone canyon leading into the desert down southeast.

Kyra's heels only had to nudge the sides of Lopo, her warm-beige faithful friend, and his trot turned into a fast canter. Riding farther from home would be crazy, but nothing could've stopped her. She didn't know yet what she would say when she caught up to him. Knowing only she had to face the beast.

Alone.

*

Over time, every stranger we meet, Leina had observed, lose their nervous caution in our company, until we're not strangers at all.

Like reverent respect diminishes as we drop our guard with our increased familiarity, so does our admiration fall away when somebody that at a distance seems larger than life turns out to be just like us when seen up close. She used to think it always to be so. Which was why she hadn't at all expected Katanya to be this irreverent this fast. The girl was shamelessly unapologetic even after the stunt she pulled, coming along as a stowaway on Leina's journey. Leina had thought herself all alone, travelling bravely all through the night, then falling asleep as she'd stopped to watch the sunrise. It was well past midday when Katanya revealed herself, casting a shadow on Leina's moment of glory.

And now the girl had the nerve to be sour, to even sulk.

Leina glared straight ahead as she heard the enervating little girl say, "Can I ask you why you stole this two-horse cart and drove it to the middle of the outer regions of nothingness?"

Leina snarled. "I never asked you to come with me, did I?"

"I'm not backing down. At least not until we come to the frontier mining town. I just want to know why you yesterday said to yourself, *'To hell with it!'* and broke away."

"It wasn't a knee-jerk decision like you make it sound."

The girl murmured, "No, more a spur of the moment."

"What's that?"

"Nothing. Go on."

"I'd had it. To be traded like cattle, sold into a loveless marriage to a person that makes me want to vomit."

"You've never met him."

Leina barbed her voice. "You don't know that, Katanya."

"Am I wrong?"

"No, but that's beside the point," Leina snapped. "You make assumptions and it's ticking me off."

"You're angry with me because I hid under the two layers of banana bunches until you were well out of your father's land. But you're angrier with him, and you did it to spite him, I'd wager."

"Don't tell me my reasons for me, I'm warning you."

"It seemed like a ready-fire-aim-effort to me, that's all."

Leina was about to raise her voice, but the word 'testy' came to her, and she held her tongue because she never wanted to be seen as that, didn't at all see herself that way.

Katanya continued, "Over an engagement to a man you'd might find is your soulmate."

"*Ha!* I read my father's letter about him, and his political views literally made me throw up in my mouth a little. Yesterday morning before work, as I received the letter and couldn't bring myself to read the first pages straight away, I went to see a beggar who had been a maid in his family before they threw her out on the street. After I gave her a generous amount of coin for her sincerity, she revealed his true nature. He's spoiled, boastful, entitled, and his father ruined her life after he made her pregnant and denied that it was his, with no family of her own to help her. How he and his father can talk without holding their noses is beyond me."

"Maybe he does, for all we know. But you just took off without properly deliberating with yourself first."

"If you thought that I didn't know what I would do, you could have had no inkling that I would make a run for it. If so, then why did you hide in the cart to go with me yesterday, while I sat in the shade and read the letter of doom?"

"Because you said earlier you feared the last page of the letter spelt out your future husband's plans for you. You saved the last page for the end of the day when it was our turn to tie the bunches while the others went home early. I saw you stalk off into the roadside palms to read in the shade, and you were in your own world and didn't see me. I was close enough to hear you speak to yourself as you made the snap judgement about the letter after you read it in full and it confirmed your fears. I heard you say to yourself that you would sell your gold necklace you don't let the boys see. I figured you would sell it at the frontier, so I hid because I knew I couldn't talk you out of it. If this was a sequenca adventure tale, then the lightness with which you made that decision wouldn't have been in it. The story would cut straight to this scene, with us arguing, skipping the scene where you talked yourself into running away."

"No, it would so have made it into the book. Buggering *epic*, it was. How I... um... God, what am I *doing* out here?"

In the sudden silence that then came, in what felt like a rare moment for somebody like Katanya, Leina thought the girl looked at her with pity she hadn't summoned. In silence she got the mares moving at the highest speed away from places she knew. The steadily increasing distance to home would make it easier for her to not be tempted to stop and turn back. They swiftly passed harrowers in the oat fields with their oxen and harrows, ploughing and soughing. Then came to wild fields, the edges of the grassland whose grass grew as thick and tall as reeds, stretching to a green horizon, beyond which lay the Forbidden.

When Leina got up to ride the cart standing up, to save her behind from the brutal treatment the uneven road subjected it to, Katanya followed suit. Relieved of the pain, Katanya let out a slow exhale, smiling thinly. "Here. Have a banana. My treat."

Leina ate it humourlessly. Her usual aloof air escaped farther from her with her effort to recover it. Something felt different. Slowly, the realization came to her. She wasn't squinting any longer. "The sun is getting low. I wonder if word of my disappearance has reached my parents by now."

That night, to the sound of their protesting stomachs, they slept by the cart, at the side of the left wheel, in a makeshift tent made with the canvas used to protect the fruit.

Leina woke as her skin was touched by the morning sun.

Katanya was already up, pacing. Any other girl's first thought, seeing Leina rise and straighten her clothes, would've been to wish her good morning, perhaps ask if she slept well. But Katanya skipped that and went right ahead with picking up where they left off. "You asked before what you're doing."

"I'm not going back, Katanya. I'm leaving the cart here. I give you one of the mares while I take the other. Go now, and you'll make it to the plantation before your parents believe the worst has happened."

Katanya's eyes dropped, blinked, and looked up again. In her voice a cautious note of hope, as she said, "What about Amaida?"

"I was wrong about her. I shouldn't have believed in the purple sky, that it will ever come. It was just foolish, childish hope and wonder. False hope. Naïve wonder. Amaida was crazy. There won't be a purple sky. The Forbidden Forest isn't special. It's just a place where brutish, primitive beings dwell. What other reason could there be for nobody's return from it?"

"Are you really sure about that?"

She gritted her teeth, hating that the little girl didn't believe her. "Yes. I can't believe in a child's fantasies. I must face reality or only know disappointment. And so I tell you that I don't believe in it any more and am embarrassed that I wanted to have faith in what Amaida told me."

"I am open to the possibility that something will happen at next summer's solstice."

"No, I tell you now that it was a figment of a crazy person's imagination. Do you want to be like her, insane? If you choose sanity, then speak rationally as an adult."

"I suppose that if I look at it rationally, then, yes, it can't be real. Nothing will happen next summer. The sky won't change colour and a forest won't just vanish, because that would break with reality. To believe otherwise would be more than a stretch. It would be childish. But where do new ideas about the nature of reality come from? Playful thought experiments, that's where. Being inventive like a child at play, toying with new possibilities. And many of the wildest ideas, though once thought crazy, turned out to be true."

"Even if she was right – and that's an enormous if – she's gone, can't tell us what it meant. And I'm running scared. So I'm telling you for the last time: Don't come after me unless you are absolutely certain you won't regret it."

Katanya appeared to mull it over, then said, as a way of explaining her hesitation, "I left home for a *reason.* I'm not rash, like you. You should've waited, given it a proper thought."

Leina sucked her index finger, and held it up to see from where the faint wind came. A deep inhale later, she said, "I trust my intuition, my instinct."

"Fear of the unknown is an instinct, but you didn't seem to trust that. Which is why you had second thoughts as darkness set in on your first day all alone away from the plantation."

"You think I had second thoughts last night?"

"Well, today I would say you have third thoughts. There's no shame in it. This is unknown terrain, and I'm your only friend here, and you don't know yourself as well as you thought, and—"

"Do *you?* You, who say you're my friend, hide everything so well – especially yourself – it must be the thing you do best."

Katanya scoffed. "It's not what I do best of all, at all."

"No? What can you do better than anyone else?"

"Nobody can avoid difficult questions better than me."

"How do you mean?"

"Look!" The girl pointed at something above. "Vultures!"

Laughter pealed out of Leina before she knew it. "That was actually hysterical. Maybe your specialty really is—*Oh,* but they really are vultures. We're frying in the sun for them. My aunt told me of Topazin Canyon under the easternmost star of the Pegasus constellation. Where a centauress looking for her brother was lured out by a farmer who wanted to show her the human world. They put him in jail for trying to protect the centauress, and his father used this beast to plough his fields."

"What does that have to do with us?"

"That canyon, it's not far from where we are. We could reach it and take shelter in its shade before noon if we set out right away. Then we can travel northward to the coast by night."

"Do you know the way to this canyon?"

"I have my brother's compass."

"You have a brother?"

"Two." As they set off, she told Katanya of them, eight and eleven years older than her, both of them teachers at the same academy and both becoming fathers at the same time, their daughters born just one day apart, more like twins than cousins.

Hours later, climbing off their horses in a thick shade under an overhang in the canyon, they slumped to the ground, too exhausted to speak. Their horses panted loudly, and all Leina had the strength to do was to open the waterskin and douse her cracking dry lips with fresh water.

Then her eyelids fluttered. She felt as if in a grainy dream. As though a see-through bridal veil of red lace slow-danced before her eyes. Was she about to faint? She had noticed it before, but only now became fully aware of the wondrous appearance of this place, as if having stepped inside an impressionist painting of a sandstone otherworld. The cliff walls and her skin alike dizzily vibrantly alive in a gentle red-orange sheen. Katanya aglow with it, too. An emberlike fuzz-feathered sketch of warm colours that let Leina see a tender beauty in the girl she had never guessed. As though shortsighted, she squinted to hone her gaze to see the truth behind the magic, and it only intensified.

She followed the red rocks to the burning sky and found a dazed realization. That the narrowness of the canyon and the slanted angle of the light made all things appear as they would if seen at close range through a spyglass. An out-of-focus spyglass semblance, how everything looked close enough to touch, while at the same time subtly blurred as if far away.

For a long moment, Leina's thoughts slowly drifted from memory to memory, each thought and feeling now curiously touched by this warm canyon light. Her eyes ever blinder to the outside world yet full of its light, her languid inner drifting found a focus deep inside, as if this was her drifting's destination all along, as her mind's eye saw Amaida again. She thought about Amaida telling her about the sky turning purple. And she thought about how this mystery had uniquely intrigued her and how Amaida by telling her about it had made her excited about living and truly glad to be alive for the first time in her adult life.

But thoughts moved slow and foggy in the heat. She needed water. Weak-bodied, they ventured inside the steep wedge, and with eerie luck almost immediately saw a glittery reflection higher up. Climbing to it, they found that rainwater had gathered in oval-shaped deep hollows in shelves of rock. After they'd both quenched their thirst, Leina refilled the waterskin. As she turned, she looked at Katanya, who peered down from the boulder-strewn broad shelf they stood on. She looked at the dirty, sorry state of the girl, in just her work clothes, shirt and shorts of a colour not much different than the boulders around and in front of her. Then Leina looked at herself, at her short-sleeved, waist-length, greyish-white cotton undershirt, her tunic of coarse wool tucked inside her belt, her rough work pants and hard leather shoes. All she carried of worth was the jewellery she almost always wore, and she'd hate to part with it. It was painful to admit, but she'd been more stupid than bold.

She weighed the waterskin in her hands, enough for the mares waiting for them a short downhill walk away. But even if there'd been enough water for a long gallop, time had already run out for her. No time left to go back, pack up properly and take the stallion Halide from her father's stable. Her parents would arrive tonight, and the journey back to Dophra from this canyon would take two days even if she'd had a racing horse.

An almost inaudible whisper from Katanya gently broke into her thoughts. "A suspicious-looking man is down there."

"Suspicious how?"

"He's hooded, and he appears to be looking for tracks."

"Step back. Let me see." Still weak and light-headed, Leina pressed her stomach against the red rock and looked down. That passage below ran parallel to the shelf where she and Katanya had found water. Leina peered down to where a river once had carved its way through the sandstone, before the age of humans. And there, in the thick shade, she saw a man with a black hood over his head though it was oven hot even in the shade. He was leading a horse with distinct speckles on its hind quarter. Three, on each side. Leina's mind cast back to being told of the man seen on the night of the murder, his horse described precisely like this.

Silent as a breeze, she edged back, put a finger to her lips. She kept absolutely still to not make a sound for as long as the man she had set out to find was within hearing distance.

Somehow, the man she thought of as Black Hood, had come to the same place as she and Katanya. Why was he here? He appeared to be scanning the ground, the sand. He must be looking for a beast. But Leina knew that the centauress had left this canyon with the naïve farmer who had wanted to save her. Did Black Hood believe there were other centaurs here, hiding, unknown to the world outside?

The man went deeper down the narrow pass whose vertical walls constricted into a shadowy gorge, less than a dozen paces wide. Though she had no idea what she could hope to discover, she began to follow him. As Katanya came after her, whispering reasons why she should stop, none of which Leina listened to, she only looked back once, to silence the girl with a glare.

They crept on after him, but as the gorge curved sharply inward, he was hidden from sight. Fear and frustration ate Leina up.

Katanya said, "Something doesn't feel right."

Leina snapped, hissing back, "Girl, will you never shut up?"

"It's Kat. And I—"

"I know your name, *Katanya*. And I will never call for you by it because you're nothing but irritating and I never asked for you to come with me. I don't deserve you ruining this for me."

Silence.

As she resumed her creeping pursuit, the girl stayed behind, not moving away but not moving after Leina either. As though nourishing hope against expectations to the contrary that Leina would accept her for who she was and come back for her. But who she was right now was too irritating to accept. Leina didn't turn around to look at her again, didn't allow herself to regret having stilled her motion like a fish whacked against a rock.

*

Into the steadily growing light of a new day, Kyra rode after the centaur, the land open enough for her not to lose him. Though in the rising heat and dust he soon turned into a red-brown dot in the grassland between the Forbidden and the red amber bare sand and rock constricting the way ahead. She kept her eyes on him and only blinked when she had to, her thoughts fixed on how she would make him regret having freed one of his kind.

All centaurs must speak, and she had to begin somewhere.

But before she saw the gorge, the centaur did disappear from view, outrunning her tired horse, poor old Lopo lacking the endurance of his younger years. Fortunately, the land became wedged in like a tilted hourglass, with steep cliffs on both sides, leading to the narrow canyon, from where there was nowhere else to go. Kyra reined her horse in absently, her attention on the distant dust cloud before her. Confident that the canyon and the desert had him cornered, she gave her horse much-needed rest. Lopo, winded and spent, snorted with appreciation. It was as Kyra fed him oats from her saddlebag that she saw the two soldiers on horseback, approaching fast.

Discretely, she lifted her arms just long enough to smell her armpits. Nothing. A small miracle, but she savoured the relief. Still, she could kill for a shower, to get out of her sleeveless dust-covered pale linen shirt and near-black riding pants, darkened by sweat. But now she saw that their uniforms were to a far greater extent in need of washing, and even from a distance, *they* smelled.

The yellow-haired, moustachioed one spoke loud to her, for the other one to hear. "Two abominations – centaurs – were seen nearby. We're of the Sixth Squadron, scouting for a troop of twenty. The ranger we spoke to said he saw the beasts make for the Forbidden, but the track of one of them led back this way. Our troop has been sent from General Urun's regiment to protect the realm against nonhuman intruders. A new decree signed by the king authorises our elimination of any trespassing half-human abominations in these parts. Now, lady, why are you riding through these parts, so far from civilization?"

"I've followed one of the centaurs. The one who illegally remains in the human world is down in one of the many gorges perforating the canyon like a maze. It can't get out."

"May I ask why you're following it, Madam?"

"It released a centauress we used as a ploughhorse."

"Did you have the sanction of the royal overseer?"

"The overseer looked the other way. The matter was brought to him, but he never called us to the court of his jurisdiction. He judged that it was better we punished it by having it work our fields than to banish it."

"The overseer's name, please."

"Frieder."

The yellow-haired man in a grey uniform sighed. "Can't stand those creatures. They spread diseases that never plagued us before they encroached on our land. We've lost good men to the pestilence that's their making." He made a face of distaste as he gazed into the fiery backdrop of crab-red sandstone cliffs jagging the eastern horizon. His eyes returned to hers, and they were grim even as his voice softened. "As soon as our troop arrives, you'll get something in your stomach for your help. Then it's time for you to go home. This is now a Crown's matter."

"You're going to kill him."

"You have my word."

As the rest of the Crownsmen in the troop arrived, they gave Kyra food and wine, took her to the canyon and set up camp around her for the night, secure that the four-legged anthropoid wouldn't flee to the desert on the other side.

She ate, drank, and then awaited the call to the captain's tent.

She wouldn't lie about why she was here.

She had her own score to settle.

*

Kyra stood on one of the lower plateaus over the canyon, with her hands on her knees, recovering her breath and vigour, slowly lifting her gaze. And standing there, by the edge of the entrance to the canyon below, she remembered it at the same moment as her sight met it again, the road down the slope, cutting through the grasslands to the last outpost at the end of the realm.

A low female voice not far behind her. "Time to go."

She turned around. There she stood, pinching her lower lip and appearing to be deep in thought, the dark-skinned soldier tasked to escort her back to her father, on the captain's order. And this soldier appeared to be boiling with anger at this decision. Edeline, her name was, and never had Kyra seen a girl who looked so old and worn while at the same time so young and innocent in her anger at the world. Though much of that anger was directed at Kyra, whose foolish endeavour would cause Edeline to be away from her troop for days as she travelled to Dophra and back, Kyra couldn't return that hard feeling. She couldn't bring herself to dislike Edeline. There was something too sweetly mysterious about her, about that puzzling ache deep in her eyes, to not want to be close to her. In the hope that such closeness would open her up just enough to feed Kyra's imaginative curiosity, by providing at least a hint of her story.

Hardly had they gotten their horses ready before Kyra felt a tug towards a place where her heart longed to be. And it was in the opposite direction of where this soldier would take her.

She had to make Edeline see that she had to ask the beast why they—

Shouts. Soldiers running out of the canyon with reports.

Commotion. Loud orders from the captain.

Through the shouting that passed on the reports, Kyra got an increasingly coherent meaning, a fuller picture shout by shout. The centaur had been sighted in a gorge within walking distance, where they could easily catch it, and it was unarmed and alone. The captain told Edeline to hold off on her task and stay behind at the camp until his return. Kyra watched all soldiers disappear inside the canyon, only she and Edeline remaining by the tents.

*

Edeline watched the campfire. Watched over the campsite. Tasked to watch everything in the area until they returned from the danger she'd been kept from. Watching all but herself. The wayward farmgirl had used a pocket mirror as she'd washed her face in the water Showy had carried out of the canyon earlier. With envy which she had hated that she'd felt, she'd watched Kyra. Wanting to be able to look at herself like that, so easily, so without complicated hurtful feelings. She'd gone to get the saddlebag with the makeup box, sitting now with it unopened by the fire. She told herself to snap out of it, to open the makeup box and pick up the mirror, to resume the old ritual, which she hadn't done since she'd broken her promise to herself.

Her hands stopped midmovement, just above the box.

She couldn't open it.

Maybe she would never be able to look at herself in a mirror again, cowed by shame for the rest of her life.

A few hours ago, as they put up their last camp outside the canyon where the beast hid, Kruso had said he'd been tired of waiting for her to talk to him. She'd told him she was tired of him being a pathetic small boy who took forever to be a real man. That had had the desired effect. He had left her alone.

How had she gotten here?

How had she become this insensitive, careless person she hardly recognised?

She used to care about others. But then she'd had no choice but to become a soldier. Forced into a profession she hated, simply because her poor family were in debt and the quickest way to pay it off was to send the oldest daughter to the military. When she had tried to argue herself out of it, her father had told her she had to grow up, and couldn't live on a dream. This was the only reality, and her four sisters and three brothers, all younger than her, counted on her here and now. After her father, a miller, had seen his life's work go up in flames. After a grassfire had reached his beloved watermill and they hadn't been able to save what had cost him a fortune to build and would have taken years to make a profit. Nobody had died, though her father had looked like a ghost and hadn't been able to talk the day after the fire, circling the ashes like a sleepwalker, before finally breaking down, on his knees, ash in his fists, as tears streamed down his soot-filled face.

But pushing her to go to the military had been a death knell for her. The mindless repetition of responses to orders and the mechanical everyday routines and the endless training, sucked the joy out of life. And she had been powerless to change where she'd headed. Finding only solace in drink, in breaking rules without getting caught.

Her war against ennui had become a selfish quest for kicks, and she was terrified that she'd reached the point of no return. She used to love herself, even admire herself. Now she couldn't say what she loved, if anything. If what she wanted at this stage was the love and admiration of others, then when she got it, she didn't feel like it was really she, the real Edeline, who received it. Meant for somebody else, the one they thought they saw when they looked at her. Their picture of her was a portrait of a stranger to her. Or somebody she'd portrayed but had forgotten along the way who it was based on, a girl abandoned by a hollow hedonist.

Once she'd had a dream. To write songs to be sung by a girl aflame with a passion for music and poetry as consuming as hers had been, when she still had burned true. Deeply wanting that dream, she'd really believed there existed such a girl, a girl just like her, who felt like she did about music and poetry.

Where had that dream gone?

Where was *she*, the Edeline she'd loved so much that she'd wanted the best things she could dream of to happen for her?

The last dream that would leave her, what still drove her to look for a way out, was to realise her and Kruso's dream. To be free of servitude and move to a happier place, far away from senseless wars and persecution of mythical beings. To open a tavern they would call *The Howling Cub*, in that faraway place, where they would foster young musicians who would perform there every night. She hated being a soldier and detested what the army represented, the things it did, but like Kruso she'd had no say in it, being poor and having to save their families from destitution. They both wanted no part in the cycle of violence, but they couldn't abandon the army—deserters were hunted down and put in jail. Their only way out was to make enough money to be able to pay to be released from their contract.

Yet with her addiction, did she dare to dream that dream any more? Maybe the best thing she could do for Kruso was to stay with the army and let him go, give him his freedom to find somebody who could offer him the happiness he deserved.

As Kyra's voice broke into her thoughts, though she spoke from just the other side of the little fire, Edeline barely heard it, like words almost lost in a storm. So far away had Edeline been that Kyra had gone quiet before Edeline perceived the words, having to listen to them in the echo of her mind to be fully aware of their meaning. That Kyra would do anything to stay.

"Why?"

Kyra shoved her hair from her face and looked up from the glowing embers at their feet. "I need to speak to the centaur, to know why it is in our world, why one of its kind had to change my brother and destroy my life."

"I have a feeling that if it sees somebody as innocent as you or your brother, it will be drawn to you somehow. If you can draw it to me, I can let you speak to it before I kill it."

Kyra held her eyes. "I'll be your bait if you tell me why you want so badly to be the one killing it."

"To have the reward I need to buy myself free from my contract and live somewhere where nobody knows me."

Kyra looked at her for a long time. A storm between them though the air was still, yet not another word offered and lost.

-7-

Cooking dinner together with his grandfather while Aurora was out buying delicacies for her two guinea pigs, Niels spoke softly, a contrast to his hands' chopping motion as he cut onions. "The first time I saw a hot-air balloon, I teared up," he said, which was funny, the onions made his eyes water as he said it. "It was so beautiful. For the first time, I knew why I was born. To be an airfarer. While for me the allure is science, I am quite certain that my sister's love affair with airfaring is that of an adventurer and explorer. But we both dream of seeing the world from above."

"This airfaring business puzzles me. As an atmospheric scientist, shouldn't you be in the air to look up, not down?"

"My neck is killing me. But seriously, didn't you have theories considered too wild, even for the fringe?"

"Certainly." Cliff stuffed his pipe and put it aside for later. "This is why I agreed to help you financially, to see if my theory about the magnetic properties of the Forbidden holds true."

"Yes. One fascinating old theory that is regaining traction right now is about the strange minerals we call lodestones, about their baffling ability to attract iron.

The first scientists discovered that when a lodestone is placed on a float in a dish of water, it stunningly always faced the same direction. Until now, people have believed that the needle of the magnetic compass always points to the Naimah star in the north because the star mysteriously attracts it. But the old theory, which I know you and your colleagues found far more rational and persuasive, is that the globe itself, under our very feet, is the source of the magnetic power. Didn't you try to test this idea?"

"I did so." Cliff glanced longingly at the pipe he'd put on the windowsill. Smoking in here had been strictly banned by Aurora, who'd said that the kitchen was a safe space for Bandit. Returning his attention to Niels, Cliff said, "I once wanted to conduct an expedition to measure our globe's magnetic power. To do my share in the ongoing collection of empirical evidence showing that all systems that allow life to exist on the globe are as complex and as fragile in their balance as the interdependent systems inside the human body. The expedition sadly never happened. But if it isn't you, then another scientist will one day try another idea and be heard. You can't stop science. It's a force that never let's go, like the pull on the compass needle."

"For most people, the invisible power pulling the compass needle without fail is an absolute mystery. But for me, an airfarer scientist admiring elegant experiments that explains the magnetic forces that permeate everything, the rational yet strange answer to the big mystery is an even bigger mystery. And balloon ascent can give us the all-revealing sight of gods."

"My dear boy, I applaud your enthusiasm but implore you to be reasonable. With balloons, attempts have been made to study the solar spectrum. Dubious results. Uncovering the dew point? Clear results, but needs to be repeated. Revealing truths about the oxygenation of the atmosphere? Another unrepeated test, thereby unconfirmed. What you find may not be repeated."

"I humbly disagree. It will. Success is a repeatable story. Measurements can be done more effectively from above. We can test what you once tried to detect. An unending electric current that is made by a strong magnetic force produced by the molten iron of the globe's inner centre as it is heated by the inmost core. A natural process, as ingenious as how trees use light to produce oxygen and how our bodies use oxygen in the process that transforms food into energy. You know, scientists have observed an atmospheric shield, built not by the inner dynamic yet lifeless structure of the globe, like the magnetic force, but by life itself on the globe's surface. But new experiments indicate that it is the magnetically charged force that holds the atmospheric shield in place. A shield that guards us from the invisible light of the sun that would kill all life if we'd been unshielded."

"I've read about this. A wondrous shield made of ozone."

"Yes. But what I seek to uncover is more miraculous still, the unmapped area that came into our world at a time no one can seem to remember, a time that perplexingly doesn't appear in history books. I will think of you when I map it."

"You already thanked me approximately a thousand times and I'd say that's sufficient. I believe in you and that you will succeed, though other balloon expeditions have been sent there, each one never coming back."

"And your belief in me hinged on the technical drawings I showed you, of the lifeline such as the world has never seen."

"Yet I don't entirely see why you young people are so obsessed with flight. Well… if I strain to remember, I recall being the same once, long ago. But I've forgotten why."

"It's what flight lets us see. Before, there used to be white spots on the map of the world. They marked unexplored areas of the continents of Tair. But after the invention of hot-air balloons in our civilization of Albad, the white spots of the wilds, even of the rainforests, either shrunk or disappeared altogether. But then there appeared a new white spot, a forest. Albadine balloons have flown over it, as you know, but it's obscured by mists."

"Yes. Explorers have attempted to map what lies beneath the white mists. Whoever goes inside it doesn't come back, as nobody before has thought of your dependable lifeline."

"And I shall be the first to know why they vanished."

"Be careful with your desire to know the answer to that, dear boy. It can become an obsession you can't turn back from. It's because you're young. Youth is a dangerous thing."

"So is hope. But hope rather than fear, science rather than faith, makes more sense and speaks of more amazing truth."

His grandfather smiled easily at this and smacked his lips.

Niels sighed to himself and his eyes lidded with dreaming. "All we know is that it's a white spot, a hidden reality. As if it doesn't exist. *Anything* can be inside that which doesn't exist."

"My dear child! I didn't know you had a mystical side!"

"Well." Niels gave his grandfather a hug, his eyes briefly closed with emotion. "I'm afraid we all do. We're only human."

*

Leina had become a shadow following a shadow. On soft feet, alone, she went on after the man who her heart told her had killed Amaida. The trot and the panting of the speckled horse in tow behind him made it easier not to be heard, and there was always a rock and a thick shadow to conceal her from view, should he look back over his shoulder. She passed branching naturally formed corridors, narrow gorges with overhanging rock that sometimes formed into sandstone ceilings and tunnels.

He disappeared from view behind a bend, and as she came around it, she saw that he'd slowed down. Positioned at a sprinting distance around ten seconds away, he slowly increased the distance as he approached a silhouette of a rider ahead.

No, not a rider.

As the silhouette came inside a thinner shadow, its shape and colour came out.

A centaur.

More than flame-red, it came, its hide red like nothing in this world was red. The only way she could describe the colour to herself, the only thing that came close to it, was to liken it to a bloodred sunset. The muscles of the animal part of him were more honed and enchanting than on any beast she'd seen. And there was a sensual grace to the look and movement of this beastly side that felt so human that it struck Leina that you forgot that it was unnatural to be made that way. Above the point on his lower stomach where the beast ended and the human side began, hairless sweat-glistening skin shone a lighter red, something more like ruby-gleaming starlight. The muscles of his naked torso stood out more defined and gorgeous than she'd ever seen in a mortal, and never even in paintings and sculptures had she seen such a generous plentiful display of energy and vigour.

As the red centaur came within full view out of the shadows, Black Hood's speckled horse took fright. Though Black Hood took a step nearer his horse to calm it, still it shied, seeing the centaur. The horse reared and tore away, taking its flight inside a forking passage to the right of Leina.

She heard Black Hood say to the half-human creature, "I'm a friend. I'll lead you out of the maze of this canyon."

Inspired by the wildness of the beast, Leina hurried before the feeling faded, and shouted, "That man can't be trusted! *Run!*"

After just a single heartbeat, the centaur flew off into a gallop, stormed past her, and Black Hood never had time to load the crossbow he'd been carrying on his back.

For the space between two shuddering heartbeats, her eyes locked with his, seeing brutal fury in them.

She spun around and ran half like a fleeing animal, struck in equal measure with madness and wildness.

*

Kruso heard a cry torn from their lungs not far away, a voice that was only just barely high-pitched enough to tell him it came from a woman. He made out the words, *"That man can't be trusted! Run!"*

Kruso motioned to the cry, to the thin gorge it came from.

Kasseia, the only female still alive in the troop apart from Edeline and Ziara, and the only one apart from Brind with the right to command, barked out, "Halt!" Then, "I said halt, Kruso! Our fight is not with them, whoever shouted that. Clearly a fight about a man, not a beast. It has been sighted at the other end of the canyon and we are all to march this way. If you take one step further that way, you're disobeying a direct order! Now get back in line. I'm second-in-command!"

Before giving himself time to lose heart, he snarled at her, "Bugger all ranks and commands!" Then spoke with lucid sincerity, explaining himself, not because he sought Kasseia's respect in her role as his superior, but so as not to injure her pride. "This is bigger than the difference between you and me!"

And I'm doing what I would have wanted to be done, had it been me.

As he got inside the thin gorge and no longer could be seen from the outside, he saw in the tight space ahead a hooded man reaching for the reins of a horse with naturally formed brown patterns on its hindquarters. The horse appeared to newly have gotten away from him. Kruso demanded, "Who are you?"

Without turning to look at Kruso, which told Kruso he knew about Kruso's troop at the centre of the canyon, the man said, "A tracker. Better than any of you grey coats." Now he turned but didn't remove the hood he wore despite the heat. "I want half of the reward that's out for killing abominations."

"I'm part of the troop sent out to take him down. The others are close behind me. I'm not sharing anything with you."

"Then I'll take the whole reward myself."

"I heard a girl cry out not to trust some man."

"Yes. A man on horseback, as you can tell by the tracks right there. After she warned me of the hustler, I scared him off with my crossbow. She thanked me and went on her way."

"What was she and that other man doing here?"

"She didn't say."

"You don't mind if I go check that she's out of harm's way, do you?"

"Be my guest. But she seemed to be in a hurry to get away from that man that clearly wasn't to be trusted."

The hooded man appeared to be right. For several minutes Kruso went deep inside the gorge that wasn't much wider than a castle corridor. After Kruso had gone on for perhaps four minutes with no trace of her, he went back, the impractically attired tracker waiting at the same spot as before.

Kruso, not wanting to let the man out of his sight, said, "I think we can come to some sort of agreement, but it is not my arrangement to make. I'll take you to my captain to see if we can't help one another."

*

Leina ran in the same direction as the centaur had. Ran until she heard Katanya call out her name, and as they ran towards one another, so out of breath was she when they met that she couldn't get a word out. "I'll tell you later," she finally said.

"I found a wide gorge with palms lining the cliff edge above. Let's find a place to rest there and discuss what's next."

There were no hoofprints in the gorge Katanya took her to.

The gorge opened up to a part of the canyon nearly as wide as its centre. Here, date palms hung overhead, and Leina could see grass up there as well. They hadn't walked for long under cliffs about ten body lengths high before something drew Leina's eyes to a drape of vines on one cliffside. She couldn't say why she did it, but she went up to it and drew the vines aside. And discovered a cave hidden behind the green natural drape.

An hour later they had watered and brought the horses up to the plateau opposite the cave, where the grass grew best. Then, together they drew the drape of vines aside once more.

Inside the cave, the centaur looked out at them.

*

Edeline and Kyra walked in silence through the ever branching gorge, going in the direction where Kyra said she'd seen palm trees. Selecting this path on the hunch that the centaur would be drawn to the only green place in the canyon Kyra had been able to spot. As they walked, Edeline thought about becoming somebody completely different, somewhere far away. Where she'd never be found. Where she'd make up any past that should have been, all the things she should have done.

They stopped as they came to the place Kyra had seen, a part of the canyon overhung by palms.

There, suddenly, Edeline saw the centaur at the other end of this relatively wide part of the canyon. She and Kyra stepped back to where the cliff wall hid them, and then Edeline peeked out. The centaur hadn't seen them, and he seemed to be watching two girls from a distance. Those girls, dressed like peasants, though jewellery glittered like faint stars from the blonde one, were clearly unaware that they were watched. Something Edeline couldn't explain made her turn to Kyra and say, "Let's go back."

"You want to give up the chase? He's right there!"

"I'll convince Captain Brind to let you stay with us."

"I would only stay with you because you promised me to help me get to him."

And Kyra pointed at the cliff wall towards the point where they'd seen the centaur hide while watching the mysterious two girls. Then her eyes flashed, seeing something in Edeline's face that Edeline didn't know she'd given away. And she asked Edeline, "What happened to you?"

"Never ask that. Let's go."

"No. You don't understand. I have to ask the centaur something I need to know."

Kyra began to swiftly move out where she could be seen, but before she made it out, Edeline jumped over her, and wrestled her to the ground. She couldn't stop herself once she got started, deaf to Kyra's hoarse protests, as she began to bind Kyra's wrists behind her back. Once she'd tightened the rope and the first knot was done and she could slightly relax her muscles, she heard Kyra pant, "Why?"

"Because I can't let you hear a word it has to say without being there by your side to hear it with you. And I can't do it, just can't hear what it will say, because if it stops being *it* and becomes a *person*, I will know this person before he dies. And if it is a person, then I will remember this moment for the rest of my life and won't be able to let it go. And all that matters to me right here and now is that I will be able to forget everything."

-8-

At the reserved mahogany table at the club, surrounded by his friends who roared with laughter, Niels wanted to hide underneath it, to take cover from their japing. *"Gentlemen!"* he finally said, requesting order like a judge by banging his fist on the dark mahogany. "Many disbelieve, like you, but for irrational reasons. Some call themselves scientists yet still cling to childish beliefs in a god. And how is this different from the uncivilized people, who believe in a sun goddess? Which tells them that the rays of the sun are only life-giving and good and can never be lethal, so why should the shield of a magnetic force help us even if it existed? I respect your views, that sunlight can't be deadly. But *everything* is deadly if it's unfiltered. Even water. Saltwater would kill us, yet when it is lifted high and pours down as rain, it becomes drinking water through a natural process. Even thoughts would make us deadly enemies, were they not lifted up and filtered before we speak, through the natural process guided by our highest selves, our conscience, purifying and tempering our worst impulses not just with reason but with *compassion*."

*

Only as Leina dared to venture a full step inside the cave did she see that the centaur had been wounded. A gash in its left flank, as if from an arrow, which must have been hell to draw out. Coagulation closed up, yet blood still dripped in a slow cadence. And judging by the look in its eyes, it was in serious pain.

It spoke words slurred by a dizzy state, telling Leina it had intoxicated itself with something, probably to brave the pain as it extracted the arrow. And the words it spoke were either poetry or half-drunk and half-feverish delirium. *"See the red cloud climb. See the horses gallop wild. How they tear the old enclosed earth asunder. In the red sun."* A pause, and Leina and Katanya's flitting eyes met and then parted, looking again at the creature, as it continued, *"Under the naked tree. Hear the sisters weep. For a thousand hooves like sky-cracking thunder. In the red sun."* A second pause. *"Within mother's farthest fields. Where peace of father heals. There hides her smile in the gentle grass of summer. In the red sun."*

Dazed by the hypnotic picture painted by those words, Leina found herself walking as though through a dream, walking to it—no, to *him*. She tore off a strip from her cotton undershirt and began to clean his wound with the water she'd brought with her. As she did this, she never heard Katanya utter a single word. She spoke to the creature as though to a human patient, didn't ask him any questions, just told him what she was doing and warned him and got him ready when she moved the wet cloth onto his wound. And the only time he spoke, it was in what she now was certain was poetry from another world. And she would never forget the fourth poem. Hearing him recite with a fetching melodious foreign accent: *"Watchful child shrouded in night. Weeping for the death of the day. Her storm clouded budding fight. Defying defeat of decay."* A short pause. *"Certain eyes, unsure heart, your sadness yours alone. Singing dreams, songless speech, bled blameless to the bone. Crying rage, torn diary page, your fever blinds the sun. Desert seed, plucked family weed, flames rise where you run."* Another pause, just as short. *"She's a storm lost in dryness. Screaming at the deaf sky. She drowns your burning shyness. Wronged life you cannot right."*

Leina looked at Katanya and Katanya glanced back. Then they both looked at the centaur. Watched him become drowsy before their eyes. And he laid down on his side. And slept.

They were just two girls—this was much bigger than them.

Both girls sat hugging their knees to their chests, staring at the frightsome enormous being. Not a sound passed between the three of them, a solemn silence that didn't seem to end, as on and on he slept. Maybe an hour crept by. Neither girl dared to even whisper throughout that time, for fear of waking him.

As he woke and rose to stand on all four of his majestic equine legs, he was dramatically different from before. Lucid. Clear-eyed. And for the first time, he spoke to them in a way that they could understand.

"You're deep inside the ever branching gorges of a canyon which has no name, though humans think they've named it Topazin. The centre is carved by a river with countless tributaries, that dried out thousands of years ago. Like a tree, these gorges branch and rebranch, with many islands of rock between each, creating a maze in which one can easily get lost and die. Smugglers and robbers used this cave, and another one I lived in once. Outside this cave, there are many gorges you can take, each leading to more gorges still, and few paths you can take lead out. But I can't show you the right paths, because if I leave, there's a good chance I will be seen, and then you'll be caught for having helped me. We will have to wait until the men give up their chase, which there's a good possibility that they will, as the canyon is perforated with so many gorges that their task is like looking for a needle in a mountainous haystack. I know this because I took refuge here after I was cast out of my tribe. I then waited at the edge of my birthplace, until I saw my sister venture out, possibly looking for me. From a distance, I saw her trust humans, saw her get trapped in your world. I freed her, and now I can't go to the edge again, to hope to see my sister come out to tell me my banishment is over, because of what I did for her.

"But to thank you both, for warning me, for tending to my wound, I will give you four gifts. When the soldiers have gone, I will lead you out of the canyon. The second gift is a secret no human knows. The third gift is that I will always come when you shout my name, and I can hear things from the longest distance, as my hearing is many, many times more powerful than yours. My fourth gift is to let you drink a drop of my blood, in which you will see your *true* selves, what you're to do to be *whole*."

Silence thudded with Leina's heartbeat. She thought about it for a long time. Then said she wanted it. Wanted to swallow a drop of his blood to know the truest wish of her secret heart.

"Why?" Katanya demanded. "Why would you want that?"

Leina gave her a sideways glance, a little smile urging for the girl's patience, then spoke to her while looking at the centaur.

"If I don't, I will always wonder about it and it will kill me, that I missed the chance to just once know true *happiness*."

Something about what she said, or how she said it, upset Katanya in a way Leina hadn't foreseen. As Katanya turned her eyes back to hers, those big eyes were shining with emotion bigger than this moment, maybe spanning her whole life, tears growing, full of light from a mysterious source not from this cave. But as Katanya then spoke, what surprised Leina most of all was the girl's anger, saying, "I thought you would discuss it with me, before you decided."

Katanya then went to the dark corner of the cave, and before she melted with the shadows there, Leina saw her close her eyes and hold her hands over her ears, not wanting any part of this or be a witness to what would happen next.

Then the strangest moment in Leina's life took place.

As he bit his wrist and offered it down to her mouth.

As she committed to what she felt at that moment.

She did it before she had time to be afraid.

Maybe a minute had passed when next her awareness came back. And it came with Katanya's voice, asking her if she did it.

"I did. He punctured a vein with his canine, and I drank."

"What did you see?"

Leina opened her mouth. But for some reason, she was too nervous to tell what she saw. "I can't tell you."

"That's not fair, Leina. You have to. Please? *Please!*"

"I'll only tell you if you do it, too."

"Never. No buggering way. Uh uh. Not a chance."

A couple of minutes later, Katanya was looking up shyly at the centaur, as he bit his other arm for her. Leina grinned widely, having succeeded in being more stubborn in her secrecy than Katanya in her pressing. And less than a minute later, Katanya opened her eyes, on her back, staring as if at the brightest stars.

Stroking the girl's hair back and watching her come awake a little more with every slow blink, Leina suddenly felt more than a little tipsy. Yet mysteriously tense at the sensation of the soft hair against her palm. She said, "I think it will be less nerve-racking if we both say what we saw at the same time."

Katanya nodded. "On four?"

They counted to four, and said the same thing: *"A beach."*

As they told one another what they had seen on the beach, the two of them in loincloths, living in a hut with every tidal wave putting a spell on them anew, the blood was intoxicating them. Leina saw it in Katanya, the dizziness Leina had already felt and that only intensified. Increasingly drunk on just one drop of the centaur's blood, which she now seemed to remember tasted just like salty red wine.

Leina demanded to know his name. He gave it.

While Katanya stood back, Leina asked, "Your name is Ruckor?"

"Ruhchor."

"Yeah, I'm not going to call you that. What do your friends call you? Ruch? Ruey?"

"Chor."

"Seriously? Pronounced that way, as in doing a 'chore'?"

"Does that mean something in particular?"

"It's a task you do routinely, that doesn't stimulate you, like doing the dishes."

"I'm sure that can be stimulating if you've never done it."

"Then it isn't a chore. I tell you, it's the worst nickname I've ever heard. I'll call you Chory."

"Big improvement. I suppose it's better than my brother's. Huhchor. People call him Huh."

"Huh?"

"Huh."

"No, I mean, huh?"

"Yes, Huh."

"Well, you can see how that would confuse normal people, can't you? Wait. You're pulling my leg, aren't you?"

"I am. And it's fairly easy to do. You only have two of them and need at least one to stay upright."

"Maybe I just pretended to fall for it and was actually the one pulling your leg."

"In that case, I have three more. But I can tell that you saw something precious when you were affected by the drop."

"We saw the same thing. Is it the future?"

"No. It's the place where you let the future go. I'm glad you don't seem to regret it. You're my first. I've heard stories."

"Do you really mean it? That you haven't done it before?"

"I wouldn't have said that it was my first time as a blood-giver if it hadn't been true. It was. And it is."

After that, even as it happened she could barely retain what they said, forgetting each new word soon after it was uttered.

And the centaur disappeared without saying goodbye. But Leina mistook the past for the future, and so she thought that she and Katanya soon would find this cave and be shocked to see him inside it, which in her confused mind hadn't happened yet, as if she moved inside a memory. And in her intoxicated state, she found she was losing herself, losing her inhibitions. Shame of her sexual nature and all her forbidden, repressed fantasies no longer made any sense at all. And the realization came without effort, that if there are rules that you can break without hurting anybody, then such rules are meant to be broken. That laws without reason, made only to conserve a static society that couldn't evolve, are immoral. That all that mattered, all she had to follow, was the guiding light of her conscience.

She saw the same discovery light up Katanya's eyes, and her heart skipped a beat and she lost her breath. How could she have been so blind? How couldn't she have seen how stunning Katanya was? And how wondersome it was, to be so stunned, knowing such beauty existed. That eyes could shine like that. That a mouth could be that exquisite. Leina felt her pulse rush in violent hot beats, felt her cheeks burn and her breath quicken. Aroused nervousness filled and filled her, because she found herself unable to look away from Katanya's lips, wanting to kiss them, yet trembled as if in the presence of a goddess, finding herself unworthy. Speechless with regret at having chosen blindness and insensitivity in Katanya's company, never having allowed herself to swallow her pride and see Katanya's true beauty, there in the soul of her eyes and the desire of her mouth.

Katanya leaned close and whispered in her ear, though they were all alone in the cave. "I don't know what's come over me, but I don't ever want to lose this. I've never wanted anything this much. It's stupid, but when you just looked at my mouth, I had a fantasy that you suddenly loved to look at me, more than you've loved the sight of anyone else, and that you wanted me to look at you the same. I want to see only you."

The whisper came hot, came just like magic and did things to Leina she had no words for, and she couldn't think, nor did she want to, just wanted this wildness, this unbendable will to know Katanya's taste. She gave herself to it, kissed Katanya fully, kissed a mouth that tasted so good that she could hardly believe her taste buds, sweeter than wine. She had to hold back the heat that had come over her like rising flames fanned and lifted by a storm. The rarest thing, for blood to burn like this, for ribs to nearly break with the beat. Fearing they might be heard and devoured by human beasts if they became too loud, she sensed the same tension in Katanya, yet neither of them could stop.

Katanya's kiss felt like the motion of a mesmeric dancer. That graceful. That flowing. Her tongue bewitching, taking Leina's breath and mind, taken up to a dizzy height to balance along the edge of ecstasy. Wholly filling her with such sensitive need, with passion taking her so out of herself, she felt the pull of the rapture that obliterates the ego, close to the earthquake inside.

Feather-light, they moved their hands to hold one another's face and neck as they kissed. Slowly, as if doing it in her sleep, Leina's other hand progressed towards Katanya's breasts, then slid to their pointed peaks. Katanya's hand moved down with equal slowness. Their sound and motion were dreamlike, they touched the other like they themselves most ached to be touched. As their fingers slipped down underneath to where they with shut eyes felt a secret blaze of need, they burned their fingers on each other at the same time. But for all that they burned, they sought more friction, more heat, yet prolonging their pleasure, never wanting to have their fill. Breathing ever bigger, ever freer, until they no longer could hold back the release of their loosened daring, and their burning, seeking skin somehow seemed to find divine melting ice, as they shuddered as one, a chill born of fire.

*

Leina woke up with the mother of all headaches. And as memory fragments hit her and she pieced them together one by one, she buried her face in her hands. She had never known she could be this mortified. All her inhibitions and shame had returned, and it all hit her in full force. She felt such embarrassment that she regretted not having taken flight when she saw Chor in the cave.

She got up on an elbow and twisted around. Katanya stirred by her side, her slow movement and sleepy, unfocused gaze telling her that the girl had slept by her side all through the night. Over by the cave opening, the centaur seemed to meditate.

They ate in silence the salty beans he supplied them with. It was good, but it didn't give her the full sustenance she needed.

Finally, she spoke to Katanya in a subdued quiet tone. "How do you feel?"

"Like my head is exploding over and over again."

"Don't you feel anything else?"

"Of course I do." Cagily, Katanya frowned, her eyes averted as she thought. "I feel different. Not confused. Just… uncertain."

"Katanya, you must know that last night, it wasn't real."

Katanya shot back an injured look, the full significance of which Leina tried but couldn't read. Then, as if a dark spell had been cast, those crestfallen eyes hardened. Yet it looked to Leina like Katanya had to muster all the strength she had just to look at Leina's face. Her words, though, fell easy with her truth, as she then quickly told Leina, "It was to me. So no, I mustn't."

"Aren't you ashamed?"

"Not in the way you are."

Katanya got up, and Leina saw how that small head must hurt with pain too big for such movement, and yet the girl moved with it. Walked away. Braved come what may.

"Where are you going?"

"To the inner recesses of the cave. To find another way out. At least that will be of some worth."

As if she was worthless.

Leina tried to save something between them, though she wasn't sure what. "I don't understand why you—"

Katanya gave an abrupt, short, sad laugh. "No, you don't understand. Why do you care? You're—" And here her voice sank down to a whisper, "—*not my friend. You'd shown it by now.*"

"What do you mean?"

An angry whisper flew once more from the girl towards Leina, like heat thrown in her face. "I told you! I told you it'd mean so much to me, to be called Kat, for you to call me by a name *I* chose like I want my friends to. And *you never did it!*"

Strange, strange girl. Wait. Does this strange girl have any friends?

"Katanya, I can't just—"

But Katanya turned and made her way into the thick, black shadows. And before Leina knew what to say, it was too late.

*

Kruso felt it all again, the time when Edeline's love for him had been new and he had been wholly new to her. Tonight, finding their tent by the canyon empty, it all came back. Coming like a true friend's kindness that sang with laughter, like lost songs of forgotten dreams of many paradises, all true; so his love for her flooded him. And his throat tightened with how he missed her, missing how she used to miss *him*. How full of promise it had been, their beginning. Losing themselves in the other, how fine their abandon. How bright the nights of endless talking; how sunny the days of insatiably discovering each other. Before the flame in her eyes little by little lost its intensity. Her eyes still glowed sometimes when she looked at him, mostly when she saw a new, unexpected side to him, but it had another meaning. Maybe he couldn't be for her what she wanted any more. He had tried to make her unceasingly excited about him again. But like blushes or tears reveal intimate private feelings you don't wish to be out in the open, who he really was betrayed him. She had at times made him the happiest he'd ever been, the times she'd shown him that even when he was himself the most and didn't hide a single flaw, she still wanted him. Wanting everything that made him *him*. Once, in bed, she'd whispered, *"I adore you."* But it now seemed she no longer saw it, whatever that person had been to her.

What he now was to her seemed to be something she couldn't love as fiercely as before, as if a big part of her love for him had been for the newness of him. But clothes that once fit you perfectly can do so again, with time and effort, reclaiming your body like rebuilding a temple. They'd once worshipped one another equally. But while he still would go down on his knees at her feet to show his devotion, he feared she couldn't do the same.

If he had been better at so many things which he suspected that she secretly wished for in a lover, then she would never have stopped wanting only him. Then her curiosity would have been so tempted by him alone if he could keep on surprising her, that she'd never wanted to look elsewhere. He worried that he had let her down one time too many, that he hadn't been able to live up to who she'd hoped him to be. A worry that felt like an infected wound, and dwelling on it only caused the pain to deepen. He had to stop, but he didn't want to give up on them, because his hope was the most stubborn thing. That he would survive his military service and lose all that estranged and win all that endeared, rediscovered, as she would see him with new eyes.

*

Katanya came back with pride in her poise, eyes full of wonder, her pained anger for the moment forgotten.

Directing the words at Chor, she said, "There's a rope attached to a rock and a mechanism to lower it and lift yourself up through an opening!"

"The smugglers hauled loot out of that gap. In the other cave I spoke of earlier, I saw riches from near and far."

"We should go there!" Katanya said, then reined in her joy.

Leina offered peace, extending sympathy with a soft look. She said, "Your family must be sick with worry by now."

"I'll go back home once I know what will happen with Chor. As for me, a stray cat, I don't fear what will happen. My father is so meek that he couldn't get himself in jail even if he wanted to. At best, he'd be given a slap on the wrist for an attempted threat that no one can imaginably take seriously."

"Ah," said Leina, a hint of laughter in her speech. "How I envy you, to have an authoritative figure who's a pushover."

They laughed so very hard then, so spontaneously madly – such freeing release in the hardness of it and such welcome rescue in the madness – that Leina couldn't say if they laughed at nothing or at everything.

"It has its perks. I love that he never lies. But I just wish that he wasn't always so afraid of stepping on anyone's toes."

Katanya told them that she had used the mechanism to let herself be pulled through the top of the cave, up to the plateau above, seeing the horses on the other side and the magnificent tall palms hanging out from the brink on both sides. Chor asked her if she'd wound up the counterweight again, and she said no, that she had climbed down the rope and come directly to them. Hearing this, he said something about going to the winch to wind it back up. Like he had last night, and like Katanya had this morning, he disappeared inside the deepest recesses of the cave.

Katanya said, "I saw smoke coming from a point above the gorge farthermost to the left."

"Must be the military Chor spoke of. Look. My father will leave no stone unturned, trying to bring me back. I can't survive out there, having left home with nothing but the clothes on my back. I have to face the music, and go back. But not until I've given Chor a chance to get back to his world."

"How do you propose we do that?"

"By convincing them to let us stay at their camp. You know, know your enemy. Then, when we've gained their trust, we go back here and tell him to make a run for it while we lead the soldiers in the wrong direction."

Katanya licked her cracked lips. "I hope we'll make it."

"Then, when he's safe, I'll go to him. I intend to make him find his human side, his good human heart. I can *change* him!"

"I just think we should be careful. No, let me explain. I never believed everything they say about mythical beings. That centaurs and all other such savage creatures are inherently evil, beings without souls. People only believe that because the only times half-humans are mentioned in religious texts are when it is to name various spawns of hell sent to tempt us, hiding their monstrosity until we either fail or pass the test. I believe this centaur can help us in ways we can't yet imagine if we help him. But we can't forget that he *is* a wild, wholly uncivilized creature."

"I know, but I'm sure the influence of my humanity will make him see the advantage of civilization against primitive foraging. I would rescue him from his nature. It could be thanks to me that he renounces his wild side if I'll be the one who moulds him into being *all* human on the inside. And I could let the world know that I've helped him find goodness in his savage heart and that they have nothing to fear. Then, when he is more human than animal, I'll present him to a more peaceful human realm, and that is how everyone will see that he's not a monster. When they'll see him as you and I have."

Katanya bit her lip, though it was painfully swollen with dryness. "Before you let your ambition run away with you, let's first see if we can see the camp from the plateau on the other side, where we left our horses."

So, that's how it was. How it came to be that this time it was they who left the centaur without saying goodbye. And they did it without yet receiving half of their promised gifts. Never doubting that both of them one day would.

-9-

Walking to the dinner party his friends were throwing to celebrate the birthday of Taleb Ashroot, a fellow student from Kullum Academy, an argument with his grandfather ran through Niels' head. His sister hadn't been invited to the party, and now his lonely thoughts turned to a particular part of yesterday's subdued argument. The part that had been about Aurora. The words his memory honed in on, in what really was more of a bickering than an argument, had come just outside the temple, in whose graveyard they'd shed a silent tear and picked up oak leaves from a low-hanging branch to put on Nita's grave. Cliff had found a suitable subject to take his mind away from his grief, which Niels understood would never fully go away.

"If I'm to give you my financial support for this project, I have some reservations about whom you are conducting it with."

"I know my sister seems scatterbrained, but she's really smart."

"She hides it well. I expected more from her."

So that was it, the reason for his grandfather's upset feelings, that Aurora had declined to come with them to visit Nita's grave. After a while, Niels had said, "Don't be so hard on her. I'm sure you wouldn't have wanted that if you'd been her."

"Being too easy on her wouldn't be best for her, either."

"I believe she'll go on to accomplish great things."

"We'll have to wait and see."

"Well, that's in her favour."

"How do you mean?"

"She's not big on waiting."

It had hit him then, the urgency, like a vital moment they needed, slipping away. Missing Aurora, it hit him all over again.

*

It was still dark when Edeline woke Kruso. Her whisper was like the fall of a calm wave. She looked amused yet solemn, somehow. Blinking himself wider awake, he said, "Where were you? I've been worrying all night. I heard on the way back that something made you abandon the task to bring Kyra to her father's farm."

"I could tell you were worried by the tone of your snoring."

"I did wait up for you."

"Is it all right if Kyra sleeps here tonight? The poor thing is frightened and I told her she could. She's just outside."

"I don't mind. We might not be here for much longer. When I searched the camp for you, the men came back and I found out that one of Ramery's arrows had wounded it earlier today. Now we'll only have to follow the tracks of its blood. What happened out there, that made you and Kyra turn back?"

"She told me of a girl, Leina, who has run away from home. She and I saw her, not far at all away from here. If you and I make common cause with Kyra and head out tomorrow with a good strong rope, we can fetch a good reward for delivering Leina to her father, instead of Kyra. We can probably only get her to go with us kicking and screaming, but it'll be worth it."

After discussing it back and forth, weighing the dangers against the merits, he agreed to go along with her plan. "But how will you explain to the captain that you returned with Kyra?"

"I'll think of something."

"You haven't thought of something yet?"

"Maybe I'll say we were surrounded by a pack of hairless desert wolves?"

"Outside the desert?"

"They could be lost."

"Well, that is something, all right, though I'm not sure what. But before I'll shut up and let you think on, I have something important to say. There's a man out by the watchfire, insisting to sleep there, out in the open." He told her how the two had met, though left out that he'd disdained an order. "But though I'm sure he told me his name – it's the oddest thing – I can't seem to remember it at all."

"So that was the man I saw come out of the captain's tent. Captain Brind must have given his blessing to let him stay the night here because then I saw him bunk down by the fire."

After talking some more about things that soon after would escape Kruso's memory, they let Kyra inside. Not very long after Kruso's awkward welcome and even more awkward questions, he laid down and turned his back to Kyra, to give her privacy as she undressed and got ready to sleep.

Next morning, his nervousness about what the captain would say proved to have been unnecessary. Edeline's story about the coal-black desert wolves was too wild not to be believed. The captain bought it, perhaps because it had been Edeline who sold it, and perhaps because his mind was occupied by a new set of problems. A bird had arrived in the night with word that the general had been delayed and wouldn't come until tomorrow at noon. The good news, Edeline said, was that the captain couldn't spare anybody and that he'd said that riding to Dophra with Kyra had to wait until the general and his men arrived. Even better news, he let the farmgirl have the sick tent to stay in until then, which she'd have for the night unless misfortune struck and the medic needed it.

He and Edeline trained archery throughout the day, awaiting an assembly with the promised announcement about how they would surround the beast like a slowly closing noose.

Later, they had a moment alone, with the others merry and loud, laughing the past away, lost in exchanged stories that hinted at many more eruptions of laughter. With no risk of being heard, they decided that as darkness set in, Edeline and Kyra would go back to where they'd seen Leina and that other girl, probably Leina's servant. After Edeline had located them, she'd return for Kruso, and the two of them would set out at midnight to capture not the beast, but a rich treasure that might be their ticket out.

Darkness crept in, and the plan was set in motion.

Two excruciatingly tense hours later, she snuck back into the camp unseen by the guard, and he wanted to hug her with the relief he felt to see her again. But he didn't. Not just because of how she looked, her optimism gone, though that was part of it. He didn't want to think about why he couldn't hug her, and then the reason why she looked so sad took over all his thoughts. She hadn't seen Leina anywhere. The footprints she'd found of the two women had led to a place too rocky to leave more tracks.

Outside their tent, men drank wine, celebrating that more wine would be theirs to celebrate with, brought with the general's best and most spoiled soldiers tomorrow. And Kruso heard them sing happy songs out there, the troop suddenly in an uncommonly untroubled mood. Probably because Ramery, their most skilled scout, had come back and said he'd found a gorge full of freshly coagulated blood and tracks of a limping centaur. The beast would surely be killed very soon, even if they needed all the general's men to search through every gorge and crevice of the entire canyon. But Kruso didn't want to take another chance, didn't want to go with Edeline to search for Leina any more. They couldn't be here when the general showed up.

"Edeline, we have to go. Tonight. You and me. This is it. General Urun is on his way and will arrive tomorrow, possibly even before noon, now that word has been sent that we've wounded the beast and that it is trapped in the canyon."

"So?"

"'So'?" He tugged his hair, and tore at it. "Urun isn't just the king's right-hand man in all military matters. In the hierarchy of the royal army, he outranks Captain Brind in the chain of commands by more chains than I care to count."

"Yes?"

"Which means that the freedom the captain briefly granted us won't be his to give for much longer. The general is taking over the mission, and anyone who leaves under his command will be hunted down and hanged as a deserter. My exemption warrant signed by the captain will be worthless tomorrow."

"I'm not like you. Not only do my family count on me to be the one to keep them afloat, I have nothing else I can master than my bow. I need to stay on to be able to eat and be healthy. Which means that I'm doing this to survive."

"If we don't run now, we'll never get the chance again. Not without dying for it."

"Even if I wanted to and was prepared to starve for it, I can't. When I couldn't find Leina, I started to think about how we're bound to a cause. We shouldn't be doing this for money."

"What cause? To chase after and kill a defenceless half-human? How noble."

"You, too, called it a beast. We can help stop the plague."

"You don't believe that."

"I'm not going to be a gutless wonder."

"Is that how you see me?"

"Look yourself in a mirror. What *do* you see?"

"It's ironic, you talking about loyalty."

"How many times do I have to say I'm sorry for that?"

"We've never really talked about it, and I've had enough of letting silence rule me. You slept with him and I have to see him every day. Our archery trainer. Why him? Why Temet? He told you once he was in love with you, telling you this though you were with me and I'd never treat you disrespectfully. After he told you this, you promised me not to be alone with him. Then he tried to hold your hand that time when it was his and your turn to wash the pots and pans. You told me you'd said you were happy with me, but on the next day, I saw you look at him like you were teasing him. And then you let *that* man kiss you, touch you, take you. It makes me want to throw up, every time I picture it. How do you think I feel when I see him standing close behind you and directing your hand on the bowstring while whispering in your ear? How could you do that to me?"

"Then I give you permission to sleep with anyone you like. Maybe that's what's going to save our engagement, for us to be even. So that I can know how you feel."

"It won't be the same. You know that I've slept with others before you, but I wasn't in love with them. Nothing will be as good as with you, because they won't be *you*. If you loved me, I'd always be better than him, because you said that though meaningless kinds of sex feel good, they don't come close to the meaningful kinds, which come with love. But how can I trust you when you say that you love me if you didn't love me enough to want me more than you wanted him that night?"

"Oh, Kruso. Don't try to make me feel guilty again."

"You have yourself to blame."

"What if we're all only as faithful as the availability of temptations? Could it be that the only reason you haven't been unfaithful yet is because the girls who you were tempted by weren't tempted by you, and so they never gave you the choice?"

"Go to hell."

He crept out of the tent then. For a moment he thought she would yell after him. That moment passed and the silence went on, and as he went on with clenched fists, seething, she was out of shouting distance, and he was not turning back.

He didn't need this.

He needed anything but this.

He needed to get out of his head.

His long strides took him straight to the canteen tent, which was big enough to fit the whole troop with some elbow room, and half of them were inside. A din, in there, a relief of loudness drowning out his thoughts, numbing his pain. So boisterous in their joking and jibing. So rowdy in their dancing and playfighting. So infectious, the wildness of their drinking songs. So joyously stupid. He joined them, and the next thing he knew he was drinking as well as singing. Sing-shouting his throat raw, every now and then remedying its swollen dryness with freshly poured wine that only made him thirsty for more.

In the nearest corner, Ziara, standing alone, eyes glittery, looking right at him. Ziara, the newest recruit, her dark-eyed attention smiling directly into his eyes with daunting soberness. Her straight dusk-blonde hair was very dark where it had been cut short, at the sides and neck. Her face was so young, as if she hadn't aged since she was eighteen. If he hadn't had Edeline, there would have been no one he would have wanted more.

Ziara stood still while all others seemed to sway as if on the deck of a boat in a storm. Her eyes moved slowly, from his eyes to his mouth, and her mouth sipped carefully, her lips suggestive, and her sun-browned warm skin gleamed with the fresh sweat of being fully alive. Jamming himself between drinking men and women damp with sweat, he closed the distance between them. His eyes were now on her hair that looked light as feathers, not crisp as Edeline's. When he'd first met Edeline, it had been her hair that caught his attention, wonderfully round, cloudy. He'd always had a mysterious fondness for girls with braids, but he didn't want to change anything about Edeline's hair, or anything else about her. But after what just had happened, he could turn his back on even his most precious memories of her. It helped that Ziara smiled like she did right at this moment. Talking to her now, hardly knowing what he was saying, he felt eager to forget, and she didn't seem to mind facilitating this wish. He found her witty, and she kept him on edge, on his toes, especially after she'd hoarsely said, "The way you dance around my questions tells me that the only dance you know is avoidance." She suggested they'd go outside for a smoke, and before he knew it, he was standing alone with her on the other side of the noisy canteen tent, deliciously inhaling from the pipe and the tobacco she shared with him. And he breathed in her scent and smiled easily.

They were a small, decimated troop, and if the gossip was tasty enough, like Edeline's cheating, everyone – including Ziara – knew about it. But it didn't feel like she was flirting with him because she pitied him. She seemed to genuinely like him, and Kruso had the feeling that if she thought about Edeline at all, it was only with the thought that what Edeline had done gave her license to do this now, this thing she wanted to. To give him this melting smile, this look of nervous energy that he seemed to remember from another lifetime. Her hand gently and briefly touched his upper arm, as if wanting to see if he felt like she'd imagined. He leaned in, and before he lightly shut his eyes, he saw that she let him come close, that her smile only intensified at his mouth nearing hers. And he kissed her, and deeply she kissed him back.

"Ziara... that felt so good."

"You're the only one who calls me by my full name, you know. With the others, it's either Zia or just Zi."

"I don't want to change anything about you." Which felt dirty to say, it being a sentiment so intimately attached to Edeline. Part of him instantly regretted it. But another part wanted Edeline to know the hell he'd gone through. And then there was the part of him that thought it was over between him and her, and this was the part that took over, that made it easier to fill his mind with only Ziara.

Seeing Ziara's reaction to what he'd just said, words once meant for Edeline alone, pushed the last image of Edeline out of his mind. Her eyes sparkled with delight, thickly sheened with what seemed to be a swift rising feeling of touched exhilaration.

Out in the tall grass, away from the camp at the mouth of the canyon, they sank down, entwined in a kiss that felt both like a thing full of sin and like the most natural thing in the world. Hidden by tall straws, embracing, she pressed herself to him, as if to show her strength. She kissed him just under his ear and her breath came hot and fast against his neck, a new sensation, and as she pressed more of herself into him, he felt against his chest her small pointy breasts prick him through her shirt, an unexpectedly thrilling newness. Then she was on her back and he followed her down, and as their breaths accelerated as one, they hastily freed themselves of their clothes, impatient, hurrying to do this before they changed their minds. Skin on skin, gliding in gleaming new sweat, he wanted her firm body closer, deeper, to drive away all tangled anger and knotted hurt. And as she slid herself carefully against him, pushed him inside her, it was the easiest thing, to slide away. Into exceeding tight heat, into flames that took the world away, his body sweetly strangled, his mind sweetly gone, slipping away with her, far from every painful memory.

The next morning, waking up with Edeline's arm around him, he felt more disgusted with himself than he'd prepared himself for. He told her, and she wasn't angry. It made him regret it all the more. When he didn't think about it, he felt empty, but when he let himself remember, all he felt was pain. Nothing had changed between them. He was hurting and she wasn't. What he said to her then he couldn't remember soon after. Mindless words, uttered just because he'd wanted to wipe the smile off her face. It had the opposite effect. Before, the weight of her carelessness felt like she'd stood on his chest. To see her smile now, despite what he'd done and said, he felt that he still had her weight on his chest. But now she danced.

It was only as she let it sink in that he saw insecurity rise to the surface, for the very first time. She opened her mouth, let it spill from her lips, there in their tent that smelled only of them, and what came out felt so tight that he could hear her suffocating sadness. But amidst the pain, a bittersweet release, as he guiltily took a dark pleasure to hear her say, "Was she better than me?"

*

After a long hour of speaking with the captain of these soldiers, who Leina heard singing loudly from the biggest tent in the camp, she went and told Katanya that they could stay here until the centaur had been caught. Katanya sat and thought about it, and Leina got out the thread and needle she'd asked for from the female soldier she'd seen by the watchfire. Where Black Hood had been sitting, eyeing her with lightless malice in his eyes.

Wait.

She stopped sewing and looked up with an inward stare. At some point, she had missed something important. Black Hood's horse had three speckles on each side. She mouthed the number to herself. Three. Why did that have such a familiar ring to it? There was something about it that she had to remember. But for some reason, it escaped her. She almost captured it, it was there, on the tip of her tongue, like a name just out of reach.

But if she could just remember where she heard something so similar, she—

Cutting into her thoughts, Katanya said, "Can we talk about what we did last night?"

"It's nothing to worry about. It only happened because we were intoxicated."

"So I'm nothing to you."

Leina was about to say something but hesitated. "I don't want to give you false hope."

"No. Only false love."

Right then, the tent flap opened, held up by the hand of a girl who looked very much like somebody Leina had seen before, more than once. Though she couldn't for the life of her say where or when. They greeted, and shook hands. The girl was tall, had solemn eyes and thick black hair gathered in a heavy braid. Speaking with a hoarse voice full of breath and spark, she said her name was Kyra, apparently from Dophra, like them. She, too, had been granted to stay in the sick tent, for now. But as the rest of the soldiers came to the canyon, a female soldier would take her and Leina and Katanya back to Dophra.

Leina began to tell Kyra why she was here, having planned to say that it must have been a full moon because madness had struck her and made her leave on a banana cart with not a coin in her pocket. But hardly had she begun her story before the tent flap was drawn aside once more, letting in blinding light. And in it, a black-hooded figure, saying, "A word in private, Madam."

Katanya flew to her side, admonished under her breath, *"Be careful. Remember Amaida."*

And as Leina stepped towards the tent opening, she heard Kyra faintly yet emphatically say to Katanya behind her, *"Amaida? The girl who raved about a crazy curse that didn't come and never will?"*

Less than a minute later, at a good distance from the sick tent, their eyes met, a challenge in his that she countered with her own, keeping her mouth shut. So he went first, smirking as he started to speak. "We both know that neither of us can tell these soldiers the real reason we're here. I can't tell them you warned the centaur because then you'd have to explain why you believe I can't be trusted. I don't know your agenda, lady, only that it isn't good. After the general and his men come later today, you and I are going to leave together, and you are going to show me to the place where the centaur is hiding."

"What makes you think I know?"

"Why else would you come to this camp, if not to try to mislead them, to help the beast? That means the beast must have been with you and gotten under your skin."

"What if I tell the captain that you killed an innocent girl? Were you there, in the guesthouse that night, hearing me say Amaida's name, hearing then about the curse? Yes, I can tell by your eyes that that was when you decided to go to her. What did she tell you? Why did you kill her? Did you believe that something she said was too dangerous for anybody to hear?"

"No. I don't believe. I know."

"I don't understand."

"Let me tell you a story. Less than a hundred years ago, an idea came to a man, took possession of his very soul. He became so convinced of it that he devoted his life to make others see it as absolutely true. The idea spread, and soon a whole population believed in that one idea. It swiftly became their truth, and they were ready to die for it. Their children drank it as their mother's milk. When the children became men and women, their leaders whipped them into a frenzy of hate for people who didn't speak their language, didn't look like them, and, most importantly, didn't share their idea. They went to war and killed as many of these other people as they could."

"What was the idea?"

"It doesn't matter what it was."

"What?"

"An idea is a cultural mutation, spreading either life or death as a new immunity or disease. With broadminded ideas come mutuality. With narrow ideas? *Singlemindedness.* If your culture wrestles with ideas of discord you might die in the wars they prompt, and kill without fear of death. And think of war as a mechanism for the destructive idea to kill other ideas, for it to be the parasite that rules its host. Its adherents will only know and only care for the idea, and after a long enough time they cannot see anything else. The idea becomes their only reality."

"What does all of this have to do with Amaida?"

"Think, lady. What I try to make you see, lady is that the Forbidden Forest isn't real. It is an *idea* that the whole world has caught, and so if they all say they see it, how can you refute them and say it isn't there? If everyone believes in it, it manifests."

"No. No, I've heard sensible people say they've seen it with their own eyes."

"If it does exist in the way it has been theorized, why does nobody come back after going inside? Had it been paradise, they would have hurried to bring back everyone they love, to share the treasure. What does that say about that place?"

"You mean it tempts because it is… *that* place? Then, the mythical beings, they really *are* demons?"

"Yes. That is their true nature, and we would see them for what they really are, should we lift the veil from our eyes. But that would require to stop believing the idea of myth being real."

"How can you think that you know that the idea you have is good and constructive when it led you to be violent with me?"

"Unlike my mentor, I hold the conviction that some diseases are good, that some destructive ideas are necessary in order to strengthen our immunity. Sometimes, taking one life is necessary in order to save many lives."

I will never, ever believe that. "Is that why you killed Amaida?"

"I couldn't allow it to spread. You know of which I speak. The sky becoming entirely purple in the middle of the day."

"Why is that idea so dangerous?"

"If that really were to happen, don't you see what that would signify? It would mean that none of this, none of us, are *real*. That there is no fate, that we are all merely corrupted by the idea of this life. And then the only thing that *could* be real would be inside the evil place you call the Forbidden Forest. People would become pilgrims, like my people, but they would go towards oblivion willingly, for an idea that would end us all."

"Who *are* you?"

"I'm the one doing the right thing. We're the good side."

"The soldiers claim—"

"They want to kill him. I'm going to use his own demonic torment against him to make him confess, and admit what he is. Hearing this, the world will amass and burn the forest, the place that spawned him. Our fire will destroy the evil that made him."

"What do you want from me?"

"One day, if we don't find the beast and these soldiers retreat, I'm going to come for you and have you lure him to me."

"My father—"

"Is powerless against my brotherhood. There's no greater power, no richer structure, than the clergy, and we are its fists."

Coming back to Katanya and Kyra, Leina told them what Black Hood had said, then told Kyra what Amaida had said.

"I think we can agree," Kyra said. "That Amaida was crazy, that the purple sky is just a fantasy, impossible in the real world."

Katanya frowned hard at the puzzle frustrating her again. The little girl shook her head as if to dislodge a nagging worry.

"But if all she said was crazy, then why did he kill her?"

And Leina truthfully said, "I don't really know."

Surprised by herself, by the unexpected significance of her sudden candidness with both herself and Katanya, Leina said nothing more. With eyes uncommonly far away even for her, Katanya softly broke the silence. "It's the strongest thing you can say sometimes, to admit that you don't really know. I think it opens you up to new inspiring perceptions because ambiguity is the best gift to imagination. Maybe you are close to the heart of the mystery, yet can only hear what makes it sing, while the lyrics will always be open to *interpretation*."

*

Kruso glared at the hooded man whose name the captain knew but wouldn't say. With a head toss, he motioned the cold-eyed man to the narrowest part of the nearest shadowy passage, soon facing him there, where nobody could see or hear them.

Kruso said, "You enjoy making girls lose colour?"

"Only rich, spoiled girls corrupted by evil sin."

"I don't fear you. You go anywhere near her or Edeline, you'll regret it, I promise. Right now, I fear nothing."

Kruso turned, and got ready to close this chapter. The man had heard him and they had nothing left to say to one another.

Kruso was already thinking of what to say to Edeline, what words would be the key to unlocking the place where they'd only had eyes and ears for each other. Where he had felt her touch in the night, her fingers smooth as grains pouring through the waist of an hourglass. The recollection made his heart pound with hyper-nervous hope. A wordless prayer in his pulse, thudding in his ear for the chance that there *was* a chance. If only he had listened to what Drein said that day by the river. That anger never helped. Oh, how he longed to have it back, the youthful innocence of the beginning, him and Edeline still new to one another, the simplicity before he let it all slip away.

A loud question thrown after him stopped Kruso in his tracks. "You don't fear the beast?"

Retreading his steps, facing the strange, hooded man again, Kruso said, "Nothing in the world is as big as your fear of it."

"You should fear divine punishment in the next world."

Kruso wrinkled his nose. "There's no next world after we die, and we're alone in this one. You can have your God. What kind of God creates people such as us, creatures of devastation? I can tell that you've never seen battle, where the good may choose to refrain from killing and yet die, and the evil may choose to kill and yet live."

"Those fated to die deserve it, as it is God's will. Only God has a choice, and He made it only once. We're merely players on a stage, in His play of fate, our script written by Him at the dawn of time. Guilt is an illusion. Only fear of God is real."

"Get this, believer. My botany teacher once gave me a book written by a fringe scientist. It states that when we try to explain how countless laws of our universe have come to be just as they are, we arrive at the conclusion that there are countless worlds. Given an infinite number of worlds, most will be lifeless and many with life will be choiceless. Yet infinity is such that there *has* to be one in which a thing as improbable as choice exists. Who's to say that we don't happen to live in that world?"

"Choice is an illusion, unbeliever. God's fate alone exists."

"Then why be a pilgrim? Why haunt those who wronged you, if they had no choice?"

"The Dark One desires evil and acts through them, and God wants us to battle evil. It's a test, all part of a grand design we can never know. And there is only one material world."

"Not so. If an all-powerful, all-predicting God doesn't exist, but freedom does, it would make us endlessly *fortunate,* as *we* would be divine, in every intention, every inspired choice that requires infinite imagination. Each time we make a choice that comes from careful weighing, whether we weigh with our mind or our heart, we imagine many different futures and let our mind or heart decide which future we would most love to live in. What brings the future of our choice into being isn't God, but our desire for something better. There's no need for God."

"I won't haunt you for your heresy. But I will prove to you that fate is real, thereby prove the existence of God."

"How could you possibly do that?"

"By killing the centaur. For I have seen a vision of my fate, in which the beast dies after I shoot a bolt through its heart."

-10-

Aurora gripped his newly ironed white linen shirt tightly. Seldom had her eyes been brighter, and rarely had she looked as awake, looking now like she sought to shake and whisk him out of a bad dream. "Oh, brother, where's your sense of *adventure?*"

"It was never about adventure. It was all about *science*. About uncloaking the mysteries of the world and seeing the truth bared behind it all. To answer by answer unlock the final answer to the question at the core of it all: What *is* this world?"

"And now you have a crisis of self-confidence, because of what? A silly birthday party where the silly guests made silly jokes about you."

"Do you think there is one word you tend to overuse?"

"Don't be silly."

"It wasn't just them. It's what everyone will say if I go on a flight and come back with results that I've interpreted wrong. My whole life will be a joke. That's why I have to give up before the dream kills me. Cliff will understand."

"You think too much about how you're perceived by a tiny part of the world in a blink of a moment in history. Think of how important this could be to the whole world for all time. With the balloon, you could hold the key of keys! You don't have to be the first discoverer of the Forbidden. You can be the one who discovers the source of our world's magnetism. What are you so afraid of?"

Anger flared up. "You act nonchalant and unafraid, like a scholar who knows too much to be unprepared or unequipped for any insult or criticism. You're clueless about how clueless you are, even about who you are. Do you even fool yourself?"

She smiled softly. "Oh, I do. That's the privilege of not knowing yourself, don't you see? You can be *anyone*."

*

Leina heard a wild commotion outside the sick tent. Squinting as she hurried out, she saw soldiers standing in a ring, laughing over what sounded like a fight between women. Presently, two of the men looking down at the fighters were chanting something Leina didn't catch, possibly in another language. As Leina pushed herself inside the throng, she saw Kyra wrestling a dark-complexioned female soldier, red dust all over them.

Leina scowled, exhausted by this emotional havoc around her, which ruined any chance for her to think clearly. She yelled at them to stop, yelled with such force that she almost didn't have to use the strength of her arms to break up the fight. With unmasked anger, she asked Kyra, "What's the matter with you?"

"With me? She's the one who jumped me. Ask her!"

In the same instant that Leina's eyes flit to the soldier and saw that she was crazed with rage, this hot-tempered young woman snarled, "You don't know me! And who are you to judge me when you have no clue what happened?"

Leina summoned as much patience as she could, then brought Kyra and the uniformed woman, Edeline, to the back of the sick tent, to get to the heart of the matter. When asked what happened, Edeline avoided her eyes, took a deep breath, and then said, "She destroyed my mother's book."

"That's not true. I only tore out the blank flyleaves at the beginning and the end of it, to use to write a letter to my family."

Leina's voice had much confusion in it as she asked, "You took her book and ripped out the few blank pages in it?"

"I didn't take it. I bought it. From the cook. Ask him. I even told him why. I'm going to send a bird with a letter to—"

"Never mind. I'll trade my ring for the book. Here."

Kyra eagerly took the ring and went and got the book and put it in Leina's hand. Leina promptly gave it to Edeline, whose tears of rage stopped falling, her eyes wet with gratitude instead.

Kyra, seeing something she hadn't expected in Edeline then, extended her hand. Edeline shook it, then turned to Leina.

"I need to give you something in return. No, I insist."

She took Leina to hers and her fiancé's tent, and there solemnly put a small mirror in Leina's hand. And said, "I saw that you have a makeup box similar to mine. I hope this mirror fits it. Or you can ask Kyra to give you her saddlebag. That ring is worth a lot more than that book."

"Not to you, I suppose."

"No. Not to me. This mirror. It was my mother's once, as well. But I want you to have it. I only need the book."

"I can't take it."

"You can, believe me. I won't let you leave without it."

*

In his much larger tent, Brind said to Kruso, "Now I have two high-strung women from Dophra on my hands. Do all High-Kalid women have such hot temper? Is it because of the economic strife Dophra experiences right now, I wonder? You know, one of the reasons why Kalid might go to war with—" Kruso's attention strayed because here his captain spoke of one of many reasons for conflicts between neighbouring realms. And it didn't take a genius to see that every reason for every such conflict, no matter where you happened to be born, had its root in an economic crisis or the threat of it. Anything beyond that only amounted to governing leaders disagreeing about who had the most right to lay claim to something of high value, which they thought would solve everything to possess. Kruso didn't see the point in trying to add anything to what had already been said by scholars whose life task it was to think about such matters, and whose books Brind clearly had studied carefully. So he listened only with half an ear, thinking of Edeline instead. Until they were back from the sidetrack, as Brind said, "But that's not why I called you in here, of course." And Brind had Kruso's ear and full attention again. "Did the peasant girl really attack your betrothed over a mere book, and did the other girl stop the fight?"

"Let's not get bogged down in details about who attacked whom and why. I was told that it was just a little scuffle. I was elsewhere. Happens between men every day, and don't you always say that the punishment should be no different when women are the offenders? Seeing as you have no punishment for brawls between men that ends with a handshake, the right thing to do here is nothing, yes?"

"Yes. It pays to be lenient and to not make an exception for women. But this is an odd affair, nonetheless. I can see why Kyra feels that life hasn't treated her fairly. But Leina is quite gruff for a girl who can have anything she points at."

"Well, Tan, Leina has every reason to carve her own path."

"Oh?"

"Yes, she's of noble bearing, a plantation dynasty heiress, but she's to marry a man sight unseen, to tie her family's fortune together with his, like a trade transaction. She told me her father wrote in a letter that the date of the wedding is already set."

"That, too, happens every day. So, she passes through the canyon to seek her fortune beyond the desert in the booming easternmost port cities of the Marbela tropics, no doubt. And now she refuses to leave before knowing the fate of the mythical being. But what am I to do with her, or with the peasant girl, for that matter? Both are adamant they'll stay here until we find the beast. I can't be responsible for her, but her father has the means to prosecute me if I send her away and the beast kills her."

"Tan, if I may suggest. Let them think what they will."

"Which is?"

"That we're here to protect the people, not to kill for the king."

"And when we do?"

While Brind waited for his answer, Kruso thought about what the pilgrim had said. That he'd seen a vision of the centaur being killed by the pilgrim's hand. Maybe that was a vision of a chosen future in another world, made by all the choices of those living in it. Not this one. Where Kruso could make his life matter because his every decision counted. He only wished Edeline's decision hadn't broken his heart and killed his joy. But infinite imagination meant endless unpredictability. Something good, which he couldn't see yet, might come with the bad.

He realised his pause had drawn out too long. But as he lifted his eyes, he saw that this could be his chance to break away. "Then I volunteer to escort them to the nearest outpost."

"If I agree to this, will you need Edeline with you?"

"Tan, the reason I volunteer is to be *without* her. We've come worlds apart. We share but a tent, no longer a life."

*

As the sun approached zenith, Leina, feeling ever more that she'd missed something, walked slowly through the camp, staring.

There it was, the horse. Three speckles.

It came to her then.

Her oldest brother, Benky, was the one who had told her, Leina, the sibling resembled him the least. He'd made her swear to never ride with a man on a horse speckled that way. The richest pilgrims rode such horses, believing three to be a sacred number, paying a fortune for a mount with three spots. Most pilgrims were fanatics, and there was one thing about them that she'd been told again and again. Never slight a pilgrim. He will bind his fate to yours to make you atone, and if you didn't do all he asked of you, he will haunt you for the rest of your days.

Haunt? A big piece of the puzzle fell into place.

She had been looking in the wrong place in her search for the killer. She recalled now what people called 'pilgrims' haunt', an old name for where they nearly always stayed on their journeys. They could be found in the guesthouse, the very place she'd been to on the night of the murder.

Terror flew into her, nearly seized her, and required enormous willpower to keep it away from her heart.

She knew he had killed Amaida and now that she'd revealed this, he would *haunt* her. And then he would kill her.

She stared at the hooded man. Her eyes secretly followed his every movement. She watched him lay down in the shade next to the soldier who had stood watch last night. To nap under a tree that she'd seen too seldom to have learned its name.

Time was running out—the general's arrival imminent.

Quietly she gripped the heaviest stone she could find.

Quietly she carried it to where he lay on his side.

And lifted it over her head to bring it down on his.

-11-

Coming wide awake from a dream of a paradisaically sensual forest, the home of a green child, Niels remembered how much time had passed. A whole year since their maiden flight in the hot-air balloon he'd devoted his life to. Before he'd given it all up.

But this vivid, strong dream, made him feel like the world he knew was ephemeral, that the fire of the sun lasted but for a blink of an eye. In this view, life was far too brief to throw away.

In the dream, this year's summer solstice had already dawned and he had walked inside that dawn, which a new legend said would be the end of the Forbidden.

What if it were true, and he would never see that place?

In the apartment that spanned the entire top floor, the place he had lived in most of his life, he walked on shaky legs to the oak-furnished library. Where he could count on his scatterbrained sister to be found, curled up with whatever book made her eagerly lose sleep. And he felt so happy to see her that he immediately asked her, "Remember what I always say to cheer you up?"

"Study harder?"

"No. Not that. I say, Sometimes you chase a dream and sometimes a dream chases you, and you're equally hard to get."

"A girl once fell in love with me and wanted to kiss me."

She never failed to out of nowhere blurt something that made him befuddled. "You never told me that."

"She said I had positive energy because I'm a dreamer. Dreams can't die, because even when dreamers die, their dreams live on, even if they never shared them because the energy of their dreaming can be felt in all they say and do in life."

"Did you?"

"Did I what?"

"Kiss her?"

"You didn't listen to anything I said, did you? I'm your sister. Do you really want to know?"

"It would change my perception of you, though our close-knit biology means that I would find it quite less than enjoyable."

"You don't know her. Besides, I don't kiss and tell."

"The less I know the better. But we got off track. What I want to say is that though I rarely remember my dreams, I just had a dream come to me that felt like being sucked away from space and time. I felt so small and insignificant, my life so short, like a wind passing through, and it gave me comfort, strangely."

"Are you saying you've changed your mind about the project? That I won't be going alone?"

"Well, I'm a reasoner, not a dreamer. I need to think."

He headed out, telling her he needed some time alone, saying to himself to stop being ridiculous. It was just a dream. That he was being as irrational as his sister and that his friends would once more hurt him with their laughter if he pursued this.

Then, a sudden downpour. He looked up, couldn't explain no matter how hard he thought about it, how the drops didn't hurt, though they fell the longest distance before they struck him. How they somehow only struck him softly. Suddenly it was to him as though he was witnessing something from the other side, from within the Forbidden, reaching out to be known, by him, a mystery never touched, never struck, now at first within *his* grasp.

Not since he'd been a boy had he talked to himself, yet did it now, in the rain. And it almost felt like his words were meant for the raindrops, so soft on his skin, like the touch of a mute friend. He said, "To hell with them. I'll do this for the *dreamers*."

*

Aurora, more vivacious than ever, vaulted into the wicker basket.

Stiffly, Niels breached a delicate question. "I thought your sweetheart would be here to see you off."

"I broke up with him yesterday."

"Oh."

"But I did it so nicely that he may not know we've broken up."

"Ah."

"Though to be fair, he may not entirely have known we've been seeing each other romantically, either, so I wouldn't worry about it."

"How nice of you to consider my feelings about your romances. Do you remember everything I taught you, every test flight we took together, all through this winter? I mean, I'm worried that all you remember are the thousands of snowballs you dropped down on people's heads from a very expensive scientifically funded balloon. It drove me so mad. You even became an expert at hiding snowballs and tricking me into believing you've given up the habit. Can you once and for all tell me why you always did that?"

"Because it was hilarious! I thought you knew!"

"Well, your aiming got uncanny by the end of it, I'll give you that."

"Are you going to stand there all day or are you going to help me cast off? Hoodlum's already inside and I can tell that he's eager to be the first guinea pig to discover the Forbidden. All you taught me won't do any good if you don't untie the anchors, so what are you waiting for? God, how I love to give orders! Though I must say, it won't be quite the same without you with me to listen to them and botch every order, per usual. But I understand, truly I do, dearest brother of mine. You don't want to risk losing life and limb, not necessarily in that order. It will be dangerous as all buggering hell. But Hoodlum isn't afraid of danger. Danger is afraid of Hoodlum."

"Aurora."
"Yes?"
"I was wrong."
"Does that mean?"
He just smiled.

*

Done with the arrow she'd been fletching, Edeline inspected her own work, sitting near the canyon at the place they used for training. Absently, she slowly lifted her hand to her mouth and squeezed her lower lip's fullness, nipping its midpoint.

In the tumultuous time when Edeline had stumbled into puberty, she had known herself increasingly intimately. And knowing herself so, she knew she would be aloof as an adult, so no one would know when they struck a nerve. To drop her guard, she would have to intimately know somebody else. That somebody, that person she'd seen another part of herself in, a part which she loved, that had been Kruso.

But now she was afraid that he couldn't see anything in her that inspired the best in him any more. She'd rather not know.

*

Trying to find rest in the shade of the tall canteen tent, Kruso vividly saw a time he ached to have back. He and Edeline when they'd kissed while washed by pouring rain on a warm, drunken, blissful night, just last summer. Saw again many other times when he'd marvelled at her body, how she held herself, every muscle and curve set in a balanced symmetry that took his breath away. A fierce look to her poise, her naturally thrust-out strong chest, a sharp toughness even to her fist-sized upward-pointed breasts that at times closely fetched a rose-thorn likeness to him. All he wanted was to pull her to him, to feel that sharp danger amid her soft warmth, and embrace all of her.

It amazed him, remembering how fiercely he had loved her.

And in that memory, he rediscovered her.

*

Something made Leina hesitate, her hands trembling under the weight of the stone over her head. She turned, lowered the stone carefully to the dry tufts of grass amid the dusty red soil, staggered away to stand and think.

Then—movement at the edge of her vision. As she turned fully back around, she saw Katanya move under the tree. It happened so fast, how Katanya, her back to Black Hood, attempted to do what Leina had stopped herself from doing. Before Leina had time to open her mouth, she became aware that Black Hood had woken and had his crossbow in his hands.

Katanya stood with the stone raised above her head, facing away from Black Hood, her eyes on Leina as if awaiting some signal to turn back around and do what Leina had been unable to.

Behind the girl, whose small arms held the big, heavy stone up to the sky, Black Hood silently lifted his back from the ground. And pointed his crossbow up at the waifish form.

As Katanya slowly turned to face him with the stone still held high over her head, Leina cried, *"He's awake!"*

Just then, Black Hood fired a bolt into Katanya's chest.

The stone fell. Katanya reeled, stumbled sideways on and on. Finally lost her balance, fell down a gravelly slope, Leina leaping after her, rolling once, twice, then skidding to a stop by Katanya's dying body that swiftly drained of blood. Leina held the girl's face, crying, "I'm sorry, so sorry. It's all my fault."

The girl looked into Leina's eyes, stopped breathing, her last breath held in for just a second.

And in that second, Leina said, *"Kat."*

*

In a nightmare of surrealness, sounds muffled and distant, and very far away, Leina heard Black Hood speak to the soldier who had been with him under the tree, telling this man not to overreact. "That girl was the beast's witch. She had it coming."

Hoarsely crying out feral rage, Leina crawled up the small slope, plucked a bolt from Black Hood's quiver and lunged at Black Hood to stab him in the face.

Out of nowhere, Kyra tackled her, sending them both flying to the yellow crispy grass on the hard, red, baking-hot soil. On all fours over Leina, Kyra panted, *"Stop it! This isn't you!"*

"You don't know me! You don't know what I can do!"

"I know you're not a killer."

What happened next was hard to explain. Somebody grabbed her and she let it happen, and gave in. Knowing it was over. She moved sluggishly, unable to speak or look a single person in the eye. Moving then for the rest of it as if in a fog, seeing nothing but the shocking memory as it kept playing out in her mind. As a soldier apprehended her. As her hands were tied behind her back. As she heard two voices, that of Black Hood and of another man, telling the captain about the girl who had tried to kill him and how he had shot her in self-defence. As somebody somewhere said she was to be taken to stand trial.

Before they put her on a horse, she broke out of the nightmare and cried out Ruhchor's name. His full name.

But it was as though he'd only existed in a dream of another, fairer world because nobody came for her.

She kept the nightmare at bay just a moment longer, just long enough to urge the soldier to stop for a second, so she could say goodbye to Kyra. And to give Kyra the last of her strength. To whisper the most important words of her life in Kyra's ear.

*

The sight of Katanya's dead body carried away by two men still fresh in her mind, Edeline stood stock-still, as Leina called Kyra to her. She saw Leina cup her tied hands over Kyra's ear and whisper something that only Kyra could hear. Kyra's face went soft with astonishment as if she came awake from hypnosis.

Edeline stared, and blinked, feeling at this raw, bewildering moment how much Kruso meant to her. How much in life she had taken for granted. The regret that then hit her nearly made her pass out. A blow leaving her speechless.

Struck mute, she beheld the scene before her: Leina taken away, her last words a whispered secret for only Kyra to know.

Edeline wondered if she would have spoken even if she could, seeing Kyra slip away while only she watched.

*

On her horse again, alone again, riding into a gorge, Kyra felt as though falling forward through burning air. Until Lopo stopped sharply without warning. He wouldn't go on. She dismounted, and had to drag him after her. As her energy was nearly all spent, Black Hood came out from around the jagged bend behind her.

"You're going nowhere, whore!" he called, smiling darkly. Pointing his crossbow at her, slowly taking aim.

Just then, on the path Lopo had shied from, the centaur came—a fast, sudden grace. Her heart leapt at the sight of him!

Lopo reared, and tore the reins from her hand. But then Lopo succumbed, heeded the centaur's slightest movement, even as the mythical being dodged the bolt that flew past its shoulder, missing it by a hairsbreadth. She didn't know it was happening until she was in the middle of it, the centaur's hands pulling her up on his back, galloping out of harm's way into a tightening gorge, only Lopo able to keep up. As he didn't seem to slow down and they were about to lose Lopo behind them, Kyra told him to slow down and wait for her horse to catch up.

Panting as he galloped on, the centaur said, "Leave him. He'll find his way home."

Her protests spilt out and now he heeded *her*, slowing down considerably while she gave him the reasons why he must. "Lopo is my dearest treasure. Without him, I have nothing." In her desperation, she attempted to yank his black, curly hair. But it was too short, the thick little coils escaping her fist. As she groped for words for the turmoil inside her, her eyes dropped to his waist, which she still held with her other hand so she wouldn't fall off at a sharp turn. Below the firmness of his waist, a bladelike sharpness to his hipbones, then a gradual softness where the human hips fused with the sensuous curves of the equine shoulders of the front legs. Unexpectedly, the image of her brother flashed inside. The words came to her. "I sold a priceless ring to buy climbing equipment that's in the saddlebag, only carrying a rope and grappling hook with me in my belt."

"You're a mountaineer?"

"I didn't buy it for me. For my brother." Presently, her horse caught sight of them and happily galloped towards Kyra's voice, as she said, "His greatest wish is to climb Mount Aira."

"I saw you at your brother's farm."

"Not my brother's. My father's."

"Lopo, is he your father's horse, too?"

"No, Lopo is all mine."

After that, he had to stop speaking, as the pace made him too short of breath. They reached a place where the narrow gorge split into three dried-out even narrower channels. Taking the one to the left, looking behind him, he slowed down to a trot. He seemed secure that the clatter of his hooves on the stony path didn't leave any tracks and that their pursuer was far behind. And the hooded man would have to be very lucky if he guessed which way they took, as this was the fourth time the gorge had branched and they'd taken paths that seemed random to her. As he caught his breath, he told her, "I heard Leina shout my name. I have to turn back for her after I've gotten you to a safe place."

"It's too late. They immediately took her away."

Her thoughts were sad and far away, suffering with Leina.

They entered a gorge where there were overhanging palms, and a cliff wall curtained by vines. The centaur said they only had to go to this cave because it was the closest one.

"What cave?"

The centaur drew the vines aside and a large, round cave opened up before her eyes.

She told him she had to answer nature's call and then find grass for her horse. He nodded, then disappeared behind the natural green curtain. After she had peed, she looked up, turned round and round, slowly spinning as she looked west, at the hidden cave, north, at where the gorge bent and disappeared eastward, south, where it bent and was gone westward, and east, where she saw grass at last, up on the plateau opposite the cave. She squinted as she followed the vertical cliff walls along the gorge, overhung by tall date palms on both sides. Slender long trunks leaning in gentle curves over her head from the very top of the cliffs. Craning her neck, she marvelled at the palms there, up in the sky. The palms on one side often mirrored how those on the other side leaned out in corresponding curves as if the palms sought to bridge the gap between them. At times, the plumes of the longest palms nearly touched the other side's similarly long-reaching ones, forming at those times a formidable green high arch above. Here, where the midday sun stood directly behind a thin arch made by two palms hanging together in a semi-circle, it looked to her eyes like a high-peaked emerald-and-gold tiara filling much of the sky.

She calmed her horse, and put her cheek against the stallion's warm-beige coat, Lopo giving a sound of pleasure as she did. She found a steep slope leading up there, and with some effort, she got her horse up to the grass, got her saddlebag off him and put him to pasture. Lopo's eyes turned big at the sight of all that green and yellow grass, such a welcome sight to him, and as she turned, she heard him blow out air from his nostrils as if with delight, as he immediately began to graze with relish.

She climbed back down, nervousness rising as she neared the cave. Inside, for the first time, she took a good look at him.

He was impossibly striking like no human could be. His face gave her feelings like her earliest sensual fantasies. His chest was like two red marble blocks, protruding in flawless symmetry over abdominal muscles so big and defined they seemed riblike. His muscular physique, both the human and the equine side, was undeniably sensual, so much so that if her eyes lingered, the mere act of gazing felt perverse. And her eyes didn't want to look away from the sublime drawn-out squares of stomach muscles under the two divinely sculpted blocks that constituted his chest. She'd thought girls only swooned in romance tales. How wrong of her.

But he wasn't normal. Nothing about him was ordinary.

As the light came thinly green through the thick vines hiding them, his eyes glittered. Nobody had looked at her with such feeling before. She was just a girl. Let it be what it was. *Heavenly.*

No—perverse! Or was this only what others had said about humans attracted to beasts, that it was unnatural? What they would say about her if they could peer inside her head, not what she would say about herself? And did they only say such things because they were afraid of all that was dramatically different, such as all love that couldn't result in offspring and a future family? Or could it be that they hated those who had what they could never have? Despising that which offered a way out of the servitude to which they'd surrendered? Hadn't she been like them, believing herself to be shackled to the duty to be a mother one day? Doomed to only ever be safe as she went from one home and family to another, handed over by her father to the future father of her children, with no hope of escaping? Could she be brave to defy these unquestioned rituals of subservience, by being unnatural to the core of her human nature? Or would she sacrifice her desire, as all who had such urges yet resisted them had sacrificed all that could have been? Would she be a victim of convention, just to conserve useless tradition? Or would she be genuinely life-affirming and embrace her own life?

All questions buzzed in her mind like a kicked hornet's nest. They all led to one certainty: *Trust your heart.*

She closed her eyes and listened hard to her secret heart.

And heard the vow of the defiant girl she once was.

Vowing to never be like her mother and grandmother. Women who had chosen safety over a struggle to leave the world a better place than how they found it. Women who had made sure they would be secure, so they never had to be courageous, never had to prove their mettle, just had to sit out a monotonous existence of lazy morals and obedient passivity.

She opened her eyes, turned, and looked deep into his. Nut-brown, his big eyes smiled back, full of humour and zest for life, gazing at her with the promise of both guilelessness and wisdom. His body moved soft with the same easy, comfortable flow as his eyes, his full form shockingly natural to her now. The close look she got at him tantalized and frightened her at the same time.

She asked him what to call him, and he said, "Chor." He asked for her name and she gave it. And it was the strangest, most wondersome feeling. Because it felt just as if she was saying her own name for the very first time.

*

An hour's ride away from the canyon, Black Hood came at a gallop to Leina and the soldier who had her in his custody.

Backdropped by vast bright-green plains lit by softening afternoon light, Black Hood said, "I'll see that she will be tried and that justice will come to her for having tried to kill me."

The soldier said, "On whose authority?"

Black Hood gave him an envelope with a gold seal. The soldier handed Leina over to Black Hood without saying another word. Black Hood smiled like an unsupervised boy discovering the allure of feeling superior, a feeling that allowed boys to see the fun in being cruel, to be bullies, then tyrants.

Now alone with the hooded man, Leina thought long and hard about the most painless way to kill herself. But then she had another thought. And it surprised her, that what took away the pain of her grief and the sadness of having lost her freedom, was to think up a plan to have the sweetest possible revenge.

*

As Chor said that Leina and Katanya had stayed overnight in this cave, tears filled Kyra's eyes. She stammered that the hooded man had killed Katanya, then wept into the crook of her arm.

He comforted her by telling her of wondrous beings of other worlds, where all myths were true and all fantastical tales really had happened, farther away than stars reach. So magical were the tales of these beings to her, that she soon wholly forgot the shock and sorrow that had made her flee from the soldiers.

Forgot more and more, until she was fully gone inside his engrossing tales of a much brighter world. There, all she could remember, all she *craved* to remember, was what he told her, wanting only to hear more, to be evermore enchanted, and couldn't wait to know how each new tale surprisingly ended.

For he told her of white pegasi and green centaurs; of half-humans with wings, called sirens, and others with horns, called aigas; of sublime giants and monstrous cyclops; of dryads and naiads, muses and graces; of four-armed and six-armed anthropoids; of underwater tribes of mermen and shoals of mermaids, constantly fighting and constantly making up; of sphinxes with female human heads and bodies of gigantic lions; of unicorns, single-horned, white, giraffe-like horses; of gorgons with snakelike hair and griffins with leonine bodies and eaglelike heads and wings; of manticores with red leonine bodies and sharp-fanged human heads.

For half the night he filled her head with tales she would never forget, and she was happy, her sorrows forgotten as if they had happened a thousand years ago.

And in return, she kept him awake by telling him a tale once told by her mother, because it was the most magical tale she knew. Told by the only voice in the world that could do it justice. And she tried to capture that voice, that enchantment her mother had had, as she told him of a beekeeper in a faraway land.

"Imagine this, a poor boy yet happy in his work, glad of his bees. A boy who one summer's night, as he is swimming in the bay by the forest near his home, sees a ship catch fire and speedily burn and explode with its cargo of strong liquor. He swims to the wreck, to board it before it sinks, burnt black in the shallows, the high waves doing battle with the flames. While his friend at the shore rides to get help, he swims inside the black ruins. In the ashes that surround him, he makes his way past the bodies of sailors burnt by such a ferocious fire that only bones remain. And as he swims as deep inside as he can, he finds in the ashes of the captain's cabin a silver medallion, its emblem a new moon above a palm.

"A month later, at the very end of summer, as he wears this medallion on a trip to a market at the nearest port, a young, luxuriously dressed and veiled woman takes him for a prince who sailed the burned ship. The young woman, uncommonly lovely, falls into his arms, says her name is Deny and that she is a princess and that she desires to take him with her to her palace on an island just past the horizon. Excited curiosity leads him to assume a demeanour he would like to see most in a real prince, letting her believe that he really is the prince she seeks. As they take to the sea, he falls in love with her and falls ever deeper in love the closer they get to her island. He suspects that she suspects that he isn't who he pretends to be, the gallant prince Leth whose beauty and majesty as a little boy had inspired songs. Her willingness to let him lie to her mystifies her to him. And upon reaching her island, the mystery deepens. Because here he overhears a sailor saying that the ship with the lost prince is a myth. The prince had never sailed any ship. He had disappeared as a child, was abducted by unknown enemies and never returned.

"On a beach, he sees a girl with a golden mask come up of the water. She doesn't remove her mask but tells him she looks just like him, with birthmarks just like he has. He can see that she has his strong physique and the exact same colour as her hair which is curled just like his. She says her name is Shyreen and that she is the sister of the lost prince, Leth, the real princess of the island, and that she has just arrived with the tall ship sent out to rescue her. Deny, who'd taken him with her and let him believe she was the princess, was really Shyreen's chambermaid. Shyreen says she sent her chambermaid to chase a riddle of her lost brother. The riddle goes that the prince is to be found on a distant shore beyond the horizon, hidden among a thousand workers and many queens. She says she had an epiphany when she saw him approach the burnt ship in which she was the sole survivor after many men died to save her. She had seen his beekeeper clothes hung on a branch on the shore and had finally understood the riddle, which became all the more clear to her as she saw his face. She had put the medallion in a place where he would easily find it, then had concealed herself in rubble of black cinders where he couldn't find her. She hadn't wanted to show her badly burned, disfigured face. He tells her he is a beekeeper, and that he has more than a thousand bees, and each honeycomb has its own queen. She nods and smiles, then says her father sent her long-lost brother to a distant land to hide, as enemies had threatened to end their bloodline. But the secret of the hiding place died with her father, as his enemies assassinated him. She had gone to the place where all the clues had led her, and just as she had neared his home, someone set the ship on fire. She tells him she left the medallion for him to have because it is truly his. Then she had gone to another island and had a golden mask made before she dared show her face to him. While she waited for the mask to be done, she'd sent her chambermaid to bring him to her island. The medallion is all that is left of their parents, as they are the last of the bloodline. And so it unfolds that the beekeeper really is the prince that he pretended to be!

"The beekeeper-prince married the chambermaid who brought him home, and they lived happily ever after."

"I wish I'd heard this tale before the day I was cast out."

"Why?"

"Because before then, I could hear about human assassins without feeling a deep pain in my heart. I did something once that gnawed at me until I helped my sister. It still hurts sometimes, when tales of murder bring back the badness in me."

"No, you're different. Unlike the other mythical beings that came after the mist-shrouded Forbidden appeared, there's goodness in your heart."

"Kyra, I need to tell you something. The reason for my banishment was that I killed, something no mythical being can do, as it goes against our nature."

She took his hands in hers. "Tell me what happened."

"Not tonight," he said, let her go, and laid down to sleep.

Listening to Ruhchor talking in his sleep that night, as the hours approached dawn, little by little Kyra pieced together the puzzle. At first, his moans had either been incoherent or in a language she didn't speak. But then he'd said the king's name, and in his dream, he rapidly and lucidly told the very king of Albad how it had come to be that he'd been cast out of his forest, thereby inadvertently telling Kyra the tale of it. How the human he unintentionally had killed, Avero, a deer-killer, had slayed a centaur, Merrun, in a jealous rage. The centaur had captured the heart Avero wanted to be his, the heart of a nymph, Naidra, goddess of a sacred glade called Naidram. Naidra had given refuge to some centauress called Nachyla who appeared to also have scorned Avero. Chor had mourned Merrun and had caught sight of Avero about to leave the human world and go into the forest of centaurs and nymphs. At the edge of the forest, Chor had tried to stop the human killer by throwing a stone at his head, as the human had tried to set fire to the nymph's tree, which would have set the whole glade ablaze and killed many other innocents. Struck by the stone, Avero had died. Chor hadn't meant to kill him. He had wanted the deaths to stop.

Seeing him sleep, his face boyish and innocent in his pain. Remembering his vulnerability as he had told her his secret. Thinking of the emotion in his voice, narrating the events of the day when he became a pariah to his own people. Thinking of herself, how she could see in him so much of so many things about herself that she once held dear, things she had forgotten.

She couldn't deny it to herself any longer.

Without meaning for it to happen, she had fallen in love.

She couldn't help it or fight it, her desire stronger than her self-control. But no one must know. Before seeing this male centaur, she'd thought her brother sick, a freak. Thinking this because everyone else did. Yet she could now admit to herself that she'd never felt disgusted at the thought of her brother with that creature. She'd tried to be repulsed, as that was how you were supposed to react, but privately, the centaurs compelled her.

Yet the whole world said it was wrong.

Taboo.

Forbidden.

And so her desire cursed her.

Because there was nothing she had ever wanted more.

As his dreams calmed and he went very quiet and peaceful, she wanted to lay right next to him, on his equine side. Close, for his animal side to spoon her. But how does a centaur spoon a human? She had once slept with a very tall man and as they'd spooned, she had joked that it had been like a teaspoon in a tablespoon. As she took matters into her own hands and laid down and fit her body with the part of him that smelled like a young strong stallion, only much better, she became a teaspoon in a ladle.

Kyra woke him as golden dawn light filtered through the green curtain of vines, colouring his red skin lightly emerald. She softly said to him, "You believed him, your father when he called you a killer."

"How do you know?"

She told him what she'd heard him dream as he'd sweated and tossed and twisted in his sleep, reliving the day of his banishment. "I'm sorry. I wanted to wake you many times, but the seduction of the mystery beckoned me too irresistibly, and I needed to hear as many details of your life's story as possible."

"It isn't my whole life, just the part that I'm ashamed of."

"*Ashamed?* You saved all those innocent beings."

"But I killed *my* innocence in the process. I must have been contaminated by this world, somehow, because where we come from, we don't have a word for murder, as it doesn't exist there. Beings such as I shouldn't be capable of killing. Yet I wanted to harm him, for him to know how it feels. How you hurt us and yourselves with your incomprehensible brute force."

"Your father hasn't forgiven you, and so you haven't forgiven yourself."

"It wasn't enough, to save my sister. I thought my father would find it in his heart to forgive me when my sister returned and told him what I had done for her. But nobody has come for me, or I would have heard them. I would hear them call my name, as I hear any centaur in any part of the canyon or the area surrounding it. Maybe my father was right. Maybe I do belong here, in the world of the broken, the human world. Maybe my goddess has abandoned me. Maybe I've abandoned *myself*."

"Don't give up on yourself. You have a good heart. You deserve to be free. *I* forgive you."

"All I wish is to go wherefrom I was driven."

"You will. But not for a long time, I'm afraid. They're hunting you. But they can't chase you across the desert. The only way out is through."

"That I can't do. I have only one year left before it will be too late. I'd rather die free than survive as a slave to fear."

At that moment, Kyra thought about her brother, Remin, and about Chyanne, Chor's sister, who had fallen in love with Remin. She thought about how her brother had been sent to jail after a farmhand had seen him kiss the centauress and had turned him in. She thought about the open cruelty of the farmers in her community, who'd been eager to stone those they called freaks, how they yielded to pressure, to that which was easiest, and nothing came easier to them than to hate and fear all that was too hard for them to understand. And finally, she thought about herself, Kyra, how she and her father had used Chor's sister as a slave, pulling the plough of their fields. And thought of the whip, coiled on the saddle of her horse.

And turned her face away in shame.

Realizing only then that along with love and trust, shame and regret are the most godlike feelings. For if she'd felt these caring feelings to the fullest before, then the tragical primal holdover of *malice* wouldn't have wrecked her poor human heart.

Part II
Summer Sunset

-12-

With the glimpse of the prosecutor stuck on her retina as he passed through the main hall of the boarding house, Tinderley bowed deeply together with the other native orphans. He, in his vast power, could look at anyone he wished, while they, placed in a neat line outside their dormitory, were prohibited to look back. Tinderley glanced at the youth next to her, Nestra, hoping to find calm clarity in an exchanged look, but Nestra kept her gaze averted, staring at the floor as they'd been taught. They all did, hooding their eyes which must be owllike to humans. But to her, human eyes were jarring in their tininess, less than half the size of Tinderley's and her kinfolk. She needed the familiarity and rightness to the look of her sisters' eyes now. It would sharpen her eyes, to see through theirs, to understand through their understanding, steadying her pulse by sharing warm gazing with them. But the precious heat of their reddish-black irises was lost in the shadows as they lowered their heads and lidded their eyes. No, she refused this. So she did it, what she'd been told she mustn't. She looked at this human – this prosecutor – and didn't look away. This human who had come to take Torest away to be judged by men like him.

A priest had died, burned to death, yes, but only because he had attacked Torest. It was an involuntary reaction. Aigas can't control their biological defence, the firemoths nestled in hidden sheathes under their ribs, which are released when their symbionts feel extreme fear in life-threatening attacks.

Torest wouldn't hurt a fly. Her kindness was made of beautiful wisdom. It was there that night when her voice had been soft and full with the aching thankfulness between them, at the first stir of Tinderley's moths. Torest had been with her all through the night, massaging her tender sheathes to ease the pain. She listened now to the memory of Torest's words after she'd thanked her. *"It's enough that you know that I do it freely, that I wanted to make the effort to do what's not expected. Gratitude, you see, comes when presumption goes away. We can't be grateful for things taken for granted. Generosity, of nature and of the heart, is never a given, and it always begins with a choice that didn't have to be made but was, a beautiful thing that didn't have to be but is. This is what humans have forgotten."*

Wearing an expensive, lavish garment to mark his elevated place in society, the prosecutor was a heavyset, broad-jawed man with narrow, openly judging eyes. And those bizarrely small human eyes were piercingly clear yet void of colour and life like a cold winter sky. But he had been an infant once, and before that not even born. Who was he to take Torest away from the tall-treed mountain that was her home in this world?

Tinderley, just like Torest, her cousin and dearest friend, had lost her mother and father six years ago, when Tinderley had been eleven and Torest twelve. The Orian colonizers had rounded up all adults, and when they, the Eldeen Clan, had refused to denounce their faith and destroy their beloved books and sculptures depicting their goddess, the soldiers razed their communal dwelling. Those who resisted, which were nearly all the parents, they shot from a narrow range with crossbow bolts. This was to rid the world of a plague, so the Orians said after the deed was done. Tinderley and the other hornless children had been spared, but as they took to the woods they were left to starve throughout the winter. Until the priest, Pascor gave them shelter and baptised them. Most children had been too little to know the date of their birthday, the smallest ones not even sure of their age to begin with. They were all born in the winter but had lost track of time and had been unaware of when their birthdays had been. None of the small ones could tell Pascor with certainty how old they were. But Tinderley and Torest, and most of the other older ones, knew their age. They didn't say it. They said nearly nothing at all. Taught to be polite, pure in thought, repeating words of scripture like nursery rhymes, yet almost never speaking their minds, certainly never questioning their lessons taught by the men of the church who now owned their land though land could no more be possessed than stars. Questioning nothing and no one, only among themselves. Torest said nothing, protesting not at all, even as they shrouded her in full-covering black and locked her in a cell with barred windows.

And Tinderley had fought with her mind but hadn't understood, couldn't. Why take only the oldest among the orphaned daughters of Eldeen? Couldn't they see that the other orphans were no different from her?

*

It had hurt Tinderley's young, fiery heart, to have made the lost-eyed human boy's heart freeze in fear, which had made him flee from them. But he had to decide for himself the meaning of what they'd let him see, she and her cousin, like two authors of a scary tale that had to be told for a secret truth to be fully understood. They'd shown him that even if she revealed herself to seem like a daughter of evil, growing horns like his demons, he still couldn't hurt her. Only then would he realise the error of his ways. Tinderley wasn't sure about herself, fearing the truth about her own heart, but she knew for sure that it wasn't in Torest's heart, as wholly aiga, to end lives that didn't explicitly threaten her. And Tinderley knew that if he had had that power to set his enemies afire, he, like Torest, wouldn't be capable of doing so.

There were other ways to bring peace and equality to the world of winter. He would find his way. And like the eternally generous goat-horned nymph of the true myth of her lost home, Tinderley would help him. Like Nerenaida's sweet sacrifice, the offering that left the nymphic muse with only one divine horn exquisitely spiralled around her leaf-braided head, like this dear nymph's broken horn overflowing endlessly with inspiration, Tinderley's help could be an ever giving gift of hope.

But first, she would help Torest, as close to her as her heart.

For they could never part ways.

For they were aigas, big-hearted wide-leaping goat-beings, shaped by tender and beloved silver-horned goddess Pirenna.

And they didn't belong here. They were of Helanra, a mountain in a world high, high in the clouds. A place shaped by Pirenna, sacrificing herself. As her daughter, Nerenaida, one day would mirror her sacrifice by giving a part of herself so humans may taste divine grace. Yet Pirenna's sacrifice was the biggest, as she had given all her flesh. To make mountain trees that granted dream wishes. To form mountain rocks that let you be near the profound ocean of stars if your wishes went deep enough. To create a place where the Eldeen Clan could let their hornless children run free until they came of age and their horns began to show, by which time they would study all the mystical symbols of the mountain forests and all the secrets of the star patterns. A place where the goat children were born and played wildly, throwing endless fits of joy, knowing no sorrow or fear. Before the divine beam sent the aigas and other mythical beings to the other side of the stars, to a colder world, far below, four generations ago. Into the world of cold-hearted humans.

To men who were blind to the light that shone in the dark.

Men who couldn't see the light of Pirenna's second creation, the sacred horns that on some nights glittered like the stars of which they were made. For goddess Pirenna had brought down two stars from whose essence she made the most beautiful and strong crescent shapes possible, and with the stardust, she made her companion. And so much did she love her companion that the companion received the potent crescent shapes to wear as awe-inspiring horns, and was also gifted with the ability to have offspring. And so the companion, the doe Aldissa, became the first mother. But some of the first bucklings and doelings were homesick and wanted to leap to the stars from which their souls came. And so Pirenna's third creation was a goat-woman she named If. If would play a magical harp and sing songs that gave the gift of a full imagination. Heart-warming songs so reminding of their home that this, the first music, made the little goat-beings want to stay on the mountain a little longer. The music always drew them back from the edge of the mountain from whence they had wanted to jump off, high, high, to reach the dazzling starlight where their souls had lived before their birth. If, the mother of full imagination brought to this half-world, was the mother, too, of all goat-beings, all she-goats and he-goats who lived as near the sacred goats of Helanra as a heart lives close to the soul. Where they one day could touch the stars. In whose light was their soul home, where the star made Aldissa and If lived, in the skies of summer days of gold. To be finally home, out of reach of all fear, made whole again, to be stars shining brightly to inspire new life into being, a new light in a newborn baby's eyes.

*

Tinderley didn't know how to feel about this human boy, the one she'd scared away before. Squatting in his tent opening, she eyed him carefully, waiting for his courage to take hold. She thought about when she had peeked through the keyhole into his small chamber, seeing him exercise without his shirt on. She had known that *he* had known that he was watched. He'd looked up from time to time at the keyhole, aware of a stranger's curiosity. A half-joking, half-sincere performance, his exercising for an unknown spectator, one only boys could enact, as girls would never feel safe enough to enjoy such a game. And now, what was it she felt, apart from being curious? Unlike most of her kin, one of her parents was human, making her more than half-human.

And the human side of her hated Janrey, though hating him much less than she did the other inquisitor youths. But the aiga side of her couldn't deny that she liked his attention. And that she harboured the least amount of hatred for him mattered because even before she'd sung in the church, she had been the one among her kind whom his attentive eyes had sought out the most. With his eyes he had figuratively caressed her curves, his gaze feeling to her at times like a hand sneakily reaching out to undress her. And with her eyes she had figuratively slapped him on the wrist, never having invited any intimacy between them that welcomed such exclusive glances.

And yet.

The invigorating novelty of him had pleased her long after she'd seen the effect her singing voice had had on him. Many times, she'd drawn him in sharp focus in her mind, accentuating every remembered expression of his bare human face. And had discovered nuances of emotion in herself, familiar yet mysterious, that her naked heart had forgotten.

And now Tinderley was looking at him looking back at her in the tent opening, looking into eyes full of pensive hesitation.

She waited for the smile to return to his serious eyes, but it didn't happen. And now she knew what had upset him so. It was supposed to be the other way around: him showing her mercy and she expressing gratitude. Yet he'd been in her power. This was why her smile had bothered him. Now that her smile was gone, it became the easiest thing in the world to intimidate him. She had aroused his curiosity like never before, and he was so eager to satisfy it, to know who she was, to hold her still and size her up. It almost seemed his life depended on it. She didn't understand this. Any of it. His eyes didn't help her. The eyes of humans were mute. Yet in his, didn't she see a willingness to learn how to speak?

After he had stood guard by the wagon for about half an hour, she came to him again. Was that the trace of a smile in the shadows at the corners of his lips, or was she imagining it?

"I'm sorry that I frightened you," she whispered.

"Are you the only one?"

"No. But Torest, though older than me, have yet to mature. We needed you to see it because *you* needed it."

He stared at her as if he had forgotten how to speak, as if words had never been farther from his mouth.

Her voice level with a calm which she didn't know where she found, she said, "You didn't reveal my secret, what has started to sprout just below my hairline, what I hide under a powder-based paste. It is important, this, that you've told no one that I have begun to grow horns."

"Not so loud!" he whispered hotly with a violent emotion whose source she couldn't trace at all. His eyes fell, as though with sudden puzzlement, and his cheeks flushed intensely, his face turning redder than she'd ever known a face could be. He appeared distraught, at a loss, as confused by this exposure of riotous emotion as she was. The most inexplicable thing about humans was that they lied. Yet the colour that had flooded his face had expressed an unmasked truth that, even if he couldn't name the feeling, showed to a precise degree what went on inside him. Being human, he couldn't use his eyes to let her in. But in the dramatic way in which his face coloured, she had a better notion of the distress he felt. It let her see the child in him, and she felt an unexpected tenderness for him. She dropped her guard. She whispered, "You didn't tell them. You were dutybound to do so, yet you didn't. Now a whole day has passed and still, you haven't said a word. Because if you did, they would put me in the cage with her."

Heat and cold seemed to chase over his cheeks in a complicated rush, his emotions a whirlpool of confusion to them both. In his blinking eyes, she saw a flutter of imaginings of what she could mean by saying this. He looked increasingly dizzy as if swept up in a vortex of underlying meanings, both thrilling and daunting. Did she herself know all her undertones? Maybe she meant more than she knew. He, in his struggle with his confusing emotions, became bigger to her, and she, seen through his eyes, grew bigger still to herself. Breathless, he threw puzzled glances from side to side, even though he knew they were alone.

She said, "I knew you wouldn't breathe a word, but you needed to know exactly why you *couldn't*."

"Y-y-you're not a demon. Please. J-just say it."

"I won't. And you know why."

He looked into her eyes, then seemed to remember his tentmate, because he swiftly looked that way, towards the tent of the most fitful sleeper of their camp. Had he told Roric he had gone to relieve Charilcor of guard duty? He blanched, as if fear suddenly ran amok through his uncertainty.

She thought about what he was risking. If he got caught, Charilcor might have to tell them about taking a bribe last night, when he visited Torest's cell and she had scratched away the paste from her forehead that had masked her true form.

She took his hand and his eyes shot back from his tent to her. She put it in his hand, the thing she had prepared in order to set her plan in motion. The wrench she'd stolen from the smith just before they left the orphanage. "Come." She led him to the wagon, and after making sure they weren't watched, she went to work on the wheel. "I'll loosen it just enough so that it will fall off on its own after a while."

"And then, when the wheel falls away?"

"Someone must be sent to fetch a repairman. You volunteer. When you reach the nearest chapel, send a message to Hillgrove that Torest is not who Carec said she was, and that everyone now worships Torest as their mistress. This will create an uproar that will reach the other youths, and it will act as the signal I told them would come. After they've followed the churchmen as they ride to intercept you, they'll liberate Torest."

His arms shot out as he whispered with out-of-breath exasperation. *"How?* You don't have weapons!"

She calmed him with her eyes. "With cunning."

He handed her his knife, and after she reluctantly accepted the gift, he said, "She could have escaped last night."

"We couldn't take a chance that we wouldn't be caught as we scaled the wall. Goddess knows how Pascor made it."

His jaw forgot to hold itself up. "Goddess?"

She just looked at him.

Next morning, after nearly an hour of travelling without the slightest sign of anything wrong with the wagon, it promptly creaked and tipped to the side, like a ship rolling under the force of a giant wave. Though the wheel didn't come loose, it couldn't rotate slantwise, making the vehicle violently brake and swerve.

But though Janrey said he could ride for help, Moracar elected Frischa to do so. As Janrey tried to make him change his mind about it, it made Moracar both angry and suspicious.

A crestfallen look in Janrey's eyes as Frischa rode off.

As they made a temporary camp at the side of the road, a frog jumped onto Charilcor's boot, comically almost as though attacking him, making him recoil. Swearing under his breath, Charilcor coldly squashed the little animal under the heel of his boot and spat three times.

Roric, the twenty-something, wheat-haired, taciturn one, who had ridden at the tail of the procession with a sullener face than usual, looked with distaste at the mangled tiny green thing. Then he wandered off, saying nothing, as usual.

Later, as darkness began to fall after Charilcor had hunted and killed rabbits which they ate in silence, Moracar began to shiver in an odd way. But the coughing he'd battled since the journey began now was gone, and he strangely looked in better health than ever, even seemed warm in his shivering. He said that the Devil was taunting him. The terribly ugly Charilcor suddenly sounded out of his mind with panicky fury. "It is her!" he accused, saliva spraying as he pointed at the cage. "We have had nothing but bad omens since the journey began! First, the crow that crowed six times in a row, which is the worst omen of all to hear. Then the wheel. Then the frog that I swear cast no shadow. She has cursed us! The unnatural shiver is the first of many dark things the omens portended!"

Suddenly Moracar stood with them, grabbing Charilcor's shoulder, "He is right," he slurred.

Even from where Tinderley sat, she could smell the stench of strong wine in his breath. They only drank this wine to be able to sleep under the worst conditions, in the deep-biting cold or in the ashen hail. But tonight, Moracar had been drinking as if there was no tomorrow and little, if anything, of his sense and reason, seemed to be left. He shivered now in a strange, violent passion. Tinderley rose, watched him half-unconscious with a shadowy daze climb up and unlock the cage and pull Torest out.

"Torest!" Tinderley cried crisply, running towards her.

But Charilcor caught up with her before she could cross over to the wagon. With just one hand, he seized her wrist, giving her such a tug that she flew several paces back and hit the ground hard, feeling pain shoot through her, twisting her face.

"I'm not afraid of you!" Moracar hissed into the cage.

"If I didn't wear the shroud you put on me, I'd spit in your face!" came in a savagely heated hoarse hiss from inside the cloth.

"You dare speak to me like that!" Moracar was beside himself with outrage. He threw himself at her, making her tumble to the frosty ground with him over her. He was unshrouding her, and Tinderley couldn't get up, could only watch as he untied her rope-bound waist that tied the shroud tightly to Torest's body. He growled over his shoulder, "Charilcor, get the axe we use to chop firewood. I'm going to take away her power which resides in her evil demon horns." He spat and swore and held Torest down with both hands until the axe came to his grip.

It all went so fast that he was already about to position himself between her knees with the axe raised to strike down on one of Torest's horns when Tinderley saw Janrey come alive and heard the boy scream at the man, "Moracar, you goddamned—" Coming at a run at the kneeling human who was seconds away from traumatizing Torest.

But Charilcor saw him charge, and too late did Janrey see the fist that flew at his face. Tinderley heard the crack as Janrey's nose broke against Charilcor's knuckles in a terrible blow that sent the boy tumbling off his feet. He landed on his back on the icy hard ground, in too much disoriented agony to get up.

Tinderley's sight blurred with tears. Somewhere she heard the sound of uncontrolled madness in the dark, as two men became drunk with their belief in the rightness of their might. She heard Moracar going berserk with it, heard it in his panting, as he yelled like a man possessed, "How she struggles, the little beast! Yes, you hold her head in place so I can get a good aim."

Blinking away the tears, she saw Janrey crawl weakly on gravelly ground, seeing it as though watching a nightmare unfold. With unmasked loathing, Charilcor was pushing the young woman's half-shrouded head down on the ground. Tinderley was screaming something. Moracar was lifting the axe over his head.

Then Tinderley saw Roric in a blur of motion, his blade swinging back and with a single forward stroke, he rendered Moracar unconscious, using the flat of his sword. Roric appeared transfixed by the sight of the motionless body lying face down on the ground after the hefty blow. Charilcor presently got up, got his blade out, got his mind made up by the sight of his fallen leader. Without a word Charilcor launched himself at Roric, drawing back his blade to swing it to end Roric.

But Tinderley then came out of the dark, into the wagon's torchlight, tearing at the silent shadow that was Charilcor. She had made her decision. She was ending this nightmare. She punched her knife through the side of his throat.

Everything stopped.

Charilcor gurgled blood, his life over by the time she drew out of him the knife Janrey had given her.

A new rage took her, as she flew like a wind of fire at Moracar and slit his throat before he regained consciousness.

"Torest," Tinderley called to her cousin through the shocked silence. "Ride back south, go past home, to Deira! Ask for the protection of Caldira! Fast—before Frischa returns!"

"Tinder!" Torest rasped sharply through her shroud, now back over her face, as Tinderley mounted her white mare with the effortless grace of a master jockey. "Don't leave me!" Torest cried out in a sob like an utterance, struggling futilely to free herself from the shroud.

But, "I'll ride for the help of the wild!" Tinderley threw back with a tight cry. "We must destroy all evidence of what happened here, or they will surely come with warriors to avenge their brethren, and this time not even the children of the wild will be spared! We'll make it look like a brigand attack!" Tinderley made her horse trot towards her cousin, threw her leather bag which Torest caught in the air. "Clothes! Food! Take it! I'm sorry, Torest, but we have to move fast." Torest's eyes flashed watery in the unusually bright starlight. Tinderley jumped down and gripped Torest's face in her hands. With her eyes, Tinderley said, *I love you.* Then, interrupting them before Torest could respond, Tinderley heard Janrey shout Roric's name, his voice sounding painfully tight with overworked tension. She turned and saw him stagger to Roric as if through a mist of pain that she knew must be pulsing out from his cracked nose.

Janrey hurriedly told Roric, "I told you earlier where my sister lives in Haydell. We'll hide there."

Roric turned to where Tinderley was calming her mare.

Janrey said, his voice so low that Tinderley could just barely hear him, "I know she told us to go to Deira, but we're only humans. If you want, you can try to stop her, though I strongly advise against it. I'll meet you at Peony's farm. I'll come as soon as I figure out a way to change my appearance. I need a new persona, a believable story that'll let us move through and out of the realm without raising suspicion."

His eyes met Tinderley's. The old Janrey was no more.

They both turned to Roric at the same time. Roric nodded and opened his mouth, but even now he spoke so silently they couldn't hear him. Yet his action spoke loud enough. As she mounted and rode off at a thunderous gallop, he rode after her.

A full hour later, standing on top of the hill that rose above the forest, she waited until Roric was so close that she didn't have to strain her voice. "Did you come after me to kill me?"

Halting his slow progression, he shook his head no.

"To tie me up and make me your captive?"

Standing very still before her, he shook his head again.

Tinderley threw out her arms. "Then what?"

Below his slim, black-clad figure, naked limbs of tall trees stretched to a cold sky. The forest around them was nameless to her, but she didn't find it daunting any more. The vast shadows within it were no longer as frightening. And she didn't distrust him. He, on the other hand, wouldn't have approached her any differently had she been a predator twice his size. Yet presently he didn't look at her solely with fear. His pale eyes unblinking with a dark fascination, as if not wanting to miss the slightest impression of her. She thought he looked at her the way you do when awed by a feral beauty that had no parallel to anything else in nature.

He took a deep, tight breath. Then, soft-voiced, speaking with a quiet caution as if fearing to disturb the very air between them, he said, "I think it's time you stopped pretending to be innocent. It's clear that your kind is anything but."

"You don't believe any more that my kind can be innocent, do you?"

"You killed two men without giving them time to say a single word. What does that say about you?"

"The symbol of your faith which you wear in a chain around your neck, a miniature stake, is an instrument of torture and slow agonizing death. What does that say about you?"

He said nothing but didn't let go of her gaze as he searched it deeply with his. But she let go of his, as her gaze dropped to his hard, leather shoes. She stood barefoot in front of him in the freezing winter-cold grass. She liked to move without making a sound, like the other creatures of the forest. Unlike bumbling humans, forever noisy, carelessly foul in their unfeeling disturbance of every reverently quiet harmony. Yet this man felt different. She acutely wished she could know what he saw when he looked at her. A beast? Or an ambiguity, a good side to her, too, that most men of his kind couldn't see? She utterly hated this new phase of her life. How could she bear it? What had she become? She could never go back to who she had been. Not without trepidation she suddenly wondered if she would ever sleep peacefully again. Could she have gone back in time, she would have incapacitated the men, then stayed her hand. Fleeing instead of fighting. Her only consolation was in this regret, telling her she wasn't like humans, who could kill without remorse, without feeling like a part of them died by the action, without losing their souls. She had to trust in the better part of herself, the aiga part, that it was stronger, that she would never be human again. Never again so taken with the passion of revenge, of justification of the brutally calculating mind, that she forgot about all the wisdom of the heart.

Finally, breath shuddering, he whispered, "Don't you feel any guilt?"

Her eyes filled with tears she no longer could fight or flee, could only surrender to. "Of course I do. I'm not like *you*."

She wished she could be as sure as she made herself sound. Her father had been human. And so, unlike Torest, who was entirely aiga, Tinderley had human murderous rage in her blood. But that night she was afraid to close her eyes, lest she would see again the shocking sight of the two men she'd killed. On the ground, motionless, their stillness horrific to her, the terror of expecting them to move though their hearts had stopped beating.

The few seconds it had taken her to tell Torest where she was going had been all Tinderley could take, being near those bodies. She'd had to ride off without staying a second longer there. But even as she'd ridden ever farther away from the place of that horrific sight, the gut-wrenching memory had chased her.

As darkness grew and she knew she had to sleep or become a wreck, she felt like raging at *everything*. She now hated humans more than ever, hated them so much she could scream. And seriously wondered if she had it in her to kill her human self.

*

Having bathed in the Water of Sympathy, Torest and Janrey embraced close to the mountaintop. But then Torest took a step back. It was as if an earthquake had opened up the ground between them and he couldn't see the gaping crack yet. If he took a step closer, she would push him back. She felt tears well up and had to fight not to burst out sobbing. "I have to leave you now," she said, simply, though she was full of complicated, conflicted feelings. He just looked at her, waiting for her to explain what she meant.

Where to begin?

Just how they'd escaped from the men whose hearts were full of hate, it felt like a fading dream. And this dream of the past few days, how Janrey's sister had gone through a crisis of change and how they'd ended up at the Caldira Cavern, it would disappear altogether, if Torest didn't look back. And she wouldn't. Not yet. That was a story for another time and place. For right now, all that mattered was this moment.

"I didn't tell you," she said. "But I've been having a recurring dream this last year. A dream of light bigger than this world, calling me home. I didn't see you with me there, but I can dream again. Next time, I can see you in that world of light. All I know is that I must go to a place south of Albad, where all mythical beings are gathering. When all of us are there, at this year's summer solstice, which is soon approaching, a beam more powerful than a thousand suns will come. All lost beings, we will ascend, leave this world for good."

"But it isn't for humans?"

"I don't know. Maybe. But I was called, and Tinderley said she dreamt the same, though the call was fainter for her." The shimmering liquid emotion in his deep-dark eyes began to thicken and tremble. She had to hurry before his emotion overwhelmed her and words failed her. "A part of me doesn't want to leave. But even if I wanted to, the call would pull me to it, and I couldn't help myself from wanting home more than anything. And I would die of misery if I stayed."

"Then take me with you!"

She shook her head. She tried to smile, but it felt like walking with your legs bound. "Good humans are needed here, to right this world. You're too vital for this world to lose you."

Suddenly, she heard somebody clear her throat, and turned around to see that Tinderley had been standing not far behind her. She couldn't say how long she'd stood there, how much she had heard. Tinderley spoke softly as she now came up to take Torest's hand. But it was into Janrey's eyes she gazed. "I won't go. I'm half-human, and that half of me, in the Water of Sympathy, sensed the pain of a human girl who is starving herself. And I can't fail her, can't fail myself. The Sisters of the Caldira Cavern can help her, save her life, and heal her emotional wounds. But they need somebody to protect her. That somebody will be me. I can't go home. Not yet. Not after what I've done."

Tinderley then kissed Torest's cheek, turned, and left.

"Won't you go after her?" he asked.

"Her mind is made up. I *knew*. The calling isn't as strong for her, being half-human." Torest found she couldn't swallow past the lump in her throat, straining against her voice. "For me, it's louder than thunder."

"Then go to it, and find peace. I will find you in my dreams. Leave this place. This winter."

"Will you try to save it?"

"You already did. What's left is a lost cause."

She heard the held-back sobs in his throat strangle him. With her eyes, she told him to stop fighting, to let it out. And he somehow heard her, though he was human. And it was a release unlike no other. Yet in it, he couldn't speak. Only hold her. And she answered his embrace by tightening her arms around him, met his kiss, took as much of his pain as she could bear, and wept with his weeping. And for the last time, they shared one another's tears.

-13-

Her first night with the centaur, Kyra had barely slept. Now, as she woke on the bed of heather that he had gathered for her, she was very drunk from her heavy sleep and wild dreams in which she had been a beloved heroine. So sleep-drunk was she that as she blinked herself awake, at first she didn't know where she was or what had happened the past few days. For a few blinks, she was even unsure how old she was, as it felt like she had slept for years. As she began to remember the events leading up to the reason why she found herself in this cave with its rounded walls and vaulted ceiling, her heart started to beat very fast.

Somewhere, there was a rustle, and as she turned, she felt the sweaty smell of her body. She'd been sleeping without removing her clothes since she came to this canyon, three days ago. At the military camp, she'd never had time to wash the clothes she still wore. Now she felt self-conscious, embarrassed by not being able to disguise the smell of dirt and old sweat stuck on her unbathed body and unwashed garments.

Chor appeared in the cave opening. She shielded her eyes from the sharp rays of the sun, as they lanced inside over his broad shoulders.

"What time is it now?" she asked him.

"Two hours past midday," he replied. "How many hours after midnight did we stay up?"

"All of them," she quipped. "Well, I did. You slept until perhaps four past midnight."

She had a faint recollection of looking at him in the soft light that made it inside the cave yesterday, as the summer sun had just begun to set. The rosy colour across his cheeks had burned redder as he had excitedly told her of beings of myths, only a few of which she had heard of before.

He showed her to a flat rock on which he'd spread a white tablecloth and placed a meal for her. He told her that everything on the flat rock came from the cave where he'd eaten and slept before coming to his sister's rescue and that he'd fetched it while Kyra was sleeping. She ravenously feasted on fruits most succulent, on beans most spicy, served with a delicious yellow juice he'd made of orange, that exotic, luxurious fruit that was so hard to get hold of north of the subtropics. As she chewed and drank, she mulled over the story he had told about himself, about why he had been cast out. She eagerly mused on it, and her mind reached the end of their conversation this morning before she'd buried her face in the crook of her arm and gone back to sleep.

Though he'd been ambiguous in what he said about a much better, much brighter world where myths are real, he had given plenty of evidence of having a rational mind. True, she thought him naïve, but so were all idealists and romantics, quite like her brother. But something he had said had made her suspicious.

As she chewed on the last bite of what was both her breakfast and lunch, her chewing motion slowed down so much that her jaws nearly stopped moving. She felt her face lose colour.

He spoke of only having a year left. What did it mean?

After having thought about it some more, she went to where he stood guarding the opening, holding the curtain of vines so that he could look out through a small gap. After thanking him for the food and beverage, she asked him why he had said that, about having only a year left.

With a sombre, husky low voice, at times even raspy, scratching out difficult words to speak, Chor revealed it all, all he had kept secret. "It is true. I have to return to the forest before midsummer next year. Never to see humans in this world again. Because on the next summer solstice, when the sun is at its zenith, the whole sky will turn purple. Goddess Naira will let all mythical beings ascend from the forest, to be swept up to its true name, *Rhodomeli,* of which what you've seen is but a rough sketch. The place which you've forbidden yourselves to enter and made yourselves fear as a place of carnal sin, will disappear with us. After the day of the purple sky, the world will be empty of myth, silent of all our songs. That cursed emptiness will be felt by humans for as long as a civilization will exist. If I don't make it to the forest before then, I will perish, won't last a day."

Kyra gaped, her pulse thudding in her ears.

And she felt a great shift inside. She had believed in him. Now she saw the truth. Like what Leina had told her about Amaida, he turned out to be crazy. She had respected him. Now she had to look away, had to watch her words for fear of having him feel judged. Trying her hardest not to pity him.

When Chor had first said he couldn't cross the desert, she hadn't pursued the matter. The larger part of why she'd let it go so easily had to do with the thing he'd said that had led her to think of how she'd treated Chyanne. But the other part of the reason she'd dropped it wasn't insignificant. She had spontaneously deduced that the less she fought him about it, the faster he would lose his stubbornness. But now she saw that it wasn't mulishness she should've worried about. He'd been crazy all along, possibly the reason why his own kin had banished him.

What had she been thinking yesterday, believing all he'd said? For a full day, she'd been chasing an illusion.

Carefully, sensitively gently, she said, "Chor. You're wrong. You have to be an adult, and live in the real world. Of course, the sky won't turn purple, and of course you have nothing to fear next midsummer. Think realistically. Nothing will happen."

He swallowed, and didn't speak. For the first time, she saw anger in his eyes. He went to the other side of the cave, his back turned to her. She came to him, treading softly yet tensely.

Levelly, he said, "Stop. Just… leave me in peace."

"Won't you explain it in a way that makes it easier for me?"

Angrily, with hooves stamping loudly, he turned around, and his voice, too, came with loud force, as he spoke to her with indignation. "Kyra, if I tell you I need to be in peace, won't you do me the courtesy of respecting my wish?"

"Chor, listen, we're eternities apart. You can't ask me to believe in any of this. And I hope you will come to your senses."

"It took all I had, to find the nerve to tell you what I just did, about the midsummer midday purple sky, yet you treated me like a child. I love you… for who you might be, a change of heart from now. I will have to *show* you. You see, there is one more secret, one about my family, unknown even to my tribe."

"You don't have to prove anything."

"No, I do. I need this. To tell you that I am a *fire being*. With the fire inside me, I can sculpt myself into any shape I desire, as long as I'm given enough time and sustenance."

Her heart fell. She had strongly felt he was crazy before. Now she knew for sure. There was no coming back from this. She would leave him as soon as he slept, and never come back.

An hour later, she still watched him sleep. Nothing had happened. Chor had said he was something she had never heard of, a *fire being,* and that his body would transform into another creature's shape in his sleep. Impossible in the real world.

He meant well and didn't know it himself, but he really was a lunatic. As she watched him sleep peacefully, changelessly, she wondered how she could have fallen for certain incredible things he had spoken of as if they were true. He had spoken of the entire midday sky turning purple and all creatures like him swept away from this world, never to return. This, she understood as she thought realistically, was inconceivable, and would never happen. She didn't belong here, part of his delusion. Suddenly she feared that part of her had gone crazy, too, infected by his warped perception. She needed to be with her own, to return to the human world. Where the cold hard dependable gravity of unchangeable reality made everything predictable and safe. Where there was nothing to fear as long as your brain guided you.

Was *everything* he'd told her crazy and she'd been too willing to believe to see it? But she could no more blame herself than him, as she had needed his fantasy so she could cope with a traumatic memory. To forget the moment when she had gone to the place where she'd heard Leina shout, seeing there a very pale, lifeless little girl in the grass, a bolt deeply buried in her chest. No wonder she had let herself escape into a dream world.

She got up, kissed his dreaming head, got dressed, and made not a sound as she moved away from him. Pushing the draping vines aside, stepped outside, letting the drape fall, making sure it closed firmly behind her. She had made her decision. And she began walking believing her path was set.

-14-

Trapped.

Caught.

Stake-bearers, the renowned militia trained and armed by the Inquisition, they'd found Torest at the place she'd sought refuge. At the sheerly jutting Blacksheer, the southernmost mountain in the Deira Hills, which stood directly north of the sea that separated Ore from Albad. The stake-bearers were about to attack, ready to kill her if she resisted capture. She had nowhere to run, cornered at the top of the world, at the peak piercing the very sky in half, where the wind was never still and always cold.

The place where she was at the mercy of a hermit woman who quite possibly was mad.

She felt death edge closer. She couldn't swallow.

Death tasted like panic.

*

Trembling, yet standing very still, Kyra no longer breathed, lost in thought of the whisper, the magic that had seemed outside time.

Several minutes later, she was inside the cave again, with no awareness of having walked back. Only faint glimpses of her legs feeling like jelly and her hands shaking like dry leaves, as she had taken the first steps back to Chor, remembering Leina's whisper.

Here she stood in the dark, her back directly to the vines and the world outside. Staring, waiting for her eyes to adjust.

She was going to focus on the best of him. Not the crazy side that lived in a delusion like a child that hadn't learned to divide dream from reality. And not the side that had killed. No, the biggest side, the side that was all kindness. She wasn't going to try to change him, remembering now that she didn't have to, that that wasn't what love truly meant. She took a deep breath, ready to give him more of herself, more than the benefit of the doubt.

She edged closer to his shadowy colossal yet gentle shape.

Closer to the certainty of Chor's sleeping body.

And her hand flew to her mouth, her heart forgetting to beat, her lungs forgetting to breathe, as she was all staring eyes.

She turned away, telling herself her mind played tricks on her. But then, slowly turning back, she had to believe her eyes.

Seeing the front legs of the animal side of him gradually shrink, a cloudlike slow gliding grace to it, how they sank inch by inch back into his body.

Seeing hair fall off on plane after plane of his back legs as they became naked limbs, ever straightening, their every tendon and bone soundlessly settling in wholly new positions.

Flamelike heat vibrated up, cell after cell burning away and sculpted anew, repurposed, rearranged, changing his shape in metamorphosis as surreal as had she seen a butterfly transform back into a caterpillar. The centaur part of his body was slowly disappearing altogether, shifting into a human form before her eyes. In a trance, she watched him slowly becoming a human.

She had to walk away for a while to collect herself. When she minutes later next stood over him, on his lower body there remained very little of him still resembling an animal.

Realization dawned. He had been telling her the truth.

Slowly he dreamt himself differently.

Waking, seeing her new discomfort as she had trouble forcing her eyes not to wander, he put his hands over his crotch.

She told him to wait and went to the cave wall by the opening where she'd put the things she'd gotten from her saddlebag. She came back with a blanket and faced away while he covered himself, her mouth almost cramping with stiffness before she gave up her attempt to smile. He thanked her, his voice sounding small, and even now, wrapped in the blanket, he looked pained, ashamed, struggling to meet her eyes. He sat very still, hugging himself. And gazing brokenly with averted distant eyes, he spoke in a quiet, weak tone past her shoulder. "I miss my body."

What this must have cost him.

His legs were incredibly wobbly, he tried to rise. He immediately fell, his leg muscles too unused to their new shape to know how to hold him up. He needed a new muscle memory, yet he wasn't patient enough to wait for that. Tried again. Fell once more. As he tried to move towards her, his clumsiness crushed her heart. His legs didn't yet have the right coordination and experience to enable him to do more than crawl, and hardly even that.

The exertion made him dizzy, he appeared close to passing out. Thinking he needed to replenish his nervous system with blood and oxygen, she told him to bend and get his head low.

After she'd made a loincloth for him out of torn cloth, she sat away from him, her back to him, giving him privacy. When she glanced back over her shoulder, he lay on his side, as he had as a centaur. His eyes were wide open as he began to shiver, miserable.

On and on, he shivered.

She crept to him, held him tightly, and gave him all her warmth.

*

They woke together at the sound of horses and barked orders not far from the cave opening. Wordless, they both stared at the vines hiding them from the outside world.

A sharp clang rang out, just outside, and Kyra's shoulders shot up with abrupt spiking tension. Then a distant shout from a man, coming from down on the other side, "Bugger! The tracks just stop here! I told you! It's as if it grew wings and flew off!"

Then, another loud voice, this one with the authoritative firmness of a leader, "Did you look behind those vines?" The voices were coming closer.

"There are vines like that draping similar places along the wall of this gorge."

"I asked if you searched behind that one, not the others. If not, do so now."

She got his arm around her neck and gripped it strongly as she lifted him up with most of his heavy weight on her shoulders. He was standing fully erect when the vines swished aside. A bearded soldier yelled to the others down below, "It's here, and it's a shifter! It's got a woman with him! I can't get a clear shot!"

She began to move away with him into the shadows as fast as she could. Pulling him with her ever deeper down the cave, breathing heavily, she said, "They won't let you live."

"But I'm a human now. I don't understand."

"Can you hear what they're saying out there?"

She saw his eyes narrow as he pricked his ears. "One of them is calling for the general to come up to the cave." He blinked. They shuffled onward, now inside a constricting tunnel, so dark they could barely see where they put their feet. "Now the general is saying that all shifters are killers." Another blink and his face fell. "The general just gave them the order to aim to kill the killer." His voice shook as he asked, "What's a shifter?"

"Shapeshifter." She saw his confusion and hurriedly explained, such a flutter to her tongue that she felt certain that this was the most rapid her speech had ever been. "*Therianthrope.* A person who shifts into an animal shape. I used to think such beings only existed in fairytales."

"Why do we stop?"

"I can't see where I'm going. It's too dark in here."

"Let me be your eyes."

He steered her body as she kept pulling him upright with his weight draped over her shoulder. She felt like a soldier pulling out a wounded brother-in-arms from the front line.

Hoarsely, he said, "It's just around the corner up ahead."

"I can't see a thing."

"Wait. Are we thinking this through? I can hear the men coming inside the cave now, and their voices are so young. Isn't it possible for them to defy the order to kill?"

"No. I know men like them, soldiers, and hunters, not paid to think and severely punished if they disobey. And to them, you're not at all human, just another prey to bring down."

"I'm putting you in danger. You could surrender, live."

"I'd rather die."

As Kyra shut out the thought of dying before the day was done, Chor did his best to maintain a semblance of balance. Showing her a way out. With his arm slung around her neck, she was half-dragging him as they came to the place where sunlight shone in from a gap directly above their heads. She looked up, almost despairing, seeing that the hole up there was as high as the bell of a city temple. There was a wooden winch with a two-handed handle with which to wind up the rock that hung at the very top. A mechanism not unlike that which sailors use to raise heavy sails. She didn't have a second to lose, so as soon as Chor gripped the knots with his hands, his feet too inexperienced to know how to stand on the knots below, she unlocked the clutch, which let out the tension of the rope. The rock dropped, lifting Chor smoothly up. As the counterweight reached the ground, she heard voices of men, by the sound of it moving slowly, fumblingly, through the lightless tunnel. In manic haste, she wound the winch to hoist the rock up, the pulley creaking with the weight, and there was a rattle that secured the rock and would hold it at the top until she released the lock of the clutch. She let the counterweight pull her up, and with her lightweight, she shot up through the chimney-like vertical tunnel like firework. It took all she had to hold onto the rope as the rock slammed below and the lift stopped while her upward momentum went on, sending her violently to the side of what now seemed like a shaft. Dust rained. Chor helped her clamber out of the gap onto a level rock.

As she lay on her back recovering her breath and strength, she heard echoes of hard shouting from the shaft, just next to her ear. The soldiers had found the lifting mechanism. She had nothing with which to cut off the rope, and couldn't hinder them from winding up the mechanism and lifting themselves up.

Seconds later, standing by the edge far above the cave opening, panting heavily, she saw her horse on the other side of the gorge that swarmed with soldiers. Without wasting time on explanations, she pulled out the rope and grappling hook she'd attached to her belt. With all the strength in her arm, she threw the hook towards the sky-high palm on the lower cliff on the other side. But her target at the top of the palm, the centre from which all fronds radiated, was too far. Even with all the power, she could muster, her muscles were inadequate for such a long throw. Sorrowfully, she hauled the hook back, and the men far down below – scrambling and shouting faintly – luckily didn't notice the metal as it scraped along the rocks as she drew it in.

"Let me," she heard Chor say behind her as he crept to her.

For a second she thought she would say no, but she helped him up, and though he couldn't yet walk, he could stand if he had one hand on her shoulder. Without a second to spare, she handed the gathered rope to him.

He grunted hard as he tossed the grappling hook, but the effort didn't seem to cost him too much, as if he had quite a lot more strength to give. And the hook flew all the way to the other side. A handbreadth to the left of where it needed to hit. He tried again. Yet overcompensated his aim, the hook dropping down half an arm length to the right. She thought it futile now but asked him to do it one more time anyway.

He did, and the hook struck the centre they'd aimed at and not even when he pulled his hardest did it budge from the sky-high palm even the slightest. "Get onto my back," he said.

"I was going to suggest that you hung onto me while I jumped. Your legs are so weak, you might break them if you—"

"No time to argue. I'm far too heavy for you to make it with me on top of you. Now, don't you hear them coming, how close they are getting? It's now or death!"

She threw her arms around his neck, and locked her hold on him with her legs by crossing her ankles against his stomach.

And he jumped, launched them out into the precipice.

And they swung from the rope hooked on top of the tall, curving palm atop the vertical cliff at the other side of the gorge.

In a smooth pendulum arc, they glided through the air, over soldiers and horses far below, through the cool wind of speed.

Their bodies seemed to soar past everything, all the way to the sky-high palm on the other side. And they landed in soft, yellow grass by one of the palm's lean roots. She rolled until the momentum of her body was over, though, inside her, she still sailed through the air. She huffed, then heard herself emit a jubilant whoop, her body making that sound wholly without her mind having a say in it. But she afforded herself a smile as she glanced at Chor, seeing him spit out grass. He grinned back and adjusted the loincloth, which after his tumbling landing had become so grass-stained that she could scarcely see its old colour.

She ran to her horse, mounted it and swerved and urged it to where Chor was crawling. Lopo neighed. She patted the back of the saddle and scooted forward to make room for him behind her.

She looked at him as he thought more than twice about it, definitely thrice, and was possibly giving it a fourth thought when she interrupted him with a litany of swearwords. Such a rave of curses in such a moment of freefalling madness, that now, a mere second after it had shot out of her like hail released by a tongue as swift as she thought, she didn't recollect which words she had used. Then, finally knowing exactly what to say to make him swallow his pride, she cried, *"It's now or death!"*

That did it. He used the power of his arms alone to climb up her stirrup and to pull himself onto the saddle. He then took a deep breath, looking most tense and lost with burning shame, before he got his leg around to the other side, finally straddling the horse. And a heartbeat after his arms went around her waist, she rode to the place where they could descend without either of the three of them killing themselves in the process.

Though she held the reins, he directed her—through a maze of narrow passages that crisscrossed and zigzagged the canyon. At one narrow bend, he became very quiet, a telltale sign that he was listening to something very far away. After a few seconds, she felt him relax. A smile in his tone as he told her they could slow down, that the soldiers on horseback had lost their track.

They went slowly ever farther away from the soldiers. After stopping to let their nerves find calm again, they didn't move until he was certain that he couldn't hear the soldiers move anywhere near them. Her mind drifted, and when he stirred her, the sun had disappeared behind heavy clouds and light had faded with the fast approach of night.

"Where are we going?" she asked him, as it now seemed to her that he had a certain destination in mind.

"There's a second hiding place, another smuggler's cave. One still full of smuggler's goods."

"How did you find it?"

"You don't want to know."

"I definitely do, *now*." A note of feigned sternness in her voice, giving him a hint that his discouragement worked like reverse psychology on her.

"I discovered it after I came upon a dead body, the carcass picked apart by vultures. In the inner pocket of his coat was a map to this cave, even harder to see from the outside than the one with the rope lift. I surmised it was a smuggler's cave and when I followed the map to the X, I happily saw that it was so. It's still full of loot, all kinds of riches stolen near and far. A den of thieves, in which I lived before I heard that my sister was in trouble. So, I'm quite certain that the man whose corpse I stumbled upon was the last thief alive who knew about it. I believe there are other corpses not far from that one, and that the thieves killed one another after they fought over the loot."

"Probably because they couldn't agree to share the treasure equally between them. Humans. Story of our lives."

"Ah, yes. Note to selflessness: Keep it up. Anyway. Inside, there are enough provisions to last three seasons."

"We're going to steal from thieves?"

"I told you, they're dead, or at least one of them would have come back long ago. As they're skeletons by now, I'm sure they won't miss anything. Yes, we'll practically be graverobbers, but we'll rob as they would have robbed. I can think of no better way of honouring them."

She saw him go abruptly tense. "What's the matter?"

"A nearing rumble of thunder, I've rarely heard its kind. We have to hurry. The whole canyon might get flooded shortly. But the cave, harder to find than you can believe, should be safe."

Chor was right. The second hidden cave was indeed harder to detect than the first one, especially in the dying light of late evening sinking into the grip of the oncoming storm. Chor said they had arrived at it, though she still couldn't see where in the cliff wall it was supposed to be. It was concealed by a tall, wide boulder that appeared as part of the cliff and hid its opening like camouflage. Just as they reached this boulder and she saw and approached the narrow entrance behind it, a hard rain began to fall. The rainstorm grew and grew. Fast, the heavy rain fell, beating chaotically, to her frantic, feverish mind sounding like a manic drumbeat intended by its drummer for an unhinged circus wheel.

Kyra looked up at clouds that could dwarf mountains.

A shiver ran through her so strong that it felt like being touched by the sky, as if the chill in the air was meant for *her*.

*

Blacksheer. The hermit Hesione's mountain. Where Hesione now had seen warriors of the inquisition climb on the ledges below. Which was how Torest presently found herself at the mountain's very edge, looking down into ever thicker clouds approaching, closing in, layer upon layer of cloud welling up near her feet. She closed her eyes, and imagined that this moment was a chapter in her story with lines between lines between lines.

In her mind she heard the voice again, Hesione's voice, the notoriously madly eccentric middle-aged hermit woman who apparently liked to dance naked believing she could create rain. Hesione had seen her haggard, emaciated figure freezing to death, lost in the mountains. Hesione had brought her up to her cave. And when the men with swords and crossbows had emerged below, she had climbed in front of Torest to the very top of the mountain, guiding her up, up, always higher up. Until they were at the peak of the mountain. With nowhere left to climb, the two of them stood in silence. There, Torest had questioned with her eyes, and Hesione, who had offered her hermitage to hide in, had revealed to be a thunder being. A mythical being too strange to be true even if they came from the world of myths, humans said.

But Torest was no human. She had to believe, or there would be nothing left of her that rang true.

Hesione said, "Do you hear that?"

"It sounds like a herd of bison stampeding down below."

"A thunderstorm building up. Do you believe me now?"

Torest nodded. Then turned her chin back out over the precipice, the vast nothingness, the ground probably so far below that to fall all the way down would probably take almost half a minute. Hitting the stony ground in the abyss, there'd be no whole bone left in her body. Even her horns would break.

Raising her strained voice loud enough to be heard over the beating wind roaring up like rage below, Hesione spoke four words and Torest wondered if those would be the last words she ever heard. Because what Hesione said was, *"You have to jump."*

*

Kyra rushed, then even rushed her rushing, as she brought Lopo to a small shelter Chor had pointed her to.

She then hurried inside the cave as he on his knees held the thick cover of hanging vines open for her. He crawled in front of her and showed her a pool deep inside. Then he lit a torch and showed her crudely made bookshelves heavy with books, many of which contained stories of piracy and plunder, yet many announcing fairytales and myths. She would love to read them all. Then, opening a large colourfully patterned wooden chest, she couldn't have been more delighted if it had been full of gold.

Outside, the rain smattered loudly on, the beat now of a drummer both mad and drunk. With this backdrop, as night closed in and hid them deeply, she taught him how to walk.

On and on it rained, as if the whole world was set to flood.

*

To Torest, as the wind ripped and clawed her face, it seemed the night air was flailing like a dying bird as big as the world.

If there was a chance that Janrey had gone against her decision to make the journey over land and sea alone, he would have followed the soldiers to this mountain, into this storm. Then he'd raced up through the chaos to reach her first. She almost fully believed it to be true. Eyes narrowed, head bowed into the gale, drenched hair whipping her cheeks, she called Janrey's name into the madness of the storm, her hoarse shout a whisper in the uproar. Though near her, Hesione gave no sign of hearing her call for help. She called once more. This time she used all the air in her lungs, throwing her voice with all her might against the overpowering muscling current of wind that had the loudness of a waterfall and the wildness of a crazed beast not knowing its own strength.

But nobody came out of the sheet of rain. Nobody answered. The ones who would next appear would be black-clad soldiers armed with crossbows. The ones who would come for her would be the ones who would kill her. Unless she did what Hesione had asked her to. She looked out into the cloud-filled abyss, and just imagining coming too close to the edge gave her vertigo. In a stiff reflex, she backed away from the edge. Then felt Hesione's hand on her wrist. Hesione sombrely said, "You have to jump at the exact moment I tell you to do it."

She looked deep into Hesione's eyes. They said, *Trust me.*

She nodded, defying panic. Swallowed. "Tell me when."

-15-

A rumbling rush filled the sky and the wide eyes of the twins in their balloon. The storm had hit as sudden as an earthquake, yet it was the sky that quaked, that yelled like primal anger at an injustice shaking the entire world. The twins had rarely held hands. For a desperate moment, they did so now. Niels recalled having heard of a similar sudden storm, a little more than a year ago, that had taken soldiers by surprise in a canyon near the Forbidden, some soldiers even dying in a flash flood. Never catching the centaur they hunted. Did the centaur and the human woman with him drown as well? Such sudden storms, did they mean death for anyone coming too close to such rage?

The thunderstorm hurtled their hot-air balloon towards a mountain that had been obscured by black night, black clouds—until this very second, as they were about to crash.

Into the deafening wind, Niels shouted, "We have to ascend to get above the storm! Toss out the sandbags!"

At the top of her voice, Aurora demanded, "How many?"

"All of them!"

In a manic, half-hysteric trance, they moved as one.

Every instant speeding faster towards the end, they hurried in the face of running out of all time they would ever have.

A dark avalanche of storm clouds, closing in, closing in like the smoke of a burning house. With no time for warning, the crack of thunder lashed closer, louder than anything. Niels felt himself pant hard, but couldn't hear it, the storm drowning him out, its rising roar bigger than any sound he could make. He whirled around, labouring to hold on, fighting to keep his balance. Angry desperation hit him in the face, as he saw his sister halt her movement. "Why are you stopping? *Throw them out!*"

"It's not working! The wind is forcing us down! Look! My God! It's full of lightning!"

"Buggering hell, we're done for."

"The mountain wall, we're heading straight at it!"

"Aurora, look at me." Through wet nostrils he pulled as much air into his lungs as he could, cold rain striking his right cheek like nails. His eyes touching his dearest one, he fought tears, and took Aurora's small hands in his. "It's been an honour to—"

Aurora stilled. "Wait." She looked out while absently taking hold of the valve cord. "What's happening?"

The wind dramatically changed direction, sharply changing their course with it. Niels flung his gaze to the mountain – to the valve cord in his sister's hand – back to the mountain – to Aurora. Wild-eyed, Aurora threw her gaze all around. The wind at Niels' right abated, and a new forceful wind coming from behind made them jeer enough to glide alongside the vertical mountain wall, instead of zooming directly into it.

Just above the rain-smattered, onion-shaped green canvas bag full of hot air, the vertical wall of rock leaned outward at a less than ninety-degree angle. The top of the balloon ever so lightly scraped against the wall of rock that shone black with the dousing wind. Niels stretched himself out of the wicker basket and looked up at the mountain's peak, seeing the overhang up there gradually becoming an out-curving buttress. Seen through strips of clouds above, the buttress presently overhung half of the balloon, and they were about to pass under it. The wind grew soft, lessening their speed considerably, then slowly seemed to come to a standstill, making Niels' mouth fall open. Pulling himself together, he said, "The wind just—stopped."

"We must be in the eye of the storm. Incredible."

Niels' eyes filled with tears of relief. "We're passing through, getting away from the vertical side of the mountain! It seems we're under the end of the buttress, doesn't it?"

Suddenly, a plunging thud from on top of the balloon.

Aurora looked as if her world had just become a sea in which she had turned into an ever-surprised creature, who – apart from breathing water and swimming for dear life – knew nothing about anything any more. "What in heaven's name was that?"

Before losing courage, Niels hurried up, braved the storm closing in on them again, climbing up the rope to the web of the giant lime-green airbag. Climbed up and up. Finally, the roundedness of the top of it. He laboured on, clamouring in the thick misty wind they travelled through. The mountain disappearing with the mist and their steadily increasing distance away from it. Clambering out of breath, one more pull, then, grunting, looking up. And believed he was dreaming. Because there, right next to the gas release valve at the topmost point of the balloon, a horned mythical being was lying on her stomach, holding so tightly to the rope-web that her knuckles whitened.

First, all Niels could feel was shock.

Then, utter confusion.

Then, utter wonder.

Then, fear.

But now, seeing that the creature was much more frightened than he was, something happened to him. He felt a gentleness come over him, a softness for this strange apparition that he couldn't explain to himself. Knew only he had to act on this feeling that beat pure and true in his tight chest.

He gave voice to that feeling. "Hold on. Don't be afraid. Girl, look at me. I'm coming for you."

*

While Chor practiced walking in the torchlight with the rain drumming ever louder outside, Kyra luxuriated in the pool deep in the shadows where he couldn't see her. Submerged in the lukewarm water while fresh cool rain poured down from above, sluicing her shoulders and arms. Her body would soon be all clean and fragrant again, and she was still alive, still young and strong. Feeling the water wash off the tension of being in mortal danger, a very different tension, a nervous hope, filled her. A beckoning fantasy about Chor, that what she'd thought she'd seen in his eyes had equalled her own desire. In an instant, the fantasy ran away with her and her heart felt overfilled, straining against her breastbone, her chest too small to hold it. Her chest rose steeply as she heaved a sigh. Then she just savoured the sweet sensation of bathing, becoming new, feeling as though shedding old skin, a much younger skin underneath.

Lathering her naked, sunburned skin with soap.

Heaven.

When he had presented her with the soap bar, she'd been so happy that she'd gently taken it and held it like a baby to her cheek. Drawing in the sweet scent of it as she rubbed it all over herself, she could kiss this soap bar, a gift like a boon from divinities of purity. She could kiss *him*.

Finding privacy behind a pillar at the back of the cave, she slipped into the treasure she'd found in the wooden chest. A thin night-blue dress of cloth as fine as a wedding gown. Delicately cut from neck to knees, an uncanny precise fit to her measure, and the silk appeared to have been sewn just for her, to closely follow every tapering and out-curving line of her.

Suddenly thunder rumbled out there. But here it was softly warm, the air smooth and easy to breathe. *Breathe. Just breathe.* But she almost couldn't let herself. Because though she felt as fresh as the newly cleaned air she breathed, she found that she ached to sweat, to mingle her sweat with his. Now that he could walk and stand on his own, she could tell that he no longer was embarrassed by his clumsy legs. And this loss of embarrassment seemed to carry a feeling of readiness as if he was ready for anything, even her wildest fantasies about the two of them. It was just that it was almost too good, too perfect. And this was why her breath trembled in and out, why she was afraid that maybe just a breath was all it took to break the spell.

They drank wine, laughed, and joked, and as the rain intensified, so did her yearning. She let it take her all the way.

At some point, after he had read a raunchy story of a pirate queen for her, she made him shut the book, looking deep into his eyes. She got up and did a twirl in her beautiful dress. Squatting back down to him, she lifted his chin with her finger, and felt the sandpapery stubble as she slid her finger along his jawline.

She knew he could sense how nervous she was – of him as of herself – though she trusted him enough to egg him on with her smile. Before he had appeared in her life, a thousand hurts had thickened her skin, a shield that desensitized her but was in the way of true reaching. The only way to her was through.

He smiled shyly. She kissed him nervously, slowly, yet hopingly, teasingly, tucking her lower lip just lightly between his.

And whispered with her eyes closed, "How am I doing?"

"So far, so good."

She gave him an open-mouthed kiss.

"Now?"

"So farther, so better."

She kissed him deeply.

And he whispered with heavy breath, "So farthest, so best."

He undressed her with his voice, then with his hands.

Feeling his naked human body against hers, she closed her eyes and felt herself slip into a dream of falling endlessly. Like holding on to a freely moving pulley suspended on an aerial runway mounted on a peak above the clouds, sliding through clouds over treetops and over waves. Her stomach endlessly dropped, her body forever in freefall, so it was, this loss of control within her control. That heavenly. The sensation of diving from the highest height down into the deepest depths. Into the place filled by the transformation of their ever-shifting shapes, her ever-deepening for his ever-extending, him changing as much outward as she inward. Just like that, after the slow lift of his hips. That endless drive into and through her, the pit of her stomach falling as fast as her ache sought its filling, a slow-teasing to how he reached and she pressed and how each begged to be pressed and reached, like an underwater chase.

She found her face smiling like when she was a little girl and had discovered for the first time the surprising exhilaration and elation of a wonder. Her fantasy granted her entrance to this wonder, a mysterious nameless joy. Not knowing yet how inexperienced she had been, so early in her life, her innocent body had been like a miracle to her, a secret promise she had been desperate to know how to fulfil. And she felt now as if she was inside that miracle, as if in a long-awaited wonderworld, as deep with heat as newly sunburned skin. Falling inside, nearing arrival of building intensity and light, filling her with the wideness of the brightest night. Her increasing weightlessness a dance at last caught by their drummed rhythm, filling her with the joy of his pressure and weight. And she opened her eyes, dared to look deeply into his and to whisper to him to not be afraid, that she wasn't going to hurt him.

Lucid thoughts melted away and only dreamlike poetry made sense. *He is a fraction away,* she felt, *from meeting the core of me, the place where I end and begin, to transgress the point of no return. The part of me that I alone can make into a tale unfolding as I like, refolding and reshaping hidden pages like petals at once opening and tightly budding anew. This drum of drums, this tale ever-changing, turning over a new leaf even as it is re-read, this ever-evolving surprise of pleasure found on the other side of pain, mingling like sweat-stinging eyes to join with tears like endings.*

*

"How in all the buggering hell did you know when to jump?" Aurora asked as politely as only she could.

Niels felt himself roll his eyes.

"The woman who helped me escape knew there was only one way I could survive. Her name is Hesione, and she revealed to me tonight that she is a thunder being."

"What the buggering hell is a—"

Niels elbowed Aurora.

"Beings who can attract and repel thunder. By drawing the thunderstorm to her, she directed your balloon directly under the best outcrop to jump from. Though I saw only clouds below, she told me to trust her, to take a leap of faith, and she knew the exact moment when I needed to leap."

Niels asked, "What's your name?"

"Torest."

"Well, Torest," Aurora said with a little lopsided smile. "I'm glad you didn't fall on your head."

Torest laughed, and after a moment, the coin dropped for Niels as well. After a short expelling of tense air in the relief of a quick laugh, Niels said, "You look like a being of myth. I'm sorry for my bluntness."

"It's fine. I'm an aiga, from a world that only exists in your myths, so yes, I truly am a being of myth. Soldiers of the church had surrounded the mountain they hunted me up to, and they were only going to wait out the storm until coming to kill me. They don't believe in myths, only in their own religion, so when they saw me, they thought I must be from hell."

One hand on her hip, the other on the side of the waist-high wicker basket, Aurora said, "Buggering hell."

"No, just hell," Torest deadpanned.

"Well," Niels said. "We can't take you down until we're across the Little Sea. I'm afraid you will be quite far from home by then."

"Where are you heading?"

"To a place in the south that hasn't been mapped. Nobody who has gone inside or flown over it has ever come back. We hope to be the first ones. The southerners call it the Forbidden."

"In that case, I don't want you to drop me off anywhere. I want you to take me with you because that's where I'm going."

Niels wondered aloud, "May I ask why?"

"It's a very, very long story. I think you should tell me yours first."

Niels proudly said, "We were told of the legendary airfarers of the north, so we pledged to build our own balloon and let nothing stop us from flying to them and learning their secrets. To then go south, to explore the place nobody has returned from. We will be the first. We're doing what we set out to do."

Aurora filled in, "We heard tales of magnificent scientists ascending to record heights. It was all we talked about, growing up. And now my brother had this idea about the longest rope anchoring us while we mapped the world's last unmapped place."

"Yes, Aurora tells it true. She's now my co-pilot and part of my scientific team. She gave me the extra push I needed to believe in myself and what I can accomplish in the world."

"We have to tell the world what we've seen on the other side. There is a legend making its journey around the world that that forest is going to disappear at the summer solstice, so we've timed our arrival to that date, to see if anything unusual will happen then." With a smooth, languid swagger to her movement, Aurora did a little slow dance while holding her shoulders, for some reason. "I hope it will."

Torest blinked with a higher focus in her eyes. "You do?"

"Yes," Aurora said and went back to lean against the side of the wicker basket, drawing one knee up to rest her heel against it in a tough-looking pose. "My brother doesn't believe anything will happen on that day, apart from our big discovery, but I want the legend to be true."

Niels cleared his throat. "In any case, we welcome you, Torest. Welcome to the first and maybe last expedition of Nita."

Aurora straightened herself in full attention. "Hear, hear. Go on, tell her, Niels!"

"That was it, actually."

Aurora slumped back, a little disappointed. "Oh. I thought you'd prepared a speech. That there would be wine."

Niels rolled his eyes. "Yes, you naturally expect the high likelihood of a mythical being dropping from the sky as you pass dangerously close to an overarching mountain, so you always have a speech ready for such a likely occasion. How silly of me."

Torest asked, "I'd love to watch you work."

Aurora said, "Just keep your eyes peeled and don't drift off."

"Wouldn't dream of it."

Aurora quipped, "That's right. No dreaming, or you'll miss it. It's about time we get to it, isn't it? I can see the coastline and the sea ahead, beyond those dispersing clouds. Buggering hell, the sea is impressive! It's not little at all."

Niels took a moment to let himself be overwhelmed by the sight of the vast water, glittering with millions of waves of light of the full moon. He then shook himself awake and got into his most serious professional mode. He took out the logbook and his pencil and eraser. "Check the instruments."

"Just a minute."

Aurora was cupping Hoodlum in one hand while in the other she held finely cut carrots. The fuzzy little thing was quite literally eating out of her hand. Niels rolled his eyes. Hoodlum looked up at him while munching, astonishingly looking just like a kid eating snacks while watching a thrilling adventurous play.

Torest laughed. "Is that a guinea pig?"

With a flushed face suffused with warmth, Aurora let Torest hold Hoodlum. Aurora smiled lopsidedly and said, "He loves to fly. He—"

Impatient, Niels said, "Aurora, please."

Torest's grin became crooked, as if she already liked Aurora so much that she unconsciously mirrored her mannerisms and idiosyncrasies. "It looks like he has a lot on his mind and you seem to be a good listener."

"Well, yes," Aurora said. "We have a special connection. As I said, before I was so rudely interrupted, he loves to fly. It makes him feel nine hundred grams lighter."

Merrily, Torest asked, "How much does he weigh?"

"Nine hundred grams. So he feels light as air, up in the air. He's having the time of his furry life."

Niels had no more patience to spare. "Aurora! Would you please check the instruments?"

Seconds of rustling activity from Aurora. "All checked."

"Altitude."

"Four thousand and eight hundred feet."

"Time."

"Forty-eight hours and twenty-nine minutes."

"Air temperature."

"Buggering twenty degrees above freezing point."

Niels shot back an irritated look, rubbing his knuckles between his chin and his lower lip as if a mosquito bite itched there. "Could you do it without the swearing?"

"What's the point?"

"The freezing point."

"No, I mean—never mind. Twenty degrees above. Hey, what about the air pressure?"

Niels put the logbook back in his coat's inner pocket. "I already logged it. I was afraid we'd forget it otherwise. Will you remind me to check it again when we're at five thousand?"

"I will. If I remember to. You'll have to remind me."

As if warming to them more than she'd initially thought she would, Torest now seemed to care as much about what happened to them as what happened to her. "Look, you two. You should bear in mind that what's in front of you, after the sea and the river, behind the veil of mist over the plains, it's the unknown. Once memory is lost, it can never be retrieved. That which you are evolving towards is innocence, tantamount to facing death and rebirth, a new life where you can't remember this life. But then you would no longer be you, and can you love somebody else as much as you love yourself? Maybe it's a leap of *folly.*"

Aurora surprised Niels then, saying, "I'd rather be a crazy shepherd than a lost sheep."

Niels said, "Aurora's right. The most important scientific discoveries have the highest possible stakes. You have to be a little obsessed and crazy to be the discoverer leading the way."

Torest took a moment to think about this, then seemed to reach some conclusion that surprised even her. She slowly spoke to them both, dispersing her glances equally between them. "To lead the way, I think… you have to have courage before you choose. And you can't have courage before you have love that allows you to sacrifice yourself. Love, I think, is an act of two parts. To love is to first pay attention to what's under the surface, then to create something passionate in the deep together. If these two halves are fulfilled, two undercurrents meet, and that love is the thing that leads you, forever novel, always expanding."

Niels looked at Aurora, and Aurora slowly turned her eyes to look back at him, and then they both directed their gazes at this strange being of myth.

It had the feeling of waking up completely rested and comfortably warm after a long, shuddering fever.

It felt just like coming home.

*

The night after the sudden, heavy rain that appeared to have violently flooded part of the canyon outside, Chor quietly sang a song to himself. A song in a foreign tongue Kyra couldn't understand, yet every word felt true to her. His singing voice was unhuman, husky, breathy, almost whispery, with a feathery quality to it, every tone full of hidden, ambiguous meanings.

She found herself fawning as the song ended. "That was… It sounded the way stars look."

"A song for Leina."

"Leina?" Hot jealousy flew into her like anger.

"She left everything behind, all comforts of civilization, and carried nothing with her but the blood singing in her veins. A vagabond of songs, she became part of mine. Now that she's gone, my inner music is melancholy. I promised I would come for her when she called my name. I should have come for her."

"You came for me," she said in half a voice.

"I'm sorry. It's just that she had a mythical power that let her change colour when she mirrored herself in others."

"Sometimes I don't know if you're talking symbolically or if the world is stranger and more complex than I thought."

He took her hand then. Slowly, languidly, he blinked, his eyelids swollen and heavy with sudden dazed abandon. His long lashes barely lifted past half the reach of his widened pupils. His blurry focus tugged at hers, drew her in and down, pulled her under, and helpless to move from this tug, she stared through his stare, lost deep in his eyes, in the resistless, unyielding pull of an undertow in a storm.

"I need my old body back," he said. "I need to be myself."

"I know. Just one more night. Please. For me?"

That night, after they had made love, he talked again in his sleep. Kyra felt like a thief, but she couldn't help herself, listening to each new whisper passing his lips. First, disjointed words. Then, something songlike, its rhythm and lyric like nothing of this world. *"From the cradle to the grave. From womb to tomb. To dust from lust. To perish from cherish."* Pause. *"The flame consumes all life and death. Until no fuel and no air follow to swallow. Only sparks of hope and dreams glow to outlive all. From the last strife to the first breath."* And after a long pause, she could hear him faintly repeat, *"Ibris."*

When he woke, sometime after midnight, she only asked him of this last word he'd said again and again while deep in sleep. And he said, "In our tongue, Ibris means *Climber*. It is the name of Silver Monkey of a sacred secret fable. If I tell it to you, the tale will bind you with the magical bond of liberty. It will free you, but only if you tie your future to its narrator."

She said, "I choose to be bound to the tale and its teller."

"You must swear to never tell a soul."

She said, "This I swear."

"Then hear the tale of Silver Monkey.

"Desiring nothing more than to know the secret in the silence of birds, for this was long before they sang, Silver Monkey climbed the Endless Tree of Illumination. Towards the goddess of infinite light, he climbed. And so he climbed ever higher, into the sky of the golden sun, where the sunglow gives the power of wisdom to see four moves ahead. And on he climbed, into the sky of the red sun, where the treasure of fire granted him speech. And on he climbed, into the sky of the green sun, where the treasure of the green nectar let him understand the mystery of melody and rhythm. On, on, ever on he climbed, finally into the sky of the purple sun, where he found the treasure of dance and song in the cloud of oblivion. But it stayed out of reach. He cried and said he would sacrifice everything to know this treasure. As he gave up his silver sheen, the cloud let him immerse in it, and by using all of his wisdom, his inner illumination became part of the outer. And in the embrace of this cloud, he saw that it would grant him weightlessness, but only if he gave up his other gifts and that this was always the true fourth move. Doing so, he gained the power to hover high above every treetop and to glide through the air as far and wide as he wished, needing only to forget in order to ascend skyward and dance with the air. Within the everlasting purple light, he gave up more and more of himself, until he became bodyless, a spirit, the silver sound of morning birdsong that wakes every world.

"But this playful and sensitive silver spirit of bountiful tropical treasures, he only inspires. The secret of what it means when birds change their song, why they break their inherited pattern, is this. Touched by overwhelming true beauty, they want to mirror it. And true beauty comes from the sun above all others, whose colour only exists in that highest heaven, where every extinct species live, the place where humans are the last to enter."

Part III
Midsummer

-16-

Eleven months after the termination of their failed mission in Topazin Canyon, Edeline received a brief dispatch in black ink, saying she'd been assigned to go back there, to the farthest east. She was now needed at the outpost nearest the Forbidden Forest, the easternmost point where the human world ended. She didn't know anybody who didn't fear that forest. Many youths had wandered into it, none coming back out. Some families of those who'd been lost inside had come to believe that the mythical beings were to blame, that they had manipulated whoever ventured inside and brought them under an evil spell, forcing them to stay as they no longer answered their own will. When faced with that place, would she, too, fear it?

She would soon find out.

Tomorrow at dawn, just four days before the Midsummer Eve Festival at her garrison town, Edeline would travel to the place that had called for reinforcement. To arrive at dusk at the grasslands and the small military campsite from which Kruso's letters to her were sent. And it didn't take long after reading this sparingly scribed order before her old feelings for Kruso welled up like tears. Feelings she hadn't confronted since they'd broken their engagement last summer. The place they were sending her to, he'd been there since the month of Tenthmoon, more than half a year ago. Knowing that she would see him tomorrow night, she could already vividly see the image of his gently smiling face, and it was almost too overwhelming to bear.

Apart from the centaur that they'd hunted well into Eighthmoon, until their resources ran out as the last summer month neared its end, no mythical being had been sighted in Albad in more than a generation. They'd taken refuge in other realms, especially after the last king's decree that only trees that humans could cultivate and monetize were worth protecting. And in the realms where mythical beings still existed a year ago, none were now left. All had returned to the Forbidden. Because they'd been called to it, they said, when asked about the reason for their simultaneous migration, though none of them either would or could say who or what had called them.

With so much unnatural activity which nobody had an explanation for, General Urun had summoned a selected few to guard the eastern border between the province of Kalid and the unknown, baffling sylvan territory. The forbidden territory from which all mythical beasts came and to which they now returned, yet where all humans inexplicably vanished.

Yet so far, not a single creature had left this forest to encroach on territories of the Albadine civilization, and no sane, civilized person would break the taboo to go inside it. And with all mythical beings from every untouched forest gone from every realm, Edeline wondered how much longer Kruso would be stationed there. It might be the last time they'd be placed together. Brought to the same place due to their experience in last year's hunt. United by outside forces, to guard the edges of the known world, until the threat was determined to be over. It might be her last chance to make things right.

Now, as she packed her things for tomorrow's deployment, as the sand in her hourglass was running out, the hour before bed, her heart beat ever faster. Because when the top of the hourglass was empty, she'd promised herself to finally try to sleep. She had already packed and repacked more times than she dared to count. Delaying having to close her eyes only to open them to the day she'd see Kruso again, a full day's ride away. Engaging her mind with thoughts about the centaur shapeshifter, to postpone all thoughts of Kruso and of how things between him and her had ended in misery.

She remembered them looking everywhere for the creature. But the tracks had disappeared and never reappeared, washed away by the massively heavy rain that had caused the flash flood in which three young soldiers had died. The last they saw of the creature had been in a cave. The men who had been there said that they had had him cornered yet that he'd miraculously escaped somehow together with the girl that was under his spell.

She tried to picture how it would end, with the creature's skull on General Urun's mantlepiece, where he said it would be his most prized trophy. She recalled the day Urun had arrived and Kruso had it confirmed that he and Edeline no longer were allowed to be indefinitely relieved of their duty.

After that first day when the general nearly killed the centaur himself, they never got any closer to finding another beast like it again, centaur or otherwise. Urun had been coldly furious. And now she would be under Urun's command once more, as Kruso already was. She would have to report to this quite scary leader when she reached the grass plains, to patrol the vast stretch between the Forbidden Forest and Topazin Canyon.

She knew that the trial against Leina had never happened. The same man who took Leina in his custody to bring her to court had stopped the judicial process against her. Perhaps he felt remorse for having killed that little peasant girl, though they said the girl would have bludgeoned him with a stone if he hadn't. Whatever the reason, the man, whose name Edeline had never learned, no longer sought justice delivered to the one he had accused of attempted murder.

These thoughts, about Leina and about mythical beings abandoning the human world, she had chosen to think about because they should matter enough for her to stop dwelling over the past. Yet her mind kept circling back to Kruso, now that she no longer could avoid how near in time it was before the space between them would shrink into nothing.

When they'd been a couple, for the longest time she'd never wanted it to end. Even now, she couldn't say why it did.

She was, of course, to blame for the parting of their way.

But what was the critical thing about *her* that had made their way divide and their relationship end?

It hadn't been jealousy, neither on her part nor his. For him, it had only been an obstacle after her infidelity, and in the end, he'd let it go. As she had weathered her pain after he'd slept with another woman. A hard-hitting, surprising pain, as she'd been the one telling him he should do it, for them to be even. Yet the pain *had* dissipated, seeing how the experience had left him empty and missing her more than ever. In truth, neither of them had a jealous, possessive nature. And so it wouldn't be a fair assessment to conclude that he'd been afraid to lose her. It was rather that he felt he'd lost her *trust*. She'd come to see too late that her private fight with alcohol addiction had hurt him more than her infidelity. That she'd struggled to save herself yet hadn't let him in. As if she hadn't thought enough of him to let him help her, let alone trust him with her secret.

Both of them were free from the greedy desire to own, they'd never been consumed with fear of losing.

As in him, there was in her a proneness to share that was so big that it left little room for any inclination of rivalry or jealousy in her life. And Kruso's love for her had been too evident for her to fear he needed anybody else to be happy. It was in how he'd looked at her, in a way he never looked at anyone else, how he'd smiled in a certain way only at her like nobody else did. And, ultimately, it was in how she'd responded in kind, in how they often with true feeling had said *'I love you'* to each other and showed each other affection.

A new thought came to her: was there something wrong with her, or with them, that neither of them had been jealous when most other couples would have been? She conducted a thought experiment. What if he had looked at another girl in the warmly affectionate way that she had thought he could only look at her? Her heart didn't protest. But it then most loudly objected as she imagined him no longer looking at *her* with love, while now looking at another girl that way. And now, as the last grain of sand fell from the top of the hourglass, it came to her.

Something Kruso once had said.

That it hadn't mattered to him if she slept with or loved anybody else, as long as he would know that she loved him no less, and could love no one more.

And so she finally saw why it had ended.

Why all good things end.

Because we never know if we are all alone.

*

Waiting for the caravan that would bring Edeline to him, Kruso thought about her last letter, in which she'd told him about Phana, her new best friend. As he gazed out over the sun-yellowed sea of grass, his eyes seeking out the vague direction where he was born, what she'd written made him think of Drein, no friend dearer to him for as long as his boyhood had lasted.

He wondered what Drein did now. He recalled the two of them that time when they'd been twelve, going into the woods, bringing just their guitars on their backs. That night up on a mound in a glade in the woods, under a summer sky that had never been more starbright, together they had *created*. Then, through a voice full of tears, Kruso had let Drein know about his father's suicide. "I'm so sorry," Drein had said, putting his guitar in the grass beside him and gently taking hold of Kruso's shoulder, as if to steady him.

Kruso had said, "The only good thing about it is that now I don't have to be afraid any more that it will happen someday. It's no longer in front of me, looming."

"Can you forgive him?"

Kruso had thought about it for several heartbeats.

"It's a choice I have to make every day, to forgive him, and some days the pain will be bigger than others. I'm not there yet, but I will be, and I hope that my forgiveness will stand." It had been awfully quiet for a long moment then. But then Drein had moved to sit right next to him, so close that he'd felt Drein's warmth. Just like when they'd been small boys and had cuddled before they'd gotten teased for it and had to stop or they wouldn't get to play with the others. Drein had put his arm loosely around Kruso's neck, and it had drawn Kruso's thoughts to good, sweet things, like bees drawn to nectar. It had made him relaxed, and sleepy, and he had laid his weary head on Drein's shoulder. A moment so beautiful that Kruso's heart had broken all over again when it ended. Hugging Drein then, he'd known even before seeing the tears in Drein's eyes that Drein felt it, too. That it would be the last time they held each other like that, one boy consoling the other by snuggling up to him, the way you only do when you trust another soul completely.

*

Though she'd been engaged to Kruso for years and had known him since her early teenage years, very seldom had Edeline smoked so that he could see. The few times she'd done it, she'd been very drunk. Since they'd broken their engagement, she'd kept her revised promise to herself: to only drink if her friends were drinking and to never drink more than them. But she had instead smoked every day. These days, if she saw somebody with a cigarette and she had no money for tobacco and paper with which to roll her own, her desire to smoke would be so strong that she could easily see herself pressing her mouth to theirs just to suck some excess smoke into her lungs.

Now, after Kruso had given her an awkward hug, as he talked to Phana, who Edeline had persuaded her new captain to include in his borderland patrol, Edeline plucked a newly rolled cigarette from her pocket and smoked in plain view.

There had been other things Kruso hadn't known about her. Things she'd only told Phana, partner in crime.

Only Phana knew that Edeline occasionally was a thief.

But there were things not even Phana knew about her. Things she couldn't resist doing when the mood struck, doing them for reasons Edeline alone could understand. Each reason was an intimate feeling, yet one she couldn't even express to herself.

Presently, she neither smiled nor frowned when he gave her a sideways glance. With a little nod, he acknowledged that he saw the cigarette in her hand, but he didn't change his smiling expression the least. She didn't know what she had wanted him to feel or how she'd expected him to react. Anything except this changelessness, as if however she changed didn't matter to him any more. In sad frustration, she turned her eyes to Phana instead and kept looking only at her best friend, to protect her heart. But then she saw how Phana looked at him, partly openly flirting. Paradoxically more provocative the more innocently she smiled. Aggressively, Edeline stubbed out the cigarette. Her lower lip was swollen between her thumb and index finger as she pulled at it. Promptly, she remembered how it had been when she and Kruso had first gotten to know one another. After they had found out the other's name, how Kruso had loved to discover her quirks and peculiarities, and how she, through his eyes, had discovered these things about herself that it had taken his first sight of her for her to notice. By seeing herself through his eyes as he fell in love with her, how she suddenly had fallen in love with herself, seeing herself as he saw her, as she'd never known she could both seem to the world and be to herself. She didn't know how to feel now, seeing her new best friend Phana like him this much, discovering him as she once had.

Being with Phana this winter and spring, was the most uncomplicated time Edeline had ever had. How at night they had experimented, exploring one another in the dark in the dormitory of the base outside Kullum, while the others slept. The sensation of her kiss, so tender yet so eager with fierce passion. How in broad daylight they'd held hands, quickly becoming thick as thieves. In Phana, Edeline had found a sister in sin, an ally in her private war against boredom. The two of them always sneaking away to light up their cigarettes surreptitiously. Always laughing appreciatively at the other's joke, their weird humour ensuring that most times only they laughed, and if others joined in, nobody laughed like them. When she had kissed Phana and felt hands touch her that weren't Kruso's, in the moment it had been a higher height of pleasure for being illicit, sinful. A thing all theirs, their own exclusive treasure, about which they alone knew. As sweet as stealing delicious, luxurious chocolate. As exquisite as taking your first drag after a long day when you could kill for a cigarette. But though she loved Phana dearly, she would never love anyone like she had loved Kruso.

Right now, remembering all he meant to her, she had to walk away, because there was a sudden swollen ball of regret growing in her throat. Welling up, jealous only of the girl she'd been, who'd been as innocent and unruined as Phana was right now. As it was Phana who now got to know him, while Edeline missed him, missed herself, like never before.

She excused herself, said she had to unpack her things and would be back in a moment. They just smiled and nodded, then talked on as she left, neither of them – the closest people in her life – suspecting a thing.

Suddenly she feared that Phana would steal her chance to win him back. Phana could do that, especially if she didn't try, which she wouldn't—it was Edeline who was the flirt, the thief.

Why had she needed to steal to feel alive?

She no longer understood her past self.

But she had never hurt anybody with her petty thefts, had she? At least not intentionally. It was a secret life, only hers, a story about her that she had only told herself. And she only took when there was excess that screamed to be balanced out, and took only from confectionary and toiletry vendors at the market and only so little – a chocolate bar here, a soap bar there – that it was no consequence to them. Where was the harm?

But what she'd taken from Kruso, his experience of self-worth, and his trust in her, it did make a difference to him. She had wounded him, and she hurt that he hurt. It had been anything but harmless.

What had she wanted from him? His pride, to counterbalance all her shame? Or for him to be the opposite of her father, who had never shown any emotion, neither love nor hate, who never laughed or cried? To be somebody with which she could oppose the man who had squandered her family's money and never said he was sorry?

Inhaling the smoke aggressively now, she had a thought that felt like melting ice running down her back. That she had become like her father, a man who thought he had to teach everyone a lesson. Hadn't she thought she had to make Kruso see a truth you can't shy from? Hadn't she thought that if he cried when she hurt him too much, it was proof that she could be loved even then, despite herself? Hadn't she seemed to herself, like her father had seemed to her, like a player on a stage who played a role so well she convinced even herself? But unlike her father, she would soften when Kruso became afraid of her, would hold him in her arms, no longer acting. She would comfort him, rock him like a baby, tell him she was sorry, needing to hear him say that he forgave her to believe it. She had rather been the one to give the pain than offering to take it. A coward.

Her love had been like that. A rage of pleasure and pain.

It wasn't right, it wasn't healthy, not how she'd been raised, taught, or trained, but it had been *hers.*

She had lived a life of self-inflicted injury, to feel all she could, offering only rapture to make up for the pain of her rage.

She couldn't be that woman any more.

*

Edeline woke up with a headache so vicious it felt like it was trying to murder her. She groaned, and groped for the nearest memory. Yet she could only recall going to the canteen tent with Kruso and Phana. She got up on an elbow and saw that she was in Kruso's tent, Kruso sitting by her mattress with tea ready for her. A deeply concerned look in his eye.

She croaked, "What happened?"

"You don't remember?"

"We went to celebrate our arrival. I seem to remember buying another bottle of wine. But it's all a blur. The last thing I remember is opening that second bottle."

"You really don't remember what happened after that?"

"Not a single thing. Did I do something bad?"

"When I lent Showy my guitar and he strummed a song you requested, you took off your shirt and danced half-naked on the table. I carried you back here."

"Oh, God. I'm so embarrassed." Her face was in her palms. She hated herself too much to cry, though she wanted to.

Softly, he said, "Hey, it's all right."

He tried to remove her hands and she wouldn't let him, didn't want him to see her face. She wasn't sure if she would ever again be able to look him in the eye. She began to crawl out and said as she went, "You don't need this. I need to go back to mine and Phana's tent."

She halted as he hurriedly said, "Phana and I told General Urun you were food-poisoned last night. He might inspect the matter. If he asks the men, they won't be able to cover for you."

She was about to say something. But no. "I can't do this."

Her heart was set. She didn't meet his eye, didn't listen to what he said, only told him they would talk later. And left him.

All through the day, she suffered hellish anguish, wishing deeply she'd never been born. She was enormously lucky that her first patrol was from noon until dusk, so she had some hours in the morning in which she could rehydrate and get more sleep. By midafternoon, her headache faded and her body was slowly learning to be her friend again. Her heart was another matter.

She waded through waist-high grass in a vast stretch of flat grassland, the red canyon barely visible on the horizon to the east.

That night, she sold the ring that had been his grandmother's. So she could buy two bottles of wine for every night for the rest of the month, planning to never be sober again.

He had never wanted the ring back after their engagement was over. And now it was in the hands of the cook, and no matter, because she had the book that had belonged to her mother, and that book was underlined and had notes written in the margins. Wisdom written in her mother's hand. Those beloved pages had made her see how intelligent her mother was, and that there's always a subtext, a way to look at things differently and reinterpret everything, once you learn to read between the lines.

She hadn't finished her second glass before Kruso took the wine bottle away from her, with his other hand drawing her with him, out of the canteen tent, out of the camp, far from any living soul, to the grass that reached his hips and her waist.

He poured out all her wine.

She slapped his face.

He took it without changing expression, a calm, hot anger that didn't grow hotter or colder after the blow to his cheek.

Suddenly realizing what she'd done, she panicked, began to ramble, and told him she was sorry, so sorry, but he interrupted her.

"Why did you leave? I could have helped you get sober."

It felt just like he had her heart in his fist and squeezed as hard as he could. She looked away and let whatever may be in her heart come. "I loved you. I loved sleeping with you, loved being with you, and there was nothing you lacked as a lover and friend, physically or emotionally. You made me happy. Life was so easy with you."

"Then why were you unfaithful? Why tear it all up?"

"Please. Don't ask me that. I don't think you can understand it if I tell you."

"No. I want to know, no matter how much it hurts. What made you do it, if you really were happy? And don't tell me a vague excuse, that you wanted to leave who'd you become, to remember who you used to be. Or that you felt that I only loved the person I wanted you to be. Tell me why you hurt *me*."

Pain flooded her. "Because I can't be good! Don't you see?"

"Wait. I never—"

"It wasn't your fault. I saw what things in my personality you loved, the good you brought out in me, and so I did those good things more and more because seeing you happy made me happy. But it got to the point when those things were all I did, all you saw, and I forgot the other sides of me that you didn't care for or that made you disappointed in me. There's so much badness in me."

"You didn't give me the chance to show you that I would still want you, for all that you are, the bad along with the good. I loved the things that I didn't agree with or that didn't fit the picture I had of you, because they were part of who you are. I hate to see you smoke, but I love that you have a private life independent of mine that doesn't need my approval, and that you're not afraid to show it. It isn't just part of the picture of you I love, but the full picture."

"But not living up to the picture you had of me, I hated it so much. I was more afraid of disappointing you than I was of giving up part of who I was. I'm not good for you. But I don't care what you think of me. I don't care about *anything* any more."

He stood silent for so long that she had to look up to see if he was crying. His cheeks were dry, but he didn't look at her. She had to know if she had heard him, so she asked him.

"Yes, I heard you. You said you don't care about anything any more, which would mean that you don't care about me. I hoped you didn't mean it. I hoped you haven't stopped caring about me. What do you want me to say? That my love isn't the same? It isn't. I know you more deeply than when I fell in love with you, almost half a decade ago. My love is different because you're different than how I imagined you. But I love every way you've surprised me, so much better than what I pictured and wished for. Listen. I can accept that you can't live with me. People who love each other sometimes can't be happy together. But if you can't love me any more, *I* can't live with myself. I don't want to live in a world where your love has an end, because my love for you knows no end."

"You just love your idea of me."

"You're wrong. Look at me. Remember that nineteen-year-old boy who came up to you and asked you what book you were reading?"

"Of course I do. He was innocent, romantic, and sensitive. Sweet. I still love him, though I can't see him any more."

He looked at her intently. "I'm still him."

"I know, and I hate myself, that I was unfaithful to him."

"But good people make mistakes, lose sight of who they are, or they wouldn't be good. If good people could only ever be good, if it would be impossible for them to do anything other than good things, then they'd never have a choice. Instead of deliberating with themselves, they'd then just act according to predestined roles without a second thought—playthings on strings, bound to a script that never changes. Without allowing mistakes to exist, you'd lack the ability to do otherwise, to do anything new and be better. That's not you. You can change."

"Is that what you think of my struggling with alcohol, that I'm a puppet who can't control myself, can't resist temptation?"

"No, but you drank a whole month's wine ration. Don't be angry, but please, just tell me why. I want to understand."

She thought carefully. It awed her, the calm that had found its way to them, like the marvel of silence after a storm. "I don't know. When I first tried it, I was seventeen and in a very dark place. It took all the pain away. I felt free. No bad feeling could touch me. It was like my life had been black and white, and now I could see colours. It meant *escape*, a way out of a world I couldn't stand to be around."

"Look me in the eye. No, don't look away. Keep looking. Once I was locked inside a cold, dark room and couldn't get out. But then somebody told me something. It saved my life."

She was lost in his eyes, desiring him anew. "What did?"

"Knowing that that feeling you described, it wasn't new. It didn't come from a place outside you. It came from *you*. *You* have felt it before, or you wouldn't know how to feel it. Sometime long ago. Without alcohol. And you need to believe in that, you need to search as hard as you can for that memory, so good that nothing can touch it. Because once you find it, *that* is the way out. Do you trust me?"

Tears stood in her eyes. She felt such love that she could hardly speak. "With my life. But I'm afraid that isn't enough."

"It's not cheap, life."

"Depends on who's living it. In my case, it will cost you dearly to believe in me and nothing at all to give up on me."

"One person's nothing is another's everything."

"Don't say that. Though what you just said really helped me, I'm still so afraid that I'm bad for you. That I'm *all* bad. That you won't be strong enough to put up with my weakness."

"I can be as strong and as weak as you."

She found her hand holding his, and found herself smiling with him. Then she remembered, let go of his hand, let go of his eyes, the hope he'd made her feel. "When we were together," she said. "I was horrid to you. Because I was self-absorbed. I've been utterly, utterly selfish. I drank less this winter, and have been a better version of myself, but yesterday I fell back into my old, idiotic habits." She sighed heavily. "You covered for me, though lying to your superior is a serious offense. I haven't thanked you, because I don't know how. Why are you so good to me?"

His voice small and frail like a boy's, he said, *"I love you."*

All her love inundated her then, flooding her entire being. Tears streamed down her cheeks, and her headache was gone, quite like magic. She kissed him deeply and said, "I love you, too. Things will be different now, Kruso. You're all I need, and I love you now more than I ever have in my whole life."

She put all her need in her eyes for him, gazed her deepest.

She sank down into the grass by his feet, suddenly exhausted.

She didn't care for safety. She just wanted to be home, somewhere. Freed. With rising desperate longing, she now saw that there was only one person who she'd ever had that feeling with. She gathered her legs under her, and hugged her knees to her chest, as if freezing, though her skin was beaded with sweat.

She heard the new tears in her voice as she whispered, "When I said I didn't care about anything any more, I lied."

He squatted down to her, and whispered, "I think you meant it the moment you said it. But you don't mean it now."

Relief washed over her. She breathed, "I want you."

Innocent, his eyes asked, and knowing, hers answered.

Now on their knees in the long grass that hid them well.

Now naked, now skin against skin, now lost in the other.

How he was careful of her pleasure, how he read her and watched her reactions. How his sensitive, responsive touch let her know that he genuinely cared about her, quite a lot.

She stared at him in her staring. In her shivering, she shivered. All through the day, the sun had beat down heavily, scalding her skin, and her skin smarted still with it, as with him. There was a tang of lemon in the air. Her toes curled. Her eyes drank a dream of sun hazed sensuous beauty. She swallowed.

She was home.

-17-

The night before midsummer day, yet in a time outside time, Edeline entered another world. Like an ambush of desire, it ensnared her, all seductive emerald green. A gorgeous forest world, sunlit jungles teeming with species such as natural history had never known. A hazy-vibrant place, with a nearsighted, gauzy mist veiling everything yet making colours joyously luminous in more shades than had ever been granted in the human world.

She took what she intended to be a little step, yet seemed to lift from the ground in a wide floating stride. Halting, she brushed off tickling beads of sweat from her arm, and as she did so she found that this place had enhanced her strength and colour. She'd been blessed with relishable muscles, their appearance such as eyes love to see and their strength such as can lift one's body along with one's spirit as it makes every physical effort buoyantly easier. She'd never loved to look at herself more than now. Her colour was even more beautiful, darker brown and warmer in tone, a shiny reddish warmth to it like polished mahogany.

As she looked up again, she saw four big moons in the green-hazed sky, each different in size, the one in the north the smallest—yet even this one was more than twice as big as her world's moon. And as she delved into the gold-green lustrous light of the forest, which was half like the northern summer forests, half like the rainforests of the equator, she wondered where and when this was. Where all was laughing joy and heady wonder, where there were four tides and countless beauty such as make the heart burst. Shutting her eyes, she breathed in fresh life, tiny dancing green stars melting spark by spark in the scent seducing her nose.

Something in the periphery of her awareness interrupted her green paradise, and she came awake in the sharp-edged brutal magnifying-glass focus of her tent. Still in the camp, in the cold, unforgiving, stinking reality with so much eye-hurting sharpness that all soft edges disappeared, and the clearer the picture was, the less she saw. And she cried, she knew not why. Only that she mourned something she had felt and seen that had faded from her memory as she woke, gone in a few blinks of her eyes. Only that she missed the feeling of it with all her heart. A dream that felt like the most magical moments of her first-ever memories in life, coming back for as long as it lasted.

Innocence of ambiguous dawning childhood—oh, where are you now?

*

The two of them bathing in fresh silky mist and warm green light new to her eyes, Leina saw Katanya again. Saw Kat light up as Leina, too overwhelmed to make a sound, mouthed her name. Saw her beam with delight to see Leina. Surrounded by sun-filled beauty that let Leina know she was safe. Surrounded by trees overflowing with verdancy in more than a thousand hues of green shot through with yellow light, by gemlike light-filled facets achingly missing from her past. Through this green resplendent prism, Leina saw that in this otherworld forest, Kat no longer was Kat. She was a divinity clothed in braided vines, ankle-deep in spongy moss. But Leina wanted her to be Kat. With wishful hope, she hugged her. And oh, as their skin touched, it really was Kat's smell she felt, and with this realization, euphoria washed over her. She stepped back to look at Kat in all her divine newness, in the misty, downy light. And her stare filled with the dazzling image, the shining smile that held the kind of beauty that lives forever. Leina didn't know where she was or what was happening, only how she felt, exhilarated, to be this lucky, to see this joy, her perception of beauty heightened the more she stared. How the gracile lines of Kat's divine dolphin-sleek legs stretched out far-sweeping long. How every tiniest surface of her shone as smooth as her face, pores imperceptible yet evident in the dewlike sweat on her skin, reflecting all colours, like a sun-made mirror. Even while intensely aware of every nuance of embodied wonder, Leina endlessly discovered new details taking her breath away, as the goddess, who was Kat, with every motion and expression changed into a new seamless painting of careful thought. As Leina saw her beauty mirrored in the forest, this green world became astoundingly miraculous to her in how it surpassed perfection. It held her rapt, awed by how such a sight reminds you that everything in life really is too improbable to be anything but a dream, so convincing that for a while, while you live, you forget that you, too, are a dream.

Seeing all this transcendent beauty, Leina felt herself burn with aliveness. Existing with an intensity she hadn't felt since life-changing beauty had first touched her heart when the world still was new and filled with mysterious meaning. The spell that binds, there to see in the undeniable yet unknowable significance of beauty stunning the universe with merely existing.

Suddenly she fell, fell down a steep slope, away from the dazzling green lustre, and then fell through the air. Falling down from a warm green sky of nameless essence. Falling from the feeling of being touched by magic, the kind of which she hadn't felt since she was very small and new to speaking and listening, and for the first time was told of wondersome star pictures. Falling from the wonder found in the moment before knowing any story in full, when imagination just explodes with possibilities like newborn galaxies, ablaze with possible stories behind every budding constellation of love and friendship. Falling until the wonder faded from view far above; falling into a cold blue sky of ordinariness; falling until all she knew was that she was fallen.

To wake up.

To slam into the memory of everything nearly ruined, erasing the dream, like a masterwork replaced by an empty frame.

*

Black Hood hadn't ruined Leina's life completely, but his threat to do so still hung over her. Sadness, she now understood, is the emptiness of unchosen memories imposed on you, when your life and purpose are not your own. Her one and only escape from the empty void of sadness swallowing her was her evergrowing obsession with the mystery of what Amaida had seen.

Leina had tried to tell herself that what Amaida had spoken of had just been a fairytale, the wild fancies of a crazy girl who'd come to believe the fantastical stories she told herself. She knew that it was foolish to pursue theorizing about it as if it was a mystery that could be solved. Yet despite herself, her mind kept returning to the enigma. It only intensified her curiosity that the only one who could illuminate her had been killed, taking her secret with her to the other side. But nowhere in all the annals and tomes of history had anything akin to it been documented. That the sky would turn purple for a moment in the middle of the day, was unheard of, something that had never happened before. It couldn't happen. But if it did, what would happen then?

Winter came and went, and a theory began to grow.

Say that it really did come to be, that it at least was possible that the world was stranger than she thought. It would be beyond significant that she would be there to see such unravelling of its strangeness, that the sky could turn into an impossible colour. In her lifetime. As if she had a fated role to play in what might lead up to that singular moment.

The sky turning purple. What could it mean?

What if it signified that the world wasn't at all what she'd been led to believe? That an untameable, vast, junglelike truth lurked behind it all, deeper and bigger than anything? What if she had been living in a tamed and tidy world of lies, made orderly against its true nature? Her world, her civilization, what if it had all been a design to make her believe she couldn't be free from it, devising this belief in her in order to make her a willing subject to schemes that wouldn't be her choice if she'd only known?

What could be on the other side of the purple sky? What might the price be to see the truth behind the veil that had been her life and her world? Growth or death? Metamorphosis and knowledge or rebirth and innocence?

It might be like a book written by divinities.

Yes. That felt *right* to her. A divine book of purple light.

What would it take to read it, to turn the page?

*

Niels found himself in a body light as air, alighting in a heavenly forest he'd never been able to imagine while awake. Golden brilliance pierced through every layer of vivid green leaves under a burning yellow sky, the sun so near it left no room for blue.

There he saw her. In the light he somehow knew was from the fast-approaching summer solstice, he saw the girl. The mystifying girl from a lost better place. In front of him, just a few trees away, a shower of green-golden light streamed slantwise onto her warm-toned amber skin, her small face big-eyed with innocent kindness and hopeful curiosity. Those eyes glowed bright green and profound, incredibly large for such a small head, yet exactly right for a face that was so catlike tapered in a triangular shape of startling symmetry. At home, she seemed this being who so strongly resembled a jungle cat to his eyes. A slender-limbed small being clothed in streaks of dirt alone, at one with this jungle's density, in its ever-changing, ever-tangling renewal, in its intensity, heat, and pressure. And he blinked before the dreamlike sight, before fuzzily green-lit brightness of grace colouring her feline features in endless shades of chlorophyll. A gentleness of each curve of the androgyne bone structure whose softness grew with his staring. And all the time the hazy surroundings met his eyes anew full of green vibrant light, colouring his skin green along with hers. The light now appeared to dance just like emerald fireflies, the air clouding rich with seed, and he moved closer to better see the wild cat-child. Deep in this seed-filled atmosphere, he moved. Through its pollen-shrouded air thick with new oxygen and pure with a honeyed fragrance. Through veils of mist full of fresh ozone smooth as wet lace. Through soft-edged textures of green mirages that beckoned and withdrew yet didn't fade. Through all this, as it all seduced like forgotten dreams full of secret music, the green wonder tantalized the eyes by making each sensually shaped leaf bleed into the smooth lushness of another.

But the cat-child grew blurrier with his every step closer. Needing to see her clearly, he moved back and found that the farther he moved, the more distinctly he saw her. He retreated from her to see more of her, yet though she grew smaller with his retreat, the lines of her body gained clarity, veil after veil falling off her. Finally, he looked straight in front of him and avoided a tree.

As he looked back again, she was gone.

He was about to turn back towards her, not caring how many veils she wore that hid her from him. But as he took his first running step, the ground became a steep slope, and even one upward step drained him. With each new step, the ground grew steeper, until it was so precipitous that he had to make his way up on all fours. But the grassy path steepened still and became a vertical wall he couldn't climb. As the ground reared up, he toppled, fell off the forest above, fell out of the sky of lucid green, into Nita, waking up. Falling out of the dream, he gasped as if after a long dive. Opening his eyes, he felt new light shine through them.

He didn't remember a single thing from the dream.

But the fast pulse of inspiration he felt as he woke, was what shone in his eyes long after the dream. What shone brightly in him with how scientific discovery made the world new again.

This he would never forget.

And far, far below him, the world passed swiftly by.

-18-

Nearly a year had passed since Chor briefly took human form. And with him, Kyra had been blessed with a baby. A daughter who shortly after her birth had transformed herself into a little centauress, as if growing into her inner image of herself. A little foal child Kyra loved more than life itself. She'd never known she could adore anything like this. The little girl had grown so big and strong so fast, the upper body now of a three-year-old human girl, though she was only three months old. Already a unique personality taking shape, clever and curious, humorous and adventurous. Kyra would die for her in a heartbeat.

Kyreen must've gotten her humour and playfulness from him. And Kyra could already see her prudence, too. She had his wise eyes. He once said, "There's nothing as big as hope when there's little of it left." Only Kyra knew these words. Like thoughts of hers that she'd written in the margins of books only she would read, private notes no one will know, exclusively hers.

Now, at the height of summer, having read a fairytale to Kyreen, Kyra sat by her side until she slept. She then strode out, climbed to the highest cliff, stood at the edge, and gazed at the sunset. Making time for herself for the first time this year. Touched by the sight of the sun that appeared to be blushing deeply, she brought back to her mind two of her favourite times when Chor had made her laugh. Smiling as she listened to those sweet moments again she eagerly let them echo back to her. That one time when she had asked him, *"Why do you so often speak in poetry?"*

And with a glint in his eye that told her he was only as much as half-serious – if even that much – he had replied, *"It helps to paint vivid pictures with words to take my mind off philosophical conundrums."*

"Conundrums?"

"Yes, you see you might blush when you're embarrassed, but then you're proud of your ability to feel shame, and so the blush rapidly goes away. But then you'd logically feel ashamed that you're so proud of this ability, and so the blush rapidly comes back. And so it would go, round and round, until we stop holding mirrors up to mirrors." And that other time, the evening after the morning when they'd exchanged tales of their childhood and she'd told him she found the comparison between their separate experiences mutually illuminating. How she that evening had gotten a high fever, her throat killing her, and she'd complained loudly, saying she'd gladly sacrifice being human to have his immune system. Saying this as he, after he had reshaped himself back into a centaur to be strong and happy again, never got sick. And when she grumbled that he took his good health for granted and didn't know

how lucky he was, as he'd never experienced how awful it was to be sick, he had quipped, *"Yes, health is wasted on the well, isn't it?"*

She would have given herself to laugh at the fond memory, if not for the nagging thought of the day that was approaching far too fast. In less than a week, the midsummer sun would rise. If Chor and his daughter didn't make it inside their forest before then, they would be stuck here. The only mythical beings left, as all others had already gathered in the forest that had called them, awaiting their goddess. Kyra hadn't understood it first, had merely thought that Chor spoke in metaphors when he equated being trapped in this world with dying. But now she knew better. If they didn't leave for the forest now, then after midsummer, both he and his daughter would lose hope and die of sorrow.

She had to save them, even if it meant her death.

She had thought that becoming a mother would change her so much that she would no longer have to be ashamed of who she had been. But she still winced at the thought of how she had openly hated and mistreated Chor's sister. Inexcusably, she had called Chyanne a demoness. She thought about it. *The idea of demons became a lazy way for me and others to externalize our wrongdoing to shirk responsibility, to avoid blaming ourselves for what we were guilty of. We cowardly hid behind this idea of demonic influence so that we could persuade ourselves that the wounds we'd inflicted weren't our fault. But what is a demon but an imaginary bad friend that conveniently appears when you need an excuse to avoid making an effort for anybody but yourself?*

But she had to focus on what was at hand. She sighed. Turning her mind to things ahead came with a fear slowly becoming as familiar as the pain of looking back. Being older and wiser evidently didn't stop you from wanting to take back past hurt you've caused, or from worrying about future hurt that might befall your family. She longed for a just, dignified *escape*.

During her pregnancy, she'd read every book in the cave's wonderful library. A month before Kyreen's birth, Kyra began to write her own fairytales and myths. She'd kept on, all through the spring, on into the summer, filling notebook after notebook. When she was in a flow of creativity, she often had to reschedule the time she had agreed to help Chor with something. Asking him those times to give her another fifteen minutes, as she'd just had a new idea and had to write it down before it disappeared.

But now, being scared to death for her daughter's life, she felt quite certain that if the forest disappeared before her daughter reached it, not only would she burn all she'd written, she wouldn't live for very long after losing her man and her child. Then there'd be nothing left of all she had created, not a trace.

It was her only chance, that the forest would welcome her.

-19-

While Aurora piloted the balloon on her own, Niels laid down to try to sleep. Torest had with poetic words painted an exhilarating picture of the Forbidden. With this picture fresh in his mind, Niels closed his eyes and pushed his wildest imagination as far as it could go. He lost himself in the feeling Torest had given him, telling Niels that all life in that mysterious forest was going to another, higher world, full of new, warm colours. Deep inside his imagination, Niels saw that place take shape. A greener place where there were worlds within worlds, some in which all would be seen in ever-changing tones of red, others where all inside was lit in glowing purple, green, yellow, and gold. He sank below consciousness and into the most colourful dreaming, but soon woke, couldn't have been gone more than a few minutes. Wide awake as the tiny dream of endless summer warmth disintegrated and fell into oblivion.

For the rest of the night, when it was Aurora's turn to get some sleep and he heard Aurora breathe heavily under both hers and his blanket, he and Torest whispered rapidly. Swiftly finding a kindred spirit in the other. By the end of the night, they were thick as thieves, and Niels felt that Torest had gotten closer to his heart than anyone outside his family. He told Torest all his secrets and in return, Torest spoke of her dreams.

Niels then hastened his words, as he saw the first ray of dawn, which he knew soon would wake Aurora. "What if the knowledge we will obtain in the Forbidden isn't meant for humans? It could be the reason why no humans leave that place because they've stolen knowledge that is sacred to know and can't go back without being thieves. That theft might spell the end of what makes that place special. You belong in that place, but for me, a human, it might be a sacrifice. An offering, like how we have to give up a large part of our lives to follow a dream all the way to the end. In my case, a dream of discovery. But I might never get to come back. And if I can, if I'm the first to return, will I be able to live with myself, stealing something that was never meant to be mine? A thing that has to be kept within certain boundaries. What if taking that knowledge out of the forest would be akin to diverting a river and stealing water from a realm that will swiftly die without it?"

"I don't think so. I believe something good will happen when we reach it, because the divinity I worship is good, as are you. In your eyes, I see the first pure bloom of youth, though you're full-grown. Your freckles, there's something, well, *intimate* about them. They make you so like your sister, and yet so different from her at the same time. I feel like you would be welcomed in the realm of myths. I'm sorry. I'm blabbering."

"No, it's fine." Niels revealed a precious secret then. "I've been corresponding with my cousin, Phana, through letters. She's a soldier who in her last letter told me something important pertaining to what you just said. She said she is to be stationed in the last outpost before the unknown territory of the Forbidden. She wouldn't dream of going inside, she wrote, because so many who had written about that place had described it as sacred. She actually described it as trespassing on sacred ground and being a graverobber. That it would be a sacrilege to take away knowledge from that which has become a symbol of the unknowable that lends itself to be whatever we most want it to be. Aurora actually still believes we will come back with knowledge from that place. But the closer we get to it, the more I feel that there's no coming back. *Ever.* And so I can tell you what Phana said in absolute confidence in her last letter. Just last year, she met a soldier who this winter had become her best friend. The two of them had shared a secret pleasure. Phana said that one of the best thrills of her life was when she and her new best friend, named Ediline – or maybe Edeline – had gone to the market near their base and had thieved, then shown each other their booty, giggling like schoolgirls over their plunder. To be so good at sneaking, at playing innocent, that they could snatch tiny goods right under the noses of unsuspecting rich vendors who could afford to part with so small a slice of their pie, so to speak. It had made her feel deliciously sinful and alive, she wrote. Such a secret is forgivable for me to disclose. I have faith that you won't pass it on. But there are secrets whose disclosure is unforgivable, if it means the ruin of faith you can't give up without forsaking faith in yourself. You see, she and that girl had another immense secret, as well, and that I've sworn not to tell and never will. If I tell it, though she may never know I did, I feel in my heart that it would be just like telling the secret of what's in the heart of the Forbidden. Something only entrusted to souls that have found themselves, and if everybody knows it, its secret would be *ruined*. So even if Aurora wants to go back, I will do my utmost to prepare her for the possibility that we can't. All I'm saying is that there's a reason why no humans re-enter our world after crossing over. And I have a feeling in my bones that it is because they know something that makes returning the last thing they want."

Many, many days later, they were revived by the bright golden morning light over the fields that lay before the cloud-shrouded forest forbidden to humans. They stopped just once before they at last ascended to cross into it, made camp by the canyon where they met a secretive, mysterious girl named Kyra.

At the height of summer, they rose to the sky. Soon they would see the top of the trees pass under inside that vision of a sensuous, undulating heat haze that made all motion slow, dreamlike, like an underwater dance. Niels gazed into the distant haze, closed his eyes, and smiled. To be this close, knowing that nothing could stop him from following his dream to the end, he found he could, at last, imagine how it would feel to enter that place, just beyond the red canyon and the yellow fields. With his eyes firmly shut and his inner world filling with colours unseen until this moment, part of him was already there.

*

The season of bloom was about to fully flower, and to Leina it seemed ages since it last had. Eternities since last summer, when she had been taken away from the canyon, after Black Hood had escorted her home to her family. She had been given her freedom, but he had left her with a warning not to cross him, or he would take her with him by force back to the canyon, to force her to draw out the beast from his hiding. Apparently believing only she could. That she had the power to summon the beast.

It had been all but unbearable, to live so close to him. Because he never left, watched her from afar, walking through her father's plantation. Forever silent, never letting her know his intention, never giving away his name. She could never ask him what his plans were. For he was known in Dophra as the Silent Monk after he had taken a vow of silence at the White Marble Monastery where he lived a reclusive life of prayer and asceticism.

But in the end, he did come for her, to the fields where her father had finally allowed her to work as a banana girl, until she married. She'd fought tooth and nail to postpone the wedding, but her father wouldn't let her push it farther away from her, and she couldn't escape the reality that it would take place at the end of the summer. And like she had accepted that she had to be married to Richmont, a spoiled, loathsome man, she yielded to Black Hood, the Silent Monk. Because she couldn't struggle, couldn't fight back, not when she knew that he would never give up for as long as he lived. And the black-hooded monk that had spoken his last words in life, that now only wrote notes to state his will, he was too strong, binding her hands and dragging her to a black horse tied to his. Her father was with her brothers in Kullum, attending some prestigious event at the academy where they taught, too far away for them to get to her in time. Part of her just wanted it to be over, worn out to live in fear of Black Hood and the trial he could bring back in motion if she didn't do what he wrote for her to.

They came to the place she'd thought she'd never see again.

Once more at the mouth of the sandstone canyon, in the burning summer heat of the desert borderlands.

Where he wrote a note in deafening, maddening silence.

He put it in his pocket, then rode on with her, apparently waiting to show it to her until they had reached wherever they were going. She chewed her lip, thinking of a thousand ways she would take her revenge after her ordeal was over and he untied her and set her free. Because now she finally was at a place where his body wouldn't be found. This time, she wouldn't waver. She would end his haunting. Thinking this as he took her to a place deep in the canyon that he appeared to have sought out once before, not long before coming for her. Finding it so easily that it came to her that he must have used all that time in the monastery to study its ancient maps, some of which showed this place when the water had streamed through the sandstone in a myriad of channels. To find a perfect spot for his dark purpose.

A dead end, one in which he could easily hide while she stood in plain view. Here, he gave her the note, and with the inheld breath she read his intention with her before he concealed himself and watched her pinioned body from the shadows. And his intention was clear, for his command was this: *Call his name*.

Black Hood pushed her. Something dear to her fell from her. She could barely hear it as it cracked. She didn't even look.

-20-

With the clatter of Kyra's horse falling in time with Chor's hoofbeat, their daughter trotting a little shyly behind them, they emerged from the gorge. As the canyon opened up dramatically wider than the gorge overhung with sky-reaching palms, Kyreen seemed wary of the open space, her eyes continuously looking up at her father to draw confidence from his calm. It was the first time Kyreen had been this far from the gorges right outside their cave, the heart of the canyon where she'd learned to gallop. Kyra swallowed the jealousy she always felt at such moments, to see her daughter's eyes with instinctive readiness dart to her father for reassurance. Then Kyra looked around her. The wideness of the opening seemed bigger than it should be, as it was less than a hundred paces across. It widened to the west, where the mouth of the canyon opened to sparse grass patches of the clayey steppe.

Kyra's skin gleamed with the high summer heat. Her calm was heedless. Nothing bad could happen on such a beautiful day.

She thought of what Chor had said when he saw Kyreen first begin to grow a second pair of legs when she'd had the equivalent of a one-year-old human's body. Seeing her change her body while dreaming of the form that most felt like her, her human toddler feet slowly as clouds becoming hooves, Chor had shed a tear, and with a voice coloured by the love, he'd said, *"The future is represented by children. The past is a place where only adults dwell."*

A sudden shout came from their left. A woman's shout, strangely familiar, calling Ruhchor's name. Kyra heard it clearly.

Chor's voice rasped out thickly, "Stay here with Kyreen."

Split-second fear stabbed ice into her chest. "It's a trap."

"I know. But it's Leina. I gave her my word."

"Don't be foolish. That was before you became a father. Neither of us are free to risk our lives now, remember?"

In a breath that squeezed his voice away, soft as a breeze in a thin mountainous bay, he said, *"You're my dream of dreams and the dream will never die."*

"Stop it. I hate when you do that."

She didn't.

"I need you like thirst needs rain and like rain needs thunder."

"Oh, damn." She kissed him. "I'll ask Kyreen to hide in the grass until you return. Just promise to be careful."

*

As Chor at a gallop came around the sharp-curving sandstone wall to the long shadowy gorge with no way out, Leina saw what the centaur couldn't. That Black Hood stood hidden at an angle where he unseen could see the centaur, and that his crossbow was loaded. He had removed his hood from his head. His head was completely hairless but not shaven so, lacking a single hair to shave off. The bald monk took aim, ready to fire, meaning to kill.

She very likely could die for this. But how could she look at herself in the mirror if she caused another's death?

Oh, her mirror. When it fell down and hit the ground, was it her world that cracked? No.

"Stop!" she thinly cried.

With an unhuman instant reaction, Chor balked, and veered to the left, sending up a dust cloud with surprising effect. The bolt came less than half a second after the sound of her cry, and as Chor skidded to a stop, the steel point crashed into the cliff wall at his side in an explosion of red sandstone rock splinters.

The dust Chor had stirred as he stopped, now rained down on her tanned skin that shone with sweat, clouding her with red-brown sand and dust. Her knees nearly gave way, and she became aware of her body trembling forcefully.

She and the centaur looked at one another with infinite emotion through the thick cloud of dust, and in the next second, he yelled, "I'll come back with a weapon! Stay strong!"

Black Hood, now unhooded, fumbled with the next bolt, and just as he had reloaded his crossbow, Chor was gone.

Black Hood's face was the ugliest sight she'd ever seen, a livid, wrinkly mask of fury. He turned, and strode through the air of dust towards her. Blinking fitfully, wiping his eyes free from dust, he emitted a series of sharp coughs and came ever nearer to where she stood with her hands tied behind her. Moving with the bolt ready to be released. She used her shoulder to scratch at her cheek, which was coated with sweat and red sandy dust.

Her voice an angrily inflamed wound, she asked him, "Will you let me live?" Though he had vowed to never speak again.

He shook his head. Raised the crossbow. Aimed the bolt at her forehead, and took one last step. Moved his finger to the trigger. Gave her no time to think, no time to close her eyes.

And so her eyes were wide open as she saw it.

From the sky dropped a wine bottle—and it hit him square on his bald head in a loud-ringing smash. Instantly the blow blasted consciousness out of him. His body thudded into the dust, next to a puddle of sparkling wine that popped and fizzed.

She would leave now, never fear him again. He might recover and survive, but to her, come what may, he was no more.

Leina cast her gaze upwards, into the sky, feeling so ready to take flight that she could easily imagine wings bursting out of her shoulder blades. It mattered not if her hands were tied. She felt released, given a new chance, and she smiled at the sky. There, directly above the dead-end crevice where she stood tied, a hot-air balloon! Quite high over where she craned her neck, three young faces looked down at her. Now they waved. One of them, a huge-eyed black-haired girl, had goatlike horns – looking nothing like handmade props – but what else could they be? Leina threw her voice to them, gave it as much as her dry throat could muster, and tore the sound with a muscular effort. *"Thank you!"*

Just then, Chor emerged with a bow and arrows. He relaxed as he saw Black Hood face down on the ground. He followed her gaze to the sky. A faint voice had just been heard shout something from the balloon, too far up for Leina to catch it. God, how she wished she'd heard it. Though she'd been outside cliques of girls whispering closely guarded secrets she'd been burning with curiosity to know, never had she wished this hard that she could know every word that hadn't reached her ears.

Chor pointed at the cracked mirror on the ground halfway between him and Leina. Edeline's old mirror, her gift to Leina. Now broken in five or six sharp shards, blinding with the sun's immediate reflection, so that she couldn't look directly at it. She faintly remembered it falling out of her pocket when Black Hood had pushed her with brutish violence in front of him.

Chor's wonderful melodious voice spoke with quiet marvel and wonder. "Its reflection must've drawn the balloon to you."

She looked up again, but now the balloon no longer could be seen for the steep cliff blocking the sky from view where she'd last seen the craft drift like a green bubble about to evaporate.

Chor cut her free and brought her up onto his back. She thanked him profusely, and he responded, a smile in his voice, "So funny, what the girl shouted up there when you thanked *her*."

"Oh, my God, did you hear it? What did she say?"

"'Hoodlum says you're welcome.' Hoodlum's her guinea pig."

"How do you know this?"

"I heard them talk expansively yesterday as they landed nearby, the twins in the balloon, the scientist and the adventurer, and the aiga they've rescued. The scientist had a dream about the purple sky. He told his sister that though he was highly sceptical that such an anomaly would occur, he'd chosen to begin their expedition to the unmapped place on this day, to be able to say that their exploration began under the midsummer sun."

"What will happen when the sky becomes purple?"

He smiled warmly. "You have to see for yourself."

"Yes, well, look at me, all dressed for the grand occasion."

Turning his head, he ran his eyes over her torn and dirty state. And holding onto his massive shoulder with one hand, with the other she made a sweeping elegant gesture like you do when you present yourself in a new glorious attire. She felt him chuckle under her. She rode easy on his back. He was taking her away from the man who had abducted her. It didn't matter if that man would once more seek her destruction after he woke up. She somehow knew that her days of being haunted would end on this day, if she so chose.

But now Chor turned his head in a way that told her he heard something she couldn't. She whispered, "What is it?"

"Albadine soldiers, between us and the forest, hiding in the grass. Yesterday, I couldn't help but listen in on the twins, who had landed not far from here to rest and restock water supplies. By the way, the breakneck speed of their overlapping dialogue was a tougher code to break than the military jargon. Anyway, I was just about to give them privacy when I heard the soldiers out there, and I switched focus from voice to voice until I had the knowledge I needed. Somebody has told them the secret of what I, who don't belong, have felt is to come today. I've felt it like a vibration before an earthquake, imperceptible to humans. But to those soldiers, it doesn't mean anything. Only a way for them to set a trap for whoever is last to pass into that place."

"Does Kyra know?"

"Of course. And she knows that there's not enough time to go around it and she trusts my judgement that we'll be safe going through. That the trap will be sabotaged and stopped."

"How do you know that?"

"I heard the strongest of the soldiers as she talked to herself in a secluded place. I heard her every promise to herself, one of them being that she won't let any harm come to innocents like us. Her name is Edeline and she'll protect us."

Now Kyra was in front of them, and though Leina hardly knew her, she jumped down and hugged her, and told her what had happened. Kyra blanched with the thought of nearly losing Chor.

"Will you come with us?" Kyra said after the two of them had spoken awhile and Leina's nerves felt less frazzled. Chor was off by the tall grass, to better listen for soldiers ahead of them.

Leina gazed into the heat haze with eyes that slowly found their way back to the dreams she'd briefly lost sight of. Resuming the hopeful dreaming she'd been deprived of while being Black Hood's hostage. "I need to tell you something, Kyra. I was wrong. Last summer, I was so afraid of changing myself that all I thought about was changing *him*. I thought I could make him human, more like me. But I've learned so much since then. I see now that I was never meant to make him less of what he is."

"I think you knew this, or you wouldn't have whispered what you did, which did change *me*. I've grown a lot as well. I'm still learning. It's good, I've come to find, change. And truthfully, I look forward to learning and changing even more."

"I'm still afraid, but I no longer let the fear rule me."

"Will you come?" Kyra asked again.

"You go ahead. I'll watch from a distance."

"Did you know," Kyra said, smiling softly. "I once watched you from a distance? I wanted to be you."

"You never begrudged us our wealth?"

"Not as long as you spent it on our *common* wealth. Excess is another matter when wealth exceeds your wisdom to spend it; you know, gold gathering dust instead of contributing to anything. The senseless vacuity of it, the mania of excess to fill the hole it's digging for itself, the emptiness of eating long after you're full. That I did hate. As would you had you been born into poverty. But I didn't want to be you because you're a rich girl. Leina, I wanted your strength. I felt so weak, so miserable. Now, all I want is to be safe, to find a safe home somewhere to love forever, and to be there when Kyreen calls for me."

-21-

Entering the tall, dense grass that stood between them and their new home, Kyra's thoughts took her back to last summer, to her first sight of Leina at Dophra's market. Her anticipation was now as obsessive as her envy of Leina then, a big, tight-wired energy, far too big to leave any room for fear. Nor could she consider that her immediate future would hold an unforeseen event that would cause her to lose Kyreen or Chor, Kyreen's father, the strange and astounding being she'd fallen in love with. Such an unfair, unthinkable future didn't exist to her even as a hypothetical scenario. While a year ago she'd fought her nerves only for herself, for having what Leina had, her nervous anticipation now was for them, to live and grow with the love she had chosen and the girl they'd been blessed with. Together as one. Always.

Because their hearts were one heart, nothing would separate them.

At first sight of the forest on the horizon, Kyreen had stopped and dressed for the happy occasion. The little centaur girl wore her yellow sundress of light cotton, whose hem hung far under the line under her hipbones where the human side ended and the equine began. Kyra had found it in one of the treasure chests in the smugglers' cave and had cut and sewn it to fit her this winter. It lifted her heart to see her daughter wearing it for their jubilant arrival in that happy place of peace. A place forever safe from soldiers hunting them in the name of civilization.

The thick heat in the windless grass was shocking. Its tense density eerie in its unbroken ferocity, like nothing Kyra had felt before, drowning every sense, the feeling of being lost in a crowd.

Chor said, "The pressure is disrupting my hearing. I can no more than you hear if we're alone in the depths of this grass."

Nothing could separate them—they were one.

She said, "Don't be afraid. We're almost home."

Sweat ran down her cheeks. Her view thin with squinting, she looked at her daughter cantering in the wavy heat and dizzy light. She saw tiny beads shine on Kyreen's face, and as Kyreen looked at her with nervousness that mirrored her own, Kyra smiled with courage that surprised her in that it didn't feel like a lie. She didn't know where she found that courage, but she saw it now light up in Kyreen's eyes as well, smiling back at her.

She wiped Kyreen's cheek at the exact spot where her own cheekbone tickled with unfallen sweat.

Kyra looked up. A drop fell from her jawbone. Inside her, two flashes. Visions, lasting less than a second each. One of love, one of hate. She saw her mother's beloved ash tree back in her old home. She saw a forest fire, a fire made by men.

She sank into thoughts about the meaning of this.

A thud woke her abruptly, her body fear-struck like a fawn the instant it sees a wolf charge from where it had crept unseen.

A bolt had gone through Chor's chest. His weight was like a hundred-year-old tree as he hit the ground in a muted boom.

She threw herself down, threw her arms around him, barely had time to see the last light in his eyes touch hers with feelings that burned with all the strength in the lifespan of the sun, before the light went out and he closed his eyes, never to be open again.

She was about to release him from her tight embrace, about to launch her body at whoever had fired the shot before they could harm her daughter, when her body exploded with pain.

She looked down and saw a second bolt, now buried in her body, saw the blood come out of her in confused waves, saw each pulse lose its way to her heart, saw life leaving her.

Her final thought as she felt the last energy of life run out of her, was of Kyreen. The laws of nature made it impossible for her to make a sound, but she did it anyway. The loudness of her heart broke the law of physical possibility, and it came out in a young mother's protective voice. Loud enough to strengthen Kyreen all through her fear and tears. Hearing herself yell,

"Kyreen, you have to run—but I'll always be with you! Now—run!"

Because their hearts were one heart, nothing would separate them.

*

Edeline ran through the waist-high, sedge-like grass.

Ran towards Kruso.

Ran through heat that burned as if the air was on fire.

Ran for all she was worth.

A thought of horrid truth flashed through her brain. That this was what nightmares were made of. All horrors, made of this, this cold blood in humans of violence. It all came to this, this hateful senseless killing.

Ahead of them lay the centaur, losing all his lifeblood. The black-haired woman in his arms, Kyra, was already dead.

Edeline's body had become desperation in motion. It couldn't end like this. Yet what could she do? It wasn't fair, but neither was the world, and she was a soldier in it, made by it.

But when soldiers kill, like now, how can it be any less a murder?

"Stop running!" Urun roared, and she didn't.

Didn't slow down until she was close enough that Kruso could hear her.

She panted with her hands on her knees.

Urun stared furiously at her, then at Kruso, and gave him once again the order to shoot. And the general impatiently pointed in a stabbing motion at the tiny being who stood ten paces away on twiggy foal legs.

"But," Kruso said, his voice small. "She's just a little girl."

Urun was livid now. "If you don't do as the Crown commands you, if you go against my direct order, you will face a very long time in jail. Are you aware of this, soldier?"

Edeline saw desperation take hold of Kruso, and his face twisted in anguish, as he moaned the protest, *"Look at her!"*

"It's just an ungrown creature, and I would've shot it myself if I didn't use my last arrow to fell the big creature. Ziara shot the woman, at my command, and now it's your turn to do your part, to finish the mission."

Edeline, Ziara, and Urun, all stared at Kruso, his arrow ready to be fired.

Edeline saw his legs shake as if his knees were about to buckle. She rasped out a hoarse yell that wouldn't have been fuller of trepidation if she'd stood face to face with God to plead for her soul's rescue. "Don't do it, Kruso!"

Kruso lowered his bow, and without thinking, she got her bow off her shoulder, strung an arrow to it.

She was the best archer in the troop, possibly in all of Kalid.

She wouldn't miss.

She would do it for Kruso.

*

"I know of your drinking, lass," Urun spat out, as if having bitten into a fruit that turned out to be rotten and sour. "Now is your chance to make up for it. Do this, and I'll let you have as much wine as you want. Take the shot, and I'll think about forgetting Kruso's insubordination."

She stared into his eyes. He didn't know why she was waiting, what it was she was about to do. It seemed strange to her that he didn't suspect it, and wholly incredible that he didn't even have the slightest premonition that something was very, very wrong. Her eyes went to Ziara, whose face was blank with shock at what she had done, then to Kruso, whose eyes were made of pain and whose speech faltered, as all he managed to get out was, "Edeline…"

The general now looked at something distant behind her, and she heard the sound of footfall at a sprinting distance coming closer. Urun said, "This is your last chance, soldier. The troop is coming and there is not one of the rest of them who wouldn't follow my order. Now, soldier, you *will*—"

"I'm not your soldier," she said and fired the arrow straight into his chest.

Utter disbelief all over Urun's face, the second it happened, as it drained of blood, going white from the trauma, the deadly wound at the centre of his ribcage. Blood pumped thickly out of him, telling her she'd hit an artery. The following second, he fell onto his back, and the arrow lodged deep in his chest trembled. His eyelids flickered like a moth at the glass of a lantern, as he in his last second awake began to lose consciousness, staring at the sky with eyes full of fear. Before his eyes lost all expression. And as the troop gathered all around and stared in a silent trance, Urun took his last breath and was no more.

Edeline lifted her gaze, then opened her mouth and shouted at the little centauress whose face was streaked with tears. *"Go!"*

And the little girl did, her hooves softly pattering like sudden summer rain. Away she ran, farther and farther, until she was out of shooting distance from anyone in the troop, and Edeline dared to breathe again. Into the Forbidden Forest, the foal-bodied little girl ran, looking over her shoulder just once before completely surrounded by trees. A look back not at Edeline, but at the centaur, and at Kyra who had died next to him. And then the centaur child, the daughter of this hunted couple, was gone from the human world forevermore.

*

The sun had reached its centremost position when the birdsong from the Forbidden Forest faded and the air stilled. The world around Leina seemed to hold its breath in an entranced, reverent spell of tranquillity. Her eyes followed the balloon as it was the only thing moving, soundlessly coming ever closer to the mist above the treetops. Something she couldn't explain took hold of her then. She had a very small window of time. She walked through the grass towards the forest. Then stopped by the trees, afraid of the feeling coming over her, that it might spell the end.

Then she saw her, the tiny beautiful centauress, Kyra's daughter. Where were Kyra and Chor? But then the tiny half-human girl waved her inside. And Leina wasn't afraid any more.

Taking the step across the tree line, she noticed that her skin shone with a new thin layer of sweat. Yet the heat wasn't oppressive, a mild quality to the air in how easy it was to breathe, how welcome, making every breath feel like a sigh of relief.

But she felt the window closing, a chance almost slipping from her hands. Heart pounding heavily, she hurried fully inside, beyond the boundary. Still alive. The tiny centauress stretched out her hand and Leina took it, and held it. The little girl looked up at the zenith shining on them both, and Leina followed the girl's gaze. And the sky opened up and in sudden breathless wonder, her jaw dropped.

She was ready to leave and never come back.

*

Riding together with Kruso to the havens beyond the desert, Edeline became aware of the growing quiet from the forest behind them. She reined in her horse and turned around, gazing at the Forbidden Forest whose birdsong had abruptly stopped.

She lifted her gaze to the high heavens, suddenly feeling drawn by something inexplicable. A shifting second light superimposing the sun's light, spanning the entire heavenly vault.

Suddenly the sky blinked.

Then changed colour.

They stared up, astonished to the very core of their being.

It wasn't a possible sky any more.

The whole sky was burning, and it burned entirely purple.

And from the midpoint of that all-encompassing purple fiery brightness, the warmest yellow light. A light such as she had never seen. In a soft beam, it came flushing down over the trees. Gently, the beam showered every bush, every tree, every branch, every bud. Everything in the forest was gold-glowing, uniting with the beam, and golden leaves glittered and golden birds sang again.

Until, not many seconds later, the sky blinked again, flickered hotly, and was once again a possible colour, blue, like before, like it had always been. The beam was gone—and all that had been part of it was shockingly gone with it. The forest had disappeared. All they could see where the trees once had been was lifeless, arid emptiness. The mist-obscured birthplace of myth, its interior that was an eternal enigma, a puzzle never solved, was no more. And Edeline felt a big hole in her heart, her sorrow as big as the wordless meaning of that place of boundless potential.

-22-

Leina found herself naked in a burning hot desert.

Crawling down a flaming red dune, too hot to put down her palms or the soles of her feet, scalding her knees and elbows.

A perfectly round pool in an oasis below, she rolled and flung herself into it. Floundered, fell, splashed, stood on all fours in the shallows, and drank. Looking up, catching her breath and wiping her mouth, rubbing her face that was dirty where it wasn't beaded with fresh water and fresh sweat. And pulling back her tousled hair that was partly soaked, partly caked, she saw. She saw the stillness, saw the lemon-yellow sky full of impossible light, saw the lobster-red ocean of sand that appeared to cover the entire world she had been swept up to, saw the four palms in the tiny green oasis she'd tumbled into, saw... the boy.

A warmly brown-skinned boy of the earliest adolescent age, sitting half-naked on his haunches, wearing only a loincloth. Tranquil as the palms, his hair jet-black, his mouth gently smiling, his eyes opaque and sharp as glimmering obsidian, taking her in.

She spoke and he didn't understand her.

He didn't rise, kept sitting in that squatting position, from time to time trying a word, none of which told her what he was thinking. Nothing in his easy, unhurried hand gestures let her know anything about him or where she was, only that he welcomed her. He gave her sandals that fit her perfectly. She thanked him, clothed herself in plaited reeds and sat with him.

He was waiting for something.

There was a harmonica tied on a string to a palm leaf.

Every now and then, a smooth breeze passed through the harmonica, the gentle wind playing different notes each time, chaotic patterns of infinite unpredictability.

The sun arced and still, he sat there, while she slept and ate the delicious ripe fruit he gave her, or swam, or answered when nature called. On and on the sunburned, and on and on she slept when she didn't try to think, but so tired, so drained, as if she had travelled from one star in the west to another in the east. She couldn't summon even the faintest guess about what had happened to her. Her memories of who she had been and what life she had lived barely surfaced, and when they did, they came up in slippery fragments that escaped her grasp like little jumping fish.

Her eyes, ears, and nose took in what felt just like the height of summer, the vibrant air full of sweet sunny memories which were one with the feeling of bursting youth. The oasis sang with birds of miraculous colours.

With soft footfall eager as the hurried music of the young birds, she walked gazing up. Passing through the alluring aroma of flowers with no name. Her heart wanted this.

Then curiosity led her through a breeze back to the boy.

The boy went to the harmonica and before she had time to speak, he repeated the pattern of notes the breeze had played.

Oh. This was what he waited for.

The wind moved with the chaos of utter randomness, and yet if you used your imagination, you could hear music in it. It inspired the boy, and he elaborated on the notes until he found a melody that equalled the feeling he got from nature's beauty. This she heard in the magical music he played on his harmonica. This she sensed in the moving pleasure of his adolescent eyes. What he felt was utterly new, chaos-born as the wind, and yet he guided his feelings like a dream whose content surprises you though you're its author. From the wind, he made music that touched and surprised him, and who could have said before he was born what would feel precisely like that to him? There is no such thing as preordained love, and the heart moves in mysterious ways.

Oh, she had the truth of it now. What is truly beautiful can never be predicted; not until it is felt and we decide from an endless variety of unpredictable notes which ones please the tenderest place in our heart the most.

She understood something unexpected. Her unhappiness had been made of separation. She'd been repelled by everybody, by their predictions of her that didn't take her heart into account. It had alienated her, their expectations of her, for her to conform to social conventions. Culture had torn her apart. What she'd been missing without knowing it, was to feel connected to everybody else. Thinking back, she sensed their unhappiness. Long it was, and brief their joy. She wished they could all be here, feel this with her, her chest expanding, lifting with it. She was starting to belong, piecing herself together again, reclaiming every forgotten dream. Nobody's heart had beat like this. This rhythm she'd found, a revolution she could dance to, a drum she could follow. Her blood sang with it, a wholly different, new song. In each surprising twist of melody, she seemed to glimpse a beginning unlike any other. A dawn remaking everything—how brighter the sky, how fairer the world it shone on.

With this understanding, she smiled, closed her eyes, and drifted away.

And awoke in a different world.

A world of depths within depths.

Of careful warmth instead of ferocious heat.

Of many layered warm colours.

So naturally happy to wake up in such a welcome place that she found herself smiling without effort, quite like when she was a child, all cheeks and pigtails when dreams and waking life had been inseparable. Like the little centauress, she woke up next to.

It sank in then, as she saw the shining green splendour around her. Amaida hadn't been crazy. The world she'd grown up in and gotten to know well, was just one of many others, and just because she didn't know these other worlds intimately didn't make them any less real and important than hers.

And so it was, how Leina's new life began the moment she came awake. As her invigorated, rejuvenated eyes sprang open, her mind lost the knowledge she woke from. What she had learned in that hazy place that was her past became intangible to her, replaced by a very different story. Yet she held the feeling tenderly in her heart. And felt she would always be protected from the anxiety and pain of the cold human world now behind her, because of that warm feeling she had dreamt as she left it all behind, easing her in before awakening. She would smile with it in the tide of her pulse and the wind of her lungs, with a deeper truth in her heart, until its beating stopped.

*

Half an hour after the moments of the purple sky, Edeline and Kruso had slowly regained the power of speech after a long, perplexed silence. The desert now spread out before their eyes, the grass gradually dwindling into nothing in front of them.

But Kruso forgot the desert, forgot his past and future and most of himself, as Edeline filled his heart and spanned his internal vision. The forest's disappearance had made him realise like never before how short life is, and that soon he too would be gone from the world. It made him feel such appreciation for Edeline and such privilege to be at her side, that he wanted to make a heroic effort to let her be who she was, even when she was self-destructive and moody, and not try to change her to make her fit his picture of her. But right now, such romantic heroism was effortless, since the miracle he had seen confirmed another miracle, the inexplicable unlikeliness of her beauty. He knew now what he'd always suspected, that her unique, unrepeatable being was too complex to ever be fully fathomed. All he had to do was to seize every glimpse of her and remember it until his dying day.

Though all was empty desert ahead of them for a long stretch, Edeline gave her surroundings a beaming smile. An exuberant abundance of hope and thrill in her luminous eyes. He leaned from his horse to hers and kissed her, and it felt like they kissed for the first time, their first real kiss as who they really were, accepting all flaws in themselves because they loved one another despite them. As she opened her eyes after the kiss, her gaze was so vulnerable open, he felt as though trust let him in.

The moment would show itself to him, he said to himself, when it was the right time to show her the treasure he'd found when she'd most need to smile.

Edeline said, "Do you think they'll ever come back?"

"No. But a part of their soul is still with us, never left."

"What do you mean?"

And Kruso knew that the moment he'd waited for had already come. Without waiting for another second, he got out the four thick books, opened them one by one, and showed her random pages of the finest calligraphy, some in black ink, but most in red.

He saw her perplexity re-emerge. "What are those books?"

He showed her the inside cover. "You see the name here? Kyra wrote all this. I found them in her saddlebag."

Hope sparked to life in her eyes. A swift look at him, then back at the books, inspiration coming alive again in the light of her eyes. A wild-playing light he'd almost given up dreaming of seeing again. "Her handwriting is extraordinary. I wonder what it is she's written in those books. Could it be diaries?"

"No. I read some of it earlier when you didn't see. These notebooks are full of myths, fairytales, poems, and lyrics. One tale is called *Dawning Wonder* and is about her and the centaur, and about twins flying in a balloon, a tiny furry hero named Hoodlum, and even a female small-horned goat-creature. Maybe we're in it, too. Maybe I can write the chapters that are missing."

"If you do, do you believe it will be a happy end?"

He slowly smiled. "I hope so. It will take a lot of work."

And slowly she smiled back. "I'm ready to begin."

Acknowledgements

I acknowledge with warm gratitude and thankfulness the help I have received from Helen Klemedsson, Tina Carlsson, Paul Stiel, Fredrik Olandersson and Erika Lönnquist, whose criticism and suggestions have been invaluable to me. The manuscript was edited by Pegasus Publishing. I thank them for their role in getting the book in the best possible shape for a life out in the open.